Praise for

THE ONLY CHILD

"Gothic fans, rejoice! . . . An addictive cycle of cliffhanger chapter endings, quick resolutions, and taut, punchy sentences."

The Globe and Mail

"Pyper upends genre conventions once again . . . a high-concept dark fantasy novel . . . Lily's journey with a monster who inspired the very literary tradition Pyper so skillfully exploits provides . . . a satisfying confrontation with darkness, both personal and mythological, that readers expect from the best horror."

Toronto Star

"A darkly entrancing tale that sweeps you off your feet from its first pages. Filled with deliriously clever nods to the grand Gothic tradition, *The Only Child* is also fiercely original, wildly provocative, and utterly satisfying, beginning to end."

Megan Abbott, bestselling author of *You Will Know Me*

Praise for

THE DEMONOLOGIST

"Smart, thrilling, and utterly unnerving. Pyper's gift is that he deeply respects his readers, yet still insists on reducing them to quivering children. I like that in a writer."

Gillian Flynn, #1 *New York Times* bestselling author of *Gone Girl*

Praise for

THE DAMNED

"A master of psychological suspense."

Lisa Gardner, *New York Times* bestselling author of *Find Her* and *Right Behind You*

"Pyper has more than mastered the art. . . . *The Damned* guarantees many sleepless nights."

The Globe and Mail

ALSO BY ANDREW PYPER

The Only Child

The Damned

The Demonologist

The Guardians

The Killing Circle

The Wildfire Season

The Trade Mission

Lost Girls

Kiss Me (Stories)

THE HOMECOMING

A NOVEL

ANDREW PYPER

PUBLISHED BY SIMON & SCHUSTER

NEW YORK LONDON TORONTO SYDNEY NEW DELHI

Simon & Schuster Canada
A Division of Simon & Schuster, Inc.
166 King Street East, Suite 300
Toronto, Ontario M5A 1J3

This book is a work of fiction. Any references to historical events, real people, or real places are used fictitiously. Other names, characters, places, and events are products of the author's imagination, and any resemblance to actual events or places or persons, living or dead, is entirely coincidental.

This Simon & Schuster Canada edition February 2019

For information about special discounts for bulk purchases, please contact Simon & Schuster Special Sales at 1-800-268-3216 or CustomerService@simonandschuster.ca.

Manufactured in the United States of America

10 9 8 7 6 5 4 3 2 1

Library and Archives Canada Cataloguing in Publication

Pyper, Andrew, 1968–, author
The homecoming / Andrew Pyper.
Issued in print and electronic formats.
ISBN 978-1-982108-97-7 (softcover).—ISBN 978-1-982108-98-4 (ebook)
I. Title.
PS8581.Y64H66 2019 C813'.54 C2018-903482-3
C2018-903483-1

ISBN 978-1-9821-0897-7
ISBN 978-1-9821-0898-4 (ebook)

For Ford

Aaron?

Yeah?

Where do you think he's taking us?

I don't know.

Isn't it—

It's weird. But Dad was weird.

You think Mom's gonna be okay?

She sent you over to pick me up so she could get her own ride, right?

Right.

So she's fine. She likes being alone. Sometimes I think she likes it better than being—

Aaron?

Yeah?

Have you ever been on this road before?

Nope. And I've never been driven anywhere by someone who won't even look at you either.

Aren't you scared?

Why would I be scared?

It's such a big forest. No houses or anything. It's like we've been driving through it since—before we woke up, before—

It's a big forest all right.

And spooky. Look at the trees. All crowded together. Like they're whispering. Or—

Listen to me, Bridge. This whole routine—it's just the old man setting the scene before the lawyer tells us what's what.

I know. But did you notice? Back there?

What?

The fence. The gate we drove through.

So?

That means all this is private property.

Okay. I've never told you this before, but when I was a kid, Dad would tell me these stories. Fairy tales, I guess. Children walking off the path and meeting up with creatures, doppelgängers, phantoms. They'd always take place in the woods around a castle called Belfountain. I never guessed it was real. That it was his.

I remember.

Really? So I already told you about—

No. Not you. Daddy told me the same stories. Except I'm not sure they were things he made up.

Why do you say that?

Because I've been here before. Because he brought me.

BELFOUNTAIN

1

WHEN MOM CALLED TO TELL ME THE NEWS, I WAS SURPRISED AT FIRST THAT Raymond Quinlan was capable of something so human as dying. We were given to understand that Dad was a man of many talents, but none we knew of was so great as his gift for disappearing. All our lives he would leave without saying when he would be back. It could be days or weeks or months. Long enough that just when you thought this time he wouldn't return, he did. Without warning, unburdened by guilt or explanations. But now he'd gone somewhere there was no coming back from, and it was almost disappointing, the end of his mysterious life coming not by way of stunning revelations or secret agents knocking at the door but the inevitable way it comes for all of us.

Less than an hour after I got off the phone with Mom, a woman called saying she was "a representative of your father's estate" and that a car would come first thing in the morning to pick me up. When I asked where this car would take me, I was told it would be a journey requiring a day away, the destination "necessarily confidential."

That “necessarily” irked me. A word my father would use to answer why he couldn’t say where he went. It implied we should appreciate the complicated circumstances behind things having to be this way, his importance, the triviality of our need to understand.

You’ll never tell us where you go, will you? I asked him once, though what I really wanted to know was if he ever missed us when he was gone.

No, Aaron. I’m afraid I won’t.

Because it’s a secret?

Yes, he answered sadly. A sadness for me, his tone made clear, not something he felt himself. *Necessarily so.*

The limo stops before I can ask Bridge more about her being here before. The driver pulls open the back door and speaks for the first time since we started out this morning, asking for our cell phones.

“Why do you want them?”

“Protocol,” he mumbles, the accent hinting at Russian, his fat palm thrust a little too close to my face.

“What do we do?” Bridge asks me.

“You expecting any important calls in the next hour?”

“No.”

“Me neither. So let’s humor them and play by the rules.”

We hand our phones over to the driver, who sticks them in the pocket of his blazer and, without another word, returns to sit in the front seat, leaving us to get out. He eases the limo away to park next to another just like it at the edge of a circular gravel area outside what must be the castle Dad spoke of in his stories.

What’s the best word to describe it? Not “castle,” certainly. Not “mansion” either, or “home” or “cabin” or “hotel.” My mind can’t stop thinking of it as a lodge, despite its enormity, the stateliness of its clean-lined, modernist construction. It’s the walls made from whole redwood logs that does it. Flat-roofed and maybe a little more than a hundred and fifty feet wide, with a facade that consists of a single floor with few windows, the structure's main features are the oversized front door with its polished brass knob and Frank Lloyd Wright–inspired metalwork of the railings. It's a building that communicates its expense through its extraordinary natural materials in place of ostentatious grandeur.

"Do we go inside?" Bridge asks.

"I don't really want to."

This is out before I can prevent it, and I can see how it troubles Bridge. How she doesn't want to enter either. She's fourteen, and I'm twenty-two years older. A gap so wide you might assume we aren't close, but we are. We've made a point of it. My job is to be her dad-in-place-of-a-dad, offering advice on the rare occasions she asks for it, and her job is to make me feel like I'm not alone in the world.

"Let's explore a bit," I add, as casually as I can.

"Which way?"

"You're the one who's been here before. You pick."

Bridge looks around. We both do. There's a utility building off to the right at the edge of the trees where I assume the tools and maintenance machinery is kept, though there are no windows to look through to confirm this. I also note how its single door is padlocked.

On either side of the parking area are a number of trailheads leading off into the trees in different directions. Four in total, each with a small sign on a metal post. I have to squint to read the words: Red, Green, Yellow, Orange. The kind of generic route names you'd find on a corporate campus. I try to peer along the trails to see where they lead, but each of them, after a couple dozen yards, takes a turn and disappears into the uninterrupted woods.

"How about Green?" Bridge says.

We start toward the closest trailhead to our right. The trees seem to grow closer together as we approach, forcing our lines of sight to press into the spaces between their trunks only to be stopped by the trees behind them, again and again. It makes me think of looking into a mirror reflected in a second mirror, so that the image within the glass repeats itself into a bending, infinite curve.

"You first," Bridge tells me, nudging my back with her elbow.

It's meant to be funny, and we both force out a laugh, but neither of us move.

A memory has come at me so hard I feel it as a punch to the top of my chest, a fist that passes through skin, grasping and cold.

There seems to be little pattern to what brings it back. The forest, in this case. One that makes me remember a different forest. The men who emerged out of it, whooping and calling out names in a language I didn't understand. The blades they swung over their heads, catching winks of the sun.

A buried piece of a different life.

Overseas.

I force myself to go forward. Two steps into the trees.

"You hear that?"

Bridge doesn't answer, only pivots to look in the direction the sound came from. Movement through the trees. Sleek and dark and coming fast.

"Another car," she says.

We watch it ease to a stop in front of the lodge, the driver opening the back door and extending his hand for the passenger's phone just as ours had done. A second later our mother steps out.

"Hey!" Bridge shouts, and runs off. There's a strange dawning of recognition on Mom's face as she watches her daughter come and throw her arms around her as if they'd been separated by an absence of years instead of hours.

I'm about to make my way to join them when the hushed woods are interrupted by another sound. Not a car this time. A shuffling approach on the trail we were about to start on.

There's a temptation to pretend I hadn't heard it and run off as Bridge had. But my mother and little sister are here, and I'm the eldest son. Despite my fear, despite the memory of *overseas*, there is this—what I am in the family: the surgeon, stable and mature, committed to helping others. I can't run even if it's what I want to do more than anything else.

I have to tell myself all this in order to turn and look.

A figure makes its way toward me. Coming up a slope so that first its head, then its shoulders and legs become visible like a body rising up out of the ground. A woman. Gangly and slight, her arms flapping birdishly out from her sides.

"Aaron!"

She sounds different from when I last spoke to her, though that was almost a year ago, at Nate's funeral. Her son. Yet I can still recognize the scratchy, sarcastic tone as Franny's. My other sister, though the truth is I've never really thought of her that way. She was always something else before that. A phone call from the emergency room or police station in the middle of the night. A poisonous fog I tried to stay ahead of. Most of the time growing up it was like Franny was only waiting until she could move out and get into truly serious trouble.

Now here she is, a year younger than me but looking a dozen years older, half jogging my way in the ungainly, loping manner of someone whose legs are asleep.

"You beat us here," I say.

"I went for a walk. But I got spooked out there all on my own. That's a lot of *trees*. Too much nothing for this city girl." She glances over my shoulder. "Is that Mom?"

"She just pulled in."

"Well, the gang's all here then."

"Some gang."

Franny stands a few feet farther from me than she ought to. Taking me in. Comparing the man in front of her to the profile of me she'd framed in her mind. How long would she have to go back into her years of hustling and needles to find a picture she could recall in any detail?

"I'd say 'Sorry about Dad,' but I'm not sure what that really means," I say.

"It means he's gone. Even more than he was when he was alive."

"That pretty much nails it."

She takes a half step closer to me. "Before we go inside, it's important for me— I want you to know something, Aaron."

"Sure."

"I'm different now."

She searches my face for doubt. And I try to hide it. To not show, through some involuntary grimace or narrowed eyes, how many times I've heard this before from her. Sometimes through tears, sometimes in furious accusation, though mostly conveyed with the same stony conviction she speaks with now. It's convincing. As convincing as it was five years ago when she told me she was pregnant, and during the days in and out of rehab after Nate was born.

For almost her entire adult life, being an addict has been Franny's sole occupation. I'm sure she'd correct me about the past tense. Even recovered addicts are still addicts, the disease in remission but never wholly erased. I'm a doctor; I know I'm supposed to embrace this understanding of why people—why my sister—would devote herself to her own destruction from the first day she sneaked a twenty from our mother's purse. It wasn't a lack of will, not a flaw of character, but the bad luck of having contracted a virus. And as a disease is never asked for, it has the power to excuse all cruelties and neglect committed along the way.

But the truth is, I can't talk myself out of seeing Franny the same way I see myself. An escape artist. I ran from my life, and she did too, if only figuratively, following a trail of fixes instead of twenty-six-mile courses through the streets of different cities.

In both cases, you collapse at the end.

In both cases, you finish where you started.

And now here Franny is telling me she's broken the cycle. Underweight and with a twitchy uncertainty to the way she shapes her face, as if constantly adjusting an emotional dial between dead and insane, searching for the human midpoint. But not stoned. Her words clear and firm even if the rest of her isn't. And as for making a change, I should know it's possible. I did it for Bridge. Maybe Franny has done it as a memorial to her own child.

"I'm on a new path," she says. "And I'm not talking about all the stuff that's happened with the government and the police and the camps—that's made it different for *all* of us. I'm talking about me. A new direction."

"I can see that."

"No, you can't. Because it's not on the outside, not something you can see. It's not just that I'm sober now. And it's not only about losing Nate. It's *me*. I've turned things around. I work in a shelter now, did you know that?"

"I think Mom mentioned something."

"Doing good work in a bad place."

"That's great, Franny. Really."

But she doesn't want to hear my words of support. This, it's clear by her rigid jaw and hands gripped into pale-knuckled fists, is a prepared speech that must be spoken aloud, regardless of the audience. She's doing it to hold herself together, to prove that she is inching beyond the range of grief, that she can exist here in what remains of our father's shadow.

"Whatever happens today—whatever Dad left for us—I'm giving it to the shelter. That's the only reason I've come. I'm going to pick up my check, get right back into that limo, and do something positive with what I have."

"I believe you," I say. And I do.

I can't attest to whether or not my sister will go back to using once she returns to the city, but I'm certain she will do this. I know what it's like to make a sharp turn, to give shape to life by way of one big move. After that, however, all bets are off.

"It's good to see you, big brother," she says, and surprises me by wrapping her scrawny arms around my neck and pulling in close. She smells of lemony soap and coconut hair conditioner and lilac body spray. She smells clean.

2

I EXPECT MOM TO BE CRYING WHEN FRANNY AND I WALK OVER TO JOIN HER AND Bridge. From the bereavement of losing her husband, yes, but also the image of seeing her three children around her, opening their arms to take her in. Normally this would be more than enough to shatter her into spare parts. But while she appears underslept and a little shaky on her feet, her face is dry, the permanently etched, meek downturns of brow and mouth hardened into determined lines.

"My babies," she says, and I'm startled to find that I'm the one fighting tears.

We stay like that for a while. The surviving Quinlans. Linked in an awkward group hug, none of us able to find words to fit the moment.

Bridge is the first to pull away.

"Something's coming out," she says.

We all turn to find the brass handle of the lodge's front door glinting as it moves in a slow rotation. It allows the additional second required to register the word Bridge had used. *Something*.

The door slides inward. It's too dark to see much of anything, so that it seems it's opened on its own like the doors to cobwebbed manors did in the Saturday-morning Halloween spoofs I grew up with.

After a pause an elderly man steps out, as if assuring himself that all eyes are on the threshold before stepping through into the wan light.

"Hello, Quinlans!"

It's probably nerves, a reflexive response to the unintentionally comic tenor of the old man's Bela Lugosi–like welcome, the strangeness of being in this place together after so long being in other places apart—whatever it is, all of us burst into laughter.

For a moment, we're a little less worried, a little less brittle. The trees themselves lend us space, leaning away as if confirming the harmless humor intended by every detail of this performance. Limos! Silent drivers who take your phones! A funny stranger beckoning to us!

Eventually we quiet, returning to politeness with cleared throats.

"Please, come in. Come *in*," the man at the door says again.

The laughter is over. Nothing of it remains. The forest has swallowed it whole. The man at the door waits, waxy, preposterous. Yet despite all this, the signs of things sliding from strange to wrong, we have no choice but to carry ourselves up the steps and slouch inside.

3

IT TAKES A MOMENT FOR OUR EYES TO ADJUST ONCE THE DOOR IS CLOSED. THERE are lights on—multiple bulbs set into a chandelier overhead, one that's made of what looks like animal bones fused together into an ornate, alien rib cage—but they're dimmed. For a time, all we can focus on with certainty is the man standing before us, a canine smile stretched tight above his chin. He's got to be the lawyer. It's the boastful accessories that give him away. The monogrammed cuff links, Ivy alumni tie, chunky Rolex. Evidence of decades spent tallying up the top-end billable hours.

He introduces himself as Mr. Fogarty. A caricaturizing surname like a minor character out of Dickens. In fact, he *looks* like a minor character out of Dickens: silver reading glasses balanced on the end of his beakish nose, small yellow teeth, the navy three-piece suit with a vest he keeps adjusting but never unbuttons despite the humidity.

He looks at each of us in turn.

"This is all of you?"

"Who else were you expecting?" Franny says.

The lawyer spins on the heels of his leather oxfords to face her. "No one in particular."

"Okay. I know it's not your fault or anything, Mr. Fogarty. But I think I can speak for all of us when I say we're not totally comfortable with being dragged out here for something we could have done far more easily downtown," I say, backing Franny up while attempting businesslike civility. "So can I suggest we get started?"

He purses his lips as if sucking on a lemon. *Let's get started* was supposed to be his line and I stepped on it.

"You're the surgeon," he says. "I understand. Eager to return to work."

"I just don't want to be here," I say, and as soon as I do, I realize how deeply I feel it—a claustrophobic's urge to escape despite the abundant space of the front hall we stand in.

"Of course. It's a difficult time," the lawyer says vaguely, and starts off around a corner, leaving the rest of us to follow.

From the front the lodge was impressive in its dimensions, but as we enter at one end of the great room, the building reveals its true magnificence. Across from us stands what must be an almost twenty-foot-high wall of floor-to-ceiling windows that frame the dappled woods, deepening as the trees rise up a gentle slope so that there is no sky to be seen, only variations of green leaves and brown deadfall. We traverse a raised walkway of varnished oak opposite the glass with steps down to a sunken living room of modular leather sofas and Turkish rugs laid over the wide floorboards, a stone hearth big enough to stand in, and finally, looking over it all at the opposite end from where we first entered, a banquet dining table made of recovered barn planks.

This is where Fogarty stands behind a chair at the head, gesturing for each of us to sit. I stay close to Bridge, taking a place between her and the old lawyer as if to fend off a potential assault. Franny takes the spot across from us, and Mom sits directly to Fogarty's left, her instinct for good manners and hospitality active even now, despite this not being her home nor the lawyer a guest.

"Let me first express my condolences," Fogarty begins, the last to pull his chair back and lower himself into it, fussily touching the papers and files laid out before him as if practicing a complicated piece on a piano keyboard. "I didn't know Mr. Quinlan well—he was exact in his directions but a fierce defender of his time, as perhaps you're already aware—but if I may say, he struck me as a remarkable individual. One of the privileges of my work is meeting highly varied people of accomplishment, and your husband and father had a way about him that will remain with me. I struggle to pinpoint the precise nature of his uniqueness, the *aspect*, in addition to his obvious intelligence, that I found so—"

"He was a remarkable man," Mom interrupts him. Her hand flutters to her mouth as if in an attempt to retrieve the bitterness of her words.

"Indeed," Fogarty says. He likes this scene—the Reading of the Will—and its demonstrations of emotion like this that he's obliged to at least appear to subdue while allowing himself to savor at the same time.

"Do you know what he did for a living, Mr. Fogarty?" Franny asks.

"You didn't?"

"We took guesses sometimes. Thought he might have been a scientist. Sometimes we wondered if he was a spy. But he wasn't really the double-oh-seven type. And do spies or scientists own places like this?"

"I couldn't speak to that," Fogarty says, "and as for my knowledge of his occupation, I haven't a clue, I'm afraid. I handled his legal affairs—well, some of them—but it wasn't necessary to know the specifics of his business."

"That's interesting. Because we all came to the same conclusion."

"Oh?"

"It wasn't necessary to know who he was," Franny says. "Because, for us, there was nobody *to* know."

Fogarty waits for more of this, but when Franny sits back, fighting the new twitch at the top of her cheek, we all look to him.

"Shall we pause a moment?" he asks, lifting an expensive-looking pen from the table and waving it in slow, hypnotizing circles. "Do we need a break?"

"No break," Mom says, her voice now froggy and thick. "Please continue, Mr. Fogarty."

"Very well. Now, the way this works is quite straightforward," he says brightly. "You've been asked here to attend the reading of Raymond Quinlan's last will and testament, and as executor of that will, I am responsible for its administration. There are a number of what might be considered unconventional codicils here, but at its heart, the document is—"

"How much?"

This question takes all of us by surprise not only by its abruptness, but by who asks it. Mom. Leaning forward so heavily her elbows rest on bloodless white pads of skin.

"Mrs. Quinlan, a proper valuation would only be accurate once the assets have been liquidated, if and when that occurs."

"How much did he have?" she asks again, then looks around the table at the faces watching her, and only now hears the brusque tone of her voice.

"Forgive me, Mr. Fogarty," she continues, softer now. "My husband kept many secrets from me during his life, an arrangement I accepted, more or less. Even when we were young and first dating, he told me there were things about him I could never know. What did I care? There was love to make up for knowledge. I signed an extensive prenuptial agreement before they were common, or so I was later told. But now that he's gone, I don't want to live with secrets anymore. I couldn't care less about the money—I have little use for it, God knows—but until today I was unaware this place existed. Quite something to keep from your wife of forty-two years, wouldn't you say?"

Fogarty replies with a lawyerly shrug.

"So now there's someone who is possessed of information sitting in front of me," Mom goes on. "Now there's *you*, Mr. Fogarty. So you can understand my eagerness to learn as much as I can, and in as specific terms as it's known."

"Yes, I can see all that. I certainly can," the lawyer says sympathetically. "Well, let me jump to the bottom line then. Mr. Quinlan's holdings weren't complicated. He had transferred his financial instruments—stocks, funds, etcetera—into a cash account only months before his death. The amount"—Fogarty glances down at his papers before looking up again—"is presently just over three million dollars."

"But that's not all of it," Mom says.

"No."

"Because there's this place. What did he call it?"

"Belfountain," Bridge says.

"Quite right," Fogarty says, glancing at Bridge with theatrical astonishment.

"Belfountain," Mom repeats distastefully, as if it's the name of her husband's mistress. "How much of it is his?"

"All of it. No partners, no mortgage."

"What's it worth?"

"Forgive the cliché, but a property of this kind is only worth what someone is willing to pay for it."

"My mother might, but I don't forgive the cliché," I say. "You know the ballpark. So tell her."

I expect a dirty look from Fogarty, but he merely casts a cool smile my way. That's when I see it. The reason I feel such hostility toward this man, and maybe why Mom and Franny feel it too: he reminds me of Dad. Not in his looks or attire, but the superiority, the withholding of information, the way he'd make you ask for everything and in the asking reveal your neediness. It's a game I told myself I'd never play again, and yet here I am, perspiring with frustration, trying to intimidate this older man whose very posture confirms his control, the compiling of every weakness he'd detected in me.

"It's six hundred acres of pristine rain forest. One of the finest undivided tracts of its kind in the Pacific Northwest," he answers at an unhurried pace. "The sleeping cabins are modest but well-built, and in entirely good repair. And of course there's the main building we sit in now, an exceptional piece of contemporary architecture. So while the assessed value of the estate for tax purposes stands at twenty-seven million dollars, I expect it would attract offers significantly higher than that if listed on the open market."

No one replies to this, not right away. It is a Life-Changing Moment in the same way, I suppose, that hearing a terminal diagnosis or your newborn's first cry is. Of course, in this case, it's only money. But that can do it too if there's enough of it. An amount that, even without doing the math, each of us hears for what it is. Safety. Freedom. Transformation.

Mom is the first to eventually speak. A woman who is close to tears at the best of times, a four-decade state of weepy readiness, awaiting the triggers of nostalgia or affection or joy, but more often reminders of the long-buried disappointment in herself.

"Why did he need it to be so big?" she asks nobody in particular. "Six hundred acres! Guest cabins. And this place, the size of a small hotel. What did he *do* here?"

Fogarty tents his fingers and sets them on the table.

"I appreciate how eccentric this must appear to you, Mrs. Quinlan," he says. "But I was his attorney, not his valet. I'm not aware of—"

"Did he have—were there *friends* who would come to stay? Were there *parties*? I mean, what kind of parties would they *be*?" she laughs, no longer addressing the lawyer, merely speaking her confusion aloud, questions that echoed up to the room's timber rafters. "He didn't have friends.

We didn't have friends! Not the kind who would come to a—to a private resort in the woods to—to *what*? Do *what*?"

"These are undoubtedly legitimate questions, but they fall outside my—"

"Seven and a half million."

All of us turn to Franny. And she looks back at us with the expression of someone who has spoken aloud without intending to.

"I'm just saying," she says. "Assuming the minimum sale price of the property, and the proceeds equally divided among the four of us." She looks at Fogarty. "Am I right?"

"I won't hazard an estimation on the math," he says, "but you are correct in your assumption of the will's stipulating an equal division of assets. As I said, despite the specific nature of the holdings coming as a surprise to you, your father provided clear legal directions, if also some rather unusual conditions."

He lets this last part hang in the air, waiting for it to snag in our minds, a tightness to his lips that I read as a tell of excitement. He's not just an arrogant old-school dandy, I see now. Fogarty is a closet sadist.

"What conditions?" I say, and make a point of squeaking my chair closer to him. I'd like to make him uncomfortable if I can. But I also want to physically buffer Bridge from the strangeness I can sense is about to be unleashed upon us.

"Your father assigns all his assets, in equal terms, to his wife and all of his children," Fogarty pretends to read from the papers in front of him, then raises his head to speak directly to me. "On satisfaction of a single request that all of you stay on here at Belfountain for thirty days."

"What are you talking about?"

"Which piece is giving you difficulty?"

"Having to stay here for a month. Why don't we start with that?"

Fogarty takes in a long breath and billows it over the table in my direction, a hot gust carrying the scents of mustard and butterscotch candy.

"Wills are expressions of wishes," he says. "And your father wished for you, your siblings, and your mother to live here together for a period of time after his passing. I can only assume it was for the purposes of collective grieving, or perhaps reconciliation. Families are families, yes? In any case, to participate in the division of funds, each of you must remain on the property for the duration of the term. Naturally, the delivery of food and supplies has been arranged for, and you'll find comfortable bedding has been—"

"What if we leave?"

This is Franny. Fogarty takes his time shifting around to face her.

"You forfeit your share of the estate," he says.

"Even for a day? I mean, there's things that need to be taken care of. We all have *lives*."

"The instructions are clear. The perimeter of the estate marks the extent to which you may travel."

"I'd like my phone back."

"That would violate the conditions. No phones, no internet. No outside contact of any kind."

"Is this for real?" Franny says, starting to stand and then sitting again as if against a swirl of dizziness. "You're talking about a prison!"

"Not at all. You're free to go at any time."

"At a cost."

"A forfeiture."

"When does the clock start?" I ask.

This provides Fogarty with the moment he's been waiting for. He pinches up the sleeve of his shirt an inch to reveal the Rolex on his wrist and clicks a button at the side, starting the timer.

"Now," he says.

4

IT GETS NOISY AFTER THAT.

Franny shrieking about calling the police, Bridge crying and me trying to comfort her while telling Fogarty where he could shove his gold watch. Most troubling of all is Mom. The unhinged sound of her hate-cackling at the last trick her husband had played on their marriage.

Maybe it is the haunting amplification of our voices through the cavernous interior of the lodge or the long drive here only now taking its toll, or the questions in our minds jostling and demanding to be asked first. Whatever it is, we all go quiet at the same time. Blustering and aflame moments ago, now exhausted, leaning into the table's edge or the backs of our chairs to hold ourselves upright.

Fogarty lowers his voice to little more than a whisper.

We listen.

He tells us that he's drafted notices to be sent to our respective schools or workplaces explaining our absences as a "family emergency." If any of us have partners or companions requiring similar explanation, he's prepared to do the same for them, but he believes none of us have significant others at present, and seeing how none of us correct him, it appears he's correct. No one will contact the authorities. No one will come looking for us.

In addition to regular deliveries of food, he's arranged for clothes in our sizes and a pair of sneakers for each of us in duffel bags he deposited in the front closet. There is no television or radio or computer anywhere on the estate's grounds, and no books or magazines to speak of, but we're assured of an "impressive collection of jigsaw puzzles" for our entertainment.

"You make it sound like a game," Franny says.

The old lawyer looks heavenward for an alternative phrase. "It's merely a request of the deceased. It lacks the competition of a game. Although, I suppose, there is an element of endurance. A test, then?"

"What happens if we all walk?" I ask.

"In that instance, Mr. Quinlan has arranged for his estate to be assigned to his alma mater."

"He'd give it all to his *college*?" Mom says.

"They'd probably name a dorm after him," Franny says.

"The amount is more than sufficient for that," Fogarty replies, taking Franny's point in earnest. "But Raymond's directions were for the donation to be anonymous."

"Of course," Franny says. "The invisible man."

Fogarty informs us that while there is technically no reason to make a final decision now—we can leave anytime and use the satellite phone in a metal box just on the other side of the gate to arrange for a ride—he will linger a short while in case any of us wants a ride back this afternoon.

"Hold on. Just *hold* on," I say, keeping him there as he seems about to slip out of the room. It takes a second to catch my breath, and I realize how exasperated I am, a helplessness that has led me to the edge of vertigo, my toes and fingertips tingling.

"Yes?"

"I don't think you understand. I'm a *surgeon*."

"I understand perfectly, Dr. Quinlan."

"There's patients—there's people counting on me."

"As I've already mentioned, your absence will be explained. You have colleagues who can cover your case list in such instances, do you not?"

"That's not the point."

"What is the point?"

I'm important. This is what I want to say. I'm a medical specialist, and these are difficult times. Some are calling it a national crisis, and who would argue otherwise? Emergency rooms across the country are over capacity with those who need to be patched, stitched, reassembled. But I say nothing. Partly because Franny speaks for me first.

"The point is he's a big deal," she says. "He's worked so hard to be one, to show his daddy what a good boy he could be, and he thinks he should be entitled to an exemption."

My sister looks at me without particular malice, only the fixed *Am I wrong?* expression of the aggrieved.

"Maybe this isn't the best time for a family therapy session," I say.

"No? When *would* have been a good time, Aaron? When I was in trouble taking care of Nate on my own and you were barely able to force yourself to return my calls? Or how about when he died? Even *then* you showed up late to the service and left early because you couldn't wait to disappear back to the hospital, where you could be everybody's savior." She cracks a wincing smile. "You know something? You're more like Dad than I thought."

Most of this strikes me as unfair. I *had* tried with Franny, taken dozens of runs at being a brother and a friend. But once she'd decided on her course, there was nothing I could do to coax her back, other than running my own life aground in the process. She might be cured now, she might be clean. But that doesn't mean she gets to rewrite the story.

Where she may not be entirely off is the disappearing act I've cultivated over the years. *I have to go*. My refrain the same as Dad's.

"I'll give you a little privacy to discuss amongst yourselves," Fogarty says, only half suppressing his pleasure at all this as he starts toward the walkway to the entry hall. But Mom stops him.

"We're staying," she says, and shifts her gaze around the table, taking her children in one by one. "All of us."

"We don't have to do this, Mom. We could challenge it. In court, I mean," I say, with a confidence I don't actually possess. "There's no way this is enforceable."

"He wanted us to stay, Aaron," she says. "Which means he wanted it for a reason."

"What reason?"

"To show us something. Reveal his secrets. Or maybe just one of them. That's enough for me."

"I don't understand."

"I've devoted my life to a stranger," Mom starts, measuring her words, "and it's left something missing in me. Just as the three of you—it's *damaged* you. So I need to see the truth. Don't you?"

It strikes me how close Mom's words are to what I told Bridge when we first got into the limo. *Some part of me felt empty before you came along. A corner the light couldn't reach.* I meant it as a consolation for her losing Dad, the comfort that might come with knowing that although she'd lost a life in the past two days, she'd saved mine over the years before this.

But now here was Mom saying the same thing. *Something missing in me*. It's fairly obvious Franny has felt the same from the very beginning. Was it true for Bridge as well? Always a note about her "perfectionism" on report cards, and worryingly friendless outside of school hours.

"Bridge?" I say, turning to her.

"I'm not going."

"Me neither," Franny says.

"Okay. Looks like we're all in," I say, checking to see Fogarty's reaction. The lawyer is already starting away with a flapping wave of his fingers, clapping down the walkway in his hard-soled shoes. We all wait for him to call back with final instructions or wish us good luck. But a moment later we hear the front door swing closed, and there's nothing more.

5

WE PRETEND TO BE LESS FREAKED OUT THAN WE ACTUALLY ARE FOR MAYBE three or four minutes before Franny goes to check out front. When she returns, she looks even skinnier than before. The limbs she'd held straight through force of will are now rolling and loose, her gait wobbly as a baby giraffe's.

"He's gone," she says. "The cars too."

"So this is real," I say.

"Yeah. I pinched myself to make sure. Like, *hard*."

There's a sense all of us share of having a lot of important things we should be doing right now, rules and assignments to be written up. But none of us move.

"He wasn't lying about the duffel bags," Franny says. "And there's a bicycle outside the door that wasn't there before. One with a wagon attached to the back."

"I'm guessing that's for the deliveries," I say. "It's up to us to go to the gate and bring back whatever gets left there."

"Why a bike? Why not a pickup truck or golf cart or something?"

"Dad wanted us to get more exercise?"

The fact is I have an immediate idea about the bike. Nonmotorized. Our phones are already gone. Fogarty was careful to mention no TV or computers or radio. It may be less about denying us connection to the outside world than it is about limiting our options. Dad wanted to leave us with everything except an easy way out. He wanted to leave us with us.

"Anyone hungry?" This is Mom. Abruptly standing and clearing away her previous displays of emotion with a sharp sniff. "Where do you think the kitchen is in this place?"

She starts off, and our eyes follow her around a partition at the end of the dining area, up a few steps to another platform that looks down not only on the great room but the walkway that runs the length of it.

"It's up here!" she calls. There's a rubbery sucking sound as she opens the fridge. "Well, look at that. Something for everyone!"

She's working so hard at restoring her role as mother, chief children feeder and normalizer, it would be heartbreaking if the three of us didn't need it so badly. That, and judging by the way we wordlessly move away from the table and closer to her voice, we actually could use something to eat.

We come up the steps to find that the kitchen is just as impressive as the lodge's other spaces. Rectangular like the great room, it runs for perhaps forty feet from the dining area to the pantry, with an industrial gas range and a butcher block of the kind you'd find in a restaurant kitchen and steel shelves holding enough stacked plates and bowls to serve a wedding. A series of three long windows look out the front where I confirm that the limos are in fact no longer there.

There's a tinted mirror at a corner of the ceiling opposite the sink, one that's angled downward to reflect whoever stands at the butcher block like the ones they have on cooking shows. I catch a glimpse of myself in it when I turn, a more lost-looking version than my usual confident self as I scrub in or do rounds with a pack of interns following behind me.

By the time we gather around Mom, she's laid out open Tupperware containers of cold roast chicken, broccoli salad, spinach dip. Picnic food. We set to spooning it onto plates, eating as we stand there together, not wanting to return to the unprotected expanse of the dining room's banquet table.

"That shit'll kill you," Franny says as I drop a handful of potato chips onto the side of my plate. "And didn't you used to run four times a week or something? No offense, Aaron, but don't you think you could lose a few pounds?"

I'm not especially tall, but despite the couple extra inches around the waist added over the last few years, I remain slight in the limb-stretched way tall people generally do. Even in my marathoner days, I would often look like someone suffering a nutritional deficiency. Back then it was because I ran too much. Now it's because I work too much.

"Don't you think you could gain a few ounces?" I say, pouring some chips onto her plate before scouring the cupboards. "Oh no. This is *bad*. No booze."

"It's for the best, believe me. Think of this as rehab."

"If you start twelve stepping me, Franny, I swear I'm out of here."

"Great! The rest of us will split your share. So, first step: admit you are powerless and your life is unmanageable."

"Now that I think of it, as of today, both are officially true."

It's teasing banter, brother and sister giving each other harmless jabs like old times. Except I don't remember us ever being this open and easy in the old times.

A family eating a meal together. For a moment we're relaxed, relieved of all the questions that demand replies. Then I look over at Bridge, and, watching her chew and swallow, the moment of ease instantly passes.

The scar along her throat reminds me how close we can come to losing everything.

For me, that's her.

From time to time, I've thought it was odd—maybe even a little pathetic—to not have any real social life other than my Tuesday get-togethers with Bridge. Should I be living a fuller life than this? Is even asking this question an obvious sign that I'm not? Then again, the people I know with spouses or kids—most of them feel the same way. There could be dozens who cared about you, or only one, and in both cases you were left to wonder if it was enough.

Bridge looks over at me. Sees—as she can always see—how I'm muscling through these kind of thoughts. She gives me a kick in the shins.

"Save any chips for me?" she says.

"Really? Now *you're* giving me flak about the damn Pringles? Here, have mine."

I offer her a chip, holding it like a communion wafer, and she comes at it, teeth bared. I pull my fingers away a quarter second before she bites the chip out of the air.

6

AS WE TIDY UP AFTER DINNER, I CATCH MYSELF WATCHING MY MOTHER AS IF SHE were someone I'd only seen pictures of, a washed-up celebrity in a checkout counter magazine, but now had the opportunity to observe up close. She would have been beautiful when my father first met her. A sophisticated face, but one from a different era. An aging screen star from the old studio system, Olivia de Havilland, say, or Joan Fontaine. It makes her appear older than she is. Not necessarily in years but in her place in cultural time. Slightly lost in the way of a foreigner who doesn't understand the local slang.

In recent years, her face has been difficult to find, as she's taken to hiding it behind longish bangs, the collars of her coats raised to her jawline. Her body is increasingly hidden too. Mom entered the Shawl Age earlier than others, abandoning dresses in favor of layered wraps. For other women, these bundled fineries might be seen as a way of expressing yourself as one moves from a certain age to another. But I don't think my mother saw it that way. For her it was protection. A suit of armor composed of cashmere and silk.

As if feeling my eyes on her, Mom turns to face me. Smiles with a widow's exhausted pride.

"It's good you never got married, Aaron," she says.

"Never say never, Mom. I've still got time."

"Take all the time you want. It will still be someone you'll never really know."

Franny and Bridge pause to observe this exchange, but from a distance, like a show on TV in a dentist's waiting room.

"That's kind of negative, don't you think?" I say, offering a quick eye roll in Bridge's direction. "You're talking about Dad. Not everyone's like him."

"It doesn't matter who it is. They'll be someone with thoughts and plans they won't share—even when they're sharing their thoughts and plans."

"Not if they love you," I say, and it sounds pitiful, even though I believe it to be true.

Mom comes over and touches my face with a hand covered in dish soap, leaving a trail of popping bubbles on my skin.

"I don't know about love," she says in her singular tone of cheerful defeat. "But marriage? It's a game. And people like us are built to lose every time."

"What do you mean, people like us?"

"The bad liars."

My parents never spoke of divorce, not in front of me anyway, yet it haunted their marriage like a missing child. They couldn't have been satisfied. They weren't together enough for that. Our family wasn't together enough for that.

Other kids at school had more outwardly objective reasons for being pushed off course in their lives. The captain of the swim team, Jake Envers, had a mother who committed suicide by idling her car in their closed garage while sitting in the back seat with a bottle of pinot grigio and all the Mother's Day cards Jake had ever given her. Mr. Illington, down the street from us, went to prison for fraud, and the rest of his family had to stand on their front lawn as they watched the bailiffs take the furniture out of their home. I could never say so, but part of me envied those kids. At least they had clear answers to "What *happened* to you?" The best I could come up with was that I had no memory of my father ever opening his arms to me.

I tried to make up for it. I clung to my mother as much as I could, for one thing. I told Franny I loved her so often she asked me to cut it out. I left letters for my father on the desk in his study, and when he came home, he would place them into a drawer, unopened.

Through high school, Franny busied herself by skidding into the slow-motion crash of her life. And dancing along with her was Mom, always a step behind, hopelessly trying to shield her daughter while, at the same time, denying there was any real problem at all.

It left me to keep us a unit. Keep us the Quinlans. That's how I saw it, anyway. Like the passenger with a fear of flying who believes she alone maintains the plane suspended in air by holding her breath, I thought I was preventing us from spiraling apart by being good. Good grades, good at sports. Avoiding trouble in all its forms. Not *too* good—I was conscious of not shaming Franny—but striking a balance between being the kind of son and brother you could be proud of while not having to think about him too much.

I declined acceptance to colleges back East and went to Washington State. Mom agreed it was a good idea. "Just in case," she said. It was what she would say every time I decided against taking a risk. *You should be here, Aaron. Just in case.* She never said what dire possibility she had in mind, but we both understood it to mean one of them dying. Franny, Dad, herself. If any of them dropped, I would come in and clean things up, make sure Bridge was taken care of. Until then, I would remain on standby.

Waiting for something terrible to happen can leave you with a lot of free time. That's why I started running. Marathons that wiped me clean. Provided the illusion of a fresh start.

I ran to get away.

But I could never get away.

There was no getting Dad back, even then. Mom was too swaddled in antianxiety pills and defense mechanisms to be fully reached. Franny was Franny. Which left Bridge. The only child in a home that felt underpopulated even on the once-a-year-or-so occasions we all found ourselves in it.

I slipped into the role of surrogate father without much effort. Not just because Bridge's real dad had resigned from the post, but because the two of us got along so well. There was an ease between us you wouldn't necessarily expect across the awkward chasm that divides a five-year-old girl from an introvert grown man. I think part of it came from the fact that I saw something of myself in Bridge. The brave solidity that, if you looked close enough, was slightly askew.

But along with this, I was curious.

How did she see our home, our mother, our father of the top secret phone calls that yanked him away from birthday parties and dance recitals and nine-tenths of the meals we'd eat? How did she seem to know him in a way the rest of us didn't?

Once the kitchen has been returned to design-magazine spotlessness, we all take a tour of the lodge. At the end of the walkway that acts as a spine for the whole building, dividing the kitchen on top from the living area below, we come to the bedrooms. There are three, each with its own en suite.

"Is it all right if I take this one?" Mom asks before sitting on the edge of the bed in the third bedroom we poke our heads into.

"Of course," Franny says. "I'll be right across the hall."

"What about you two?"

"I want to check out one of the cabins," Bridge answers before I do.

"You can't stay out there all on your own," Mom says, making a move to rise but finding she doesn't have the strength.

"I won't be alone," Bridge says, and elbows me in the side. "Aaron will be with me."

After I carry Mom's duffel bag to her room and tell her and Franny good night, Bridge and I head out the front door, each of us with our own bags strapped over our shoulders, to once again choose between the four trails into the woods.

"How about Orange," I say. "Anything but Green. I don't like Green."

"Orange it is."

What I hope will be enough dusky light to see by instantly snuffs out as soon as we start into the trees. There are LED headlamps included in each of our packs, and we stop to put them on, clicking the beams to their brightest setting. The light pushes back against the encroaching charcoal night like a yellow fist.

We walk along a trail that, after the first fifty yards, narrows so that we have to proceed single file. Me ahead and Bridge behind, both of us crunching over twigs and fallen leaves more loudly than I would have thought possible even if we were jumping up and down in steel-toed boots.

"Hard to believe we're the only four people on all this land," she says.

I prevent myself from saying it, because I don't want to frighten her and because I have nothing to back it up with. But the truth is it doesn't feel like we're the only ones here. It could be other people, waiting. Or not. Whatever it is, it doesn't feel hidden. It feels like everything around us. Belfountain. The trees themselves seem to observe us with an interest bordering on hunger. The ground softening under our steps, testing its hold on us with tiny grasps of our heels.

"The time you were here with Dad," I say. "What did the two of you do?"

Bridge likes to wear her hair in a ponytail. When she turns to look at you—as she looks at me now—the hair follows a half second later, perching atop her shoulders as if interested to hear what you're about to say for itself.

"Just hike around," she says.

"Did he say anything?"

"Not really. He was kind of rambling, y'know? I was only five or something like that. Everything he said sounded like philosophy."

"Or riddles."

"Same thing."

"Do you remember anything from what he was rambling about?"

"One thing, I guess," she says. "We were walking along a trail like this one and we came to the end. There wasn't a cabin or anything. It just stopped. Dad stopped too. Asks me this question. Looking at me, totally serious, y'know? Like he was searching for the answer himself."

"What was the question?"

"'Where does the path lead after it ends?'"

I let the words tumble around in my head until I can't tell if they're familiar to me or I've just made them seem so.

"What do you think he meant?"

"It was Dad. How do I know?" Bridge says. "Something about coming to the end and deciding whether to go ahead and make a new trail or go back on the one already there."

"Sounds like a Hallmark card."

"The way I'm saying it, yeah. But the way *he* said it—it sounded like this Big Idea. Everything he said, especially that day—Me! Dad! Alone together!—seemed big." She pauses. "It's strange, but when I try to think of him, it's hard to even remember what he looked like."

I'd heard of this before. The way even the most significant people fade in the memory of those who live on after they die, the physical being of the person translated from photographic portraiture into a collection of feelings, words, scents, or touches. Yet no matter how normal I know it to be, as I try to summon a picture of my father's face to mind, there's little other than the thick-framed glasses, an on-again, off-again moustache, ears that revealed long filaments of hair when he stood with the sun behind him.

There's still the sound of his voice though. Still the sense there was something missing about him that went deeper than him being gone so much. Not just an absence. An erasure.

I stop walking, and Bridge, head down, bumps into me. I turn around and she's readying a laugh, as if I caught her off guard on purpose, but one look at my face and she sees I'm not joking.

"Geez, Aaron," she says. "What's up?"

"I want to ask you something. And I want you to know that whatever your answer is, it's between the two of us."

She crosses her arms. "Okay."

"Dad never hurt you or anything, did he?"

"Hurt?" she repeats, dwelling on the word, as if it belonged to a language she only partly spoke. "You mean like abuse?"

"Not violence. Not, you know, hitting. The other kind. Anything that was wrong."

I expect her to have to think about her answer, align her memory with her standards of certainty, but she replies right away.

"No," she says. "What about you?"

"I'm pretty sure not. But the *pretty sure* nags at me a little. More now that he's gone."

Bridge steps closer. Rises on tiptoes to press her finger to my temple. "What's going on in there?"

"That's what I'm not a hundred percent about. When I think of him sometimes, it's like I've hypnotized myself. Or maybe he hypnotized me. Isn't that the way some of the survivors of bad stuff describe it? Like it's a shape they can barely make out through a fog?"

Bridge lowers onto the flats of her feet again and looks out into the snarled curtains of forest as if scanning for something there, a visual puzzle that asked you to stare at a pattern until a second pattern showed itself. After half a minute, she shakes her head, looks back up at me.

"Just because there's a fog around us doesn't mean there's anything in it," she says, stepping around me and carrying on up the slope of the trail.

7

THE TRAIL THAT HAD BEEN LEVEL AT FIRST NOW SLOPES DOWNHILL, A CHANGE that makes it easier to walk with our packs but also pulls a deeper darkness over us. From out of the forest comes something new. A thrumming. Mostly unheard when vibrating at the bottom end of its range and prickly as static at the top. Insects. But something else too. Alive in ways that reach beyond the animal or vegetative kinds of life. An intelligence.

I don't ask Bridge if she hears it too. I don't want to make her afraid. And I don't want to make me more afraid if she doesn't.

It's hard to guess how far we've gone. Four hundred yards? Six hundred? I'm about to suggest heading back. Not just to sleep in the lodge for the night but to head back to the city at first light. The words are there, my lips shaped to speak them, and then our headlamps find the square outline of a cabin.

"Cozy," Bridge says, walking around me, opening the single door and disappearing inside.

Illuminated only by the swinging circles of our headlamps, the room looks merely unfamiliar: a scratchy-looking sofa, amateur forest landscapes hanging crooked on the walls, a round pine table covered with black knots like worrisome moles. But once we find the light switch, a pair of tabletop lamps spill gold up the walls and I see that Bridge was right. It's cozy.

"I'll take this room," she announces, already having turned on the lights in the small but workable kitchen, the bathroom, and each of the two paneled bedrooms with windows the size of shoebox lids over the headboards.

I drop my bag in the room next to hers, and I'm about to see if there's toothpaste and soap in the bathroom when I notice the closet door is open an inch. Was it that way when we came in? Something about it strikes me as intentional. An invitation to see what's inside.

"Hey! Check this out!"

Bridge comes in holding something in the palm of her hand. A circular, solid brass lid that she lets me click open.

"A compass," I say.

"Pretty cool, right?"

"Where'd you find it?"

"In a box in my closet. I'm actually really into geography and stuff like that at school, and we did orienteering last summer at my camp. Remember? But the compasses we used were crap compared to this one."

"Like it was meant for you."

"I'm definitely *keeping* it, so yeah. Why don't you look in yours? Maybe you got something too."

I know before I step over and pull open the closet door, just as Bridge knew it too. There will be another box and inside of it will be something just for me.

"Yours is bigger than mine," Bridge says when she sees the cardboard box wrapped with a single white bow on the closet floor. "Why don't you open it?"

I bend and hold the box in my hands a moment, measuring it for movement from inside more than for its weight, before untying the bow and lifting its lid.

"Shiny," Bridge says.

A running shirt and matching shorts. The super-lightweight kind I used to buy when I was serious about races, every gram I reduced from what I wore resulting in a theoretically improved pace. The fabric bright neon orange, dazzlingly reflective even in the cabin's dull light. Beneath these, my brand of running shoes, and in my size.

"This one's mine all right," I say.

"Don't you like them? You look *scared* or something."

"It's just strange. Don't you think?"

"That Daddy left us gifts?"

"Not the gifts. But that they were in the right cabin, the right room, before we even decided where we were going to stay the night."

Bridge considers this blankly before frowning.

"Well, I *like* mine," she says, and scuffs back into her room, closing the door before I can explain how that's not what I meant at all.

Before we fall asleep, Bridge speaks to me through her door. Something I've heard a hundred times. A strange kind of lullaby that calms her just as it does the same for me.

"It was July up at the lake," she says, and pauses, as if this is the story's title. "So hot the waves were like syrup. You and I standing at the edge of the shore's highest boulder, doing that countdown we thought was so funny. *One-ah*, *two-ah*, *three-ah . . . diarrhea!* Airborne long enough to wonder if we'd ever come down. Then everything went dark."

"But I was there."

"You were there. My big brother. We pulled ourselves up onto the floating dock. Started on the picnic we'd floated over in the rowboat. Laughing and eating and jumping around. Playing Peter Pan."

"You were nine."

"I was Wendy. And you were Hook, slicing the air with a dill pickle. We were having fun—and then we weren't. I could tell something was wrong from the look on your face. Before I knew I couldn't breathe."

"You ate too fast."

"Or laughed too much. Either way, you did what they told you in med school."

"The Heimlich."

"But it doesn't always work. It *didn't* work. All I'm thinking is *I'm dying*. But I'm almost okay with it, you know? Almost accepting. I'm watching you jump into the rowboat and pop open the tackle box like it's happening in a movie. You flicking through the rusted hooks and lures and pulling out a silver X-Acto."

"Less than ideal."

"*Much* less than ideal. But even when I figured out what you were about to do, I was fine with it. I trusted you. Even as I laid down on the dock and you cut a line through my throat, you told me with your eyes that you were my brother, that I would be fine."

"That's what I was praying for."

"And I am. I *am* fine."

That's how it ends.

A true story of panic that's somehow more calming than any song, and soon everything is quiet.

I'm awakened by a voice.

It's not that—it's something animal, it must be—yet it arrives as a human utterance, however shattered and alien. Outside the walls of the cabin. Distant, but piercing. A shriek of alarm that comes with the first blaze of pain, as long as the breath I hold in my chest.

When I finally exhale, it's gone. The night and the bedroom's darkness are comingled, endless.

I try to tell myself it was only some small, wild thing in the woods calling out in its death, the soundtrack to the forest's nocturnal cycle of hunting and hiding, but then it comes again. Unmistakable now.

My sister Franny. Screaming into the trees.

8

THE NIGHT PASSES OVER ME LIKE A VEIL.

I remember this feeling. The sensation of running without looking at the ground, each stride a launch into the air, its molecules ready to break apart and admit me to whatever lay beyond. A bargain between myself and the universe that, if I was fast enough, I could put gravity behind me once and for all.

Back then, I ran to be free of being.

Now I run toward my sister's voice.

I'd gotten out of bed and put on the shoes and neon shirt and shorts that came in the gift box without thinking about it. My body is fully in charge for the first time in years and it feels right.

Before I left, I shouted at Bridge to stay inside and lock the door. Will she do as I told her?

She will or she won't, my heart tick-tocks in reply.

Every question in my mind is spoken through the swing of my legs.

There's time or there's not.

I'm aware of cresting the slope up from the cabin and speeding faster down the other side, following Franny's voice more than the trail. I haven't hit a sprint like this since I was training for real, and now my lungs catch fire at the same time I fly out of the trees.

She's nowhere to be seen.

I carry around the lodge's closest corner, the saplings snuggled up to the walls slashing my cheeks and taking bites from my hands like attacking, unseen birds.

The pain stops the same time I do. My body making one last decision—*Don't go any closer*—before handing control back to my mind.

My sister is alone.

Standing in the powdery rectangle of light that comes through the wall of windows at the rear of the lodge. Staring into the trees with the stillness of someone who's just been shown something whose existence they would have never thought possible. It occurs to me only now that she's not screaming anymore.

"Franny?"

She doesn't turn. It forces me to walk closer, my eyes jumping between her and the spot she's focused on in the darkness.

I touch her shoulder.

"Aaron?"

She doesn't jump, doesn't face me. Only this word.

"I'm here."

She throws herself into me and I hold her. I'd like to go inside, but I've forgotten how, at certain moments, being in a family is a performance. Right now I'm the older brother who must appear fearless, so we stay like this.

"There was a man," she says when she finally steps out of my arms.

"Where?"

"Out there." She sweeps her limp fingers across the line of trees. "He was *staring* at me."

"What did he look like?"

"Tall. I couldn't really see his face. But I could see his mouth. Made me think of Mrs. Grainger, my third-grade teacher. If she saw a kid with his mouth hanging open like that she'd say, 'Are you trying to catch flies?' That was funny. But whoever *this* was? He wasn't funny at all."

"Did he say anything?"

"No," Franny says. "Once he knew I saw him, he came closer. Not really walking. Sort of—so slow, like he was *floating*. Like he—"

"Shh."

I look and listen. Not expecting anyone to walk out toward us, but hoping to detect some evidence of retreat, the returning swing of a disturbed branch or thud of a boot on the hollow earth. We stay that way for perhaps a full minute. The only thing my eyes catch on is something glowing on the ground a few feet away. A tongue of gray curling out of its orange mouth.

"Shit, Franny. Were you smoking?"

"Why the hell else would I be out here?" Her face sours, and she's the teenaged Franny again, ready to fight or lie or threaten. Do whatever was required to get away with it. "Are you *judging* me?"

"No. I just don't want you to set the whole state on fire."

She laughs at this, one that turns into a cough. "Too late. Haven't you been watching the news? The whole country's on fire."

I step over and crush Franny's cigarette butt under the heel of my shoe. When I look up from making sure it's out, I catch a glimpse of motion through the trees. A figure—or parts suggestive of a figure—that's there and then, in no more than a stride or two, soundlessly gone.

"Aaron? What's wrong?"

"Nothing."

"You saw something, didn't you?"

I turn to my sister. "I didn't see anything."

It's impossible to say if Franny accepts this or not. I spend virtually all of my waking hours working with other doctors and surgeons and lab technicians whose jobs require the straightforward exchange of blunt opinions. I'm not used to withholding troubling news. Which maybe makes Mom right. Makes me a bad liar.

Franny starts back toward the glass rear door of the lodge without saying anything more.

"Mom isn't up?" I call after her.

"Thick walls and Zoloft. I guess they really do the trick."

"What do you think it was, Franny?"

She looks back at me.

"I don't know, big brother. I didn't like it. And I don't think it liked me either."

She lingers, so I go ahead and say it. It's meant only as a harmless consolation, but instead the words come out too loud, too sure, striking into the night as a provocation.

"There's nobody there."

Franny snorts.

I should have done more for my sister; I know this. We both do. It's why I forgive her the angry glaze she pours over most of the words she directs my way. I don't forgive myself so easily. Bridge says everybody has a "thing," a defining talent or passion or problem. If she's right, then mine is an allergy to witnessing people in pain. I think of it as that—an allergic reaction, itchy and stinging—because to see suffering triggers it in me. It's why I became a doctor. But while as a surgeon I can work to diminish my patients' discomfort, Franny's kind is different. It comes not from physical damage but as a reaction to invisible assaults, the sense of not being wholly loved, not entirely wished for. I know because it is the kind of pain that afflicts me too.

Franny slips inside. I watch her pass through the living room and turn off the dimmed pot lights. The windows turn to blackboards smudged with the chalk of a quarter moon.

There.

It's not a sound that makes me look up. My response is automatic in the way one turns to see whatever has snapped a branch underfoot.

Someone's there.

So far off it's only the irregularity of the human shape against the backdrop of branches and tree trunks that renders it visible. Not the figure I might have caught a glimpse of as I put out Franny's cigarette.

An old woman.

Hunched, arms hanging too low at her sides, the gray aura of frizzled hair. She wears what may be a hospital gown or frayed bathrobe open at the front so that, as she sways slightly from side to side, the material shifts to reveal the downturned points of her breasts.

I want to run back the way I came. To prove courage to myself, I walk instead. But as soon as I've turned my back on her, my legs stretch their stride without my being able to hold them back, and my body is in charge again, building speed, carrying me away on the instincts of retreat.

9

I DON'T RETURN TO BED THAT NIGHT.

After telling Bridge a muted version of the truth—Franny being Franny, she'd gone out for a smoke and scared herself silly all alone in the woods—I promised her she was safe here with me. Whether it was this assurance or the weight of her fatigue, she was snoring like a puppy by the time I pulled her door closed.

There's an overstuffed leather chair in the cabin's living room, and I stay there until dawn, dozing off only to be rewarded with a foul dream I can't recall that left me coughing for air.

The old woman in the trees. Not a dream because I can see her and I'm awake. Not a dream because she was there.

But she wasn't. There's another line of thought reminding me of this. At once calm and bullying. *No matter what you saw, it wasn't real.* Words spoken in my father's voice.

I push it away as best I can. Listen for footsteps outside the cabin's walls. Get up half a dozen times to check that the tab on the handle is turned up in the locked position. Each time I do, I put my ear to the wood and try to feel if something else does the same on the other side.

When the light finally grows from the color of weak tea to limestone against the window's curtains, I knock on Bridge's door.

"You up?"

A moan sounds from the other side. "You're *waking* me up to *ask* if I'm up?"

"That's a yes?"

Once Bridge has pulled on some fresh clothes—a pair of jeans and a Yale sweatshirt, Dad's college, another gift from the grave more thoughtful than any he'd given in life—we head out into the forest's mist in search of coffee.

She's a tough kid. Not quick to cry when she falls out of the trees she still loves to climb or takes a kick to the shins on the soccer pitch. But that's not the kind of toughness I'm thinking of as I look at Bridge now. Hair a shiny auburn, the elongated green eyes and gap-toothed smile that communicate how she sees the comical aspects behind even the most earnest gestures. The kind of person people will fall easily, if perilously, in love with. She's laughingly told me stories about boys at school who already have, though she admits she doesn't know why. I have an idea. It's not because of her looks, not really. It's because they want to know what she's thinking.

"How'd you sleep?" I ask as we make our way along the trail, a steeper climb toward the lodge than I remembered it being in the night.

"Okay, I guess."

"Better than nothing. So, remind me of your position on bacon. I noticed some—"

"Aaron? What really happened with Franny last night?"

"I told you. She thought she saw something, but there was nothing there."

"How do you know that?"

"I looked."

"And you don't believe her."

"It's not that." I work to find the words that might get me out of saying what I don't want to say. "Franny is in recovery, on top of a whole world of grief. You might be able to recover from addiction, but I don't think you ever recover from something like what happened with Nate."

"I guess not."

"It wouldn't be surprising if someone who'd gone through that might hallucinate a bit here and there."

Bridge stops. I carry on for another couple strides before stopping and turning myself.

"You don't believe that," she says.

"Really? How are you so sure?"

"Because you don't sound like you. You sound like Dad. And because you think you might have seen something out there too."

How do parents do it? How do they stay ahead of their kids, cut them off at the pass, shield them from whatever they need shielding from? Either I'm too inexperienced at it to know, or all parents fail the same way I'm failing now.

"You're right," I say. "I don't think Franny was hallucinating. But just because she saw something doesn't mean it was anything bad. We're in the middle of hundreds of square miles of rain forest. There's still bears and deer and I don't know what else out here. It could've been anything."

Bridge absorbs this, stone-faced, before catching up and taking my hand.

"Don't lie to me again," she says.

"I won't."

"What we're doing here—this whole thing—won't work if we can't believe each other."

I squeeze her hand three times. Our code. We haven't used it in a while—we haven't held hands in a while, as she's moved into the physical aversions of teenagerhood—but she understands.

One squeeze means *I'm here.*

Two squeezes mean *I love you.*

Three squeezes mean *It's just me and you.*

We developed the code over the time we spent sitting side by side in the backs of taxis during our Tuesday get-togethers. Sometimes we go to the movies; sometimes I take her to her soccer practice or ballet. But there's always time to grab dinner, time to talk. While we both enjoy these meetings, I've come to rely on them probably more than she does. Her calling me out on the lies I tell myself is of greater use than the counsel I can offer about how to handle boys or teachers or bullies.

I'm about to say something along these lines when we come to the top of the slope. There, in the distance, the rectangular outline of the lodge appears through the tangled mass of trees.

I start toward it, but Bridge remains where she is.

"My turn," she says.

"Your turn what?"

"To be honest about something."

"Okay," I say, turning back to face her.

"The last few Tuesdays I haven't been able to make it to our dinners. Right?"

"You had rehearsals. The school play."

"They weren't rehearsals, Aaron."

"Where were you?"

"At the doctor."

"Why would—"

"I was being treated. But it's over. They say it's—it's *over.*"

She's trembling. But I don't go to her. Not yet.

"Treatment for what?"

"Childhood leukemia. You know what that means. You're—"

"Oh my God."

"The doctor. Chemo. Four rounds. The oncologist pretty much said I'm in full remission."

"Pretty much."

"Yeah."

She doesn't have to say the chances of recurrence are on the high side. She knows. We both know.

"Why didn't—you could have—"

I try to speak the one question that needs answering first, but I'm fighting against throwing up. So she answers it for me.

"That's why I wanted you to go. The whole Doctors Without Borders thing. I wanted you to get away from here and help overseas," she says, and it's so painful to hear the apology in her voice, but she shakes her head when I take a step closer. "You were always talking about *doing something*, Aaron. Well, that was something. Saving people who never thought anybody cared enough to save them. And I knew if you stayed here, you'd just be with me all the time. Waiting in the waiting rooms, waiting for results. Waiting to see if any of it worked."

"What's wrong with that?"

"Because I'm all you have. And if the treatment didn't—if I wasn't *here* anymore, I wanted you to have something else."

She puts her arms around me. I hold her and feel the life in her and imagine part of my own life transferring into her, strengthening her blood so it can better fight the alien cells drifting in it.

Because I'm all you have.

That this is true doesn't shock me. What leaves me standing there, empty and still, is the realization that she blames herself for injuries I suffered. *Overseas*. The changes in me that came after. The never being what I was before.

"It was nobody's fault," I manage to say, pulling away from her so I can see her face. "It sure as hell wasn't yours."

"I know that in my head. But it doesn't feel that way. I see what it's done to you, Aaron. And it—"

"No. *Please—*"

"It was me who made you go."

"You didn't make me. You were trying to shield me. And what happened over there happened *to me*, not as a consequence of anything you did. Promise me you'll try not to carry that, okay? Because it's bullshit if you do."

"Okay."

"And no more holding things back. The big things, anyway. It's like you said. This whole thing won't work if we can't believe each other. Right?"

Bridge nods. Uses the sleeve of her hoodie to dry my cheeks. Sniffs the air.

"Someone's up before us," she says.

"How do you know?"

"There's a fire."

10

MOM KNEW, OF COURSE.

She was the one to take Bridge to chemo treatments, sit with her in the doctor's offices, ask the questions phrased in ways that opened the door widest to optimistic interpretation. Mom kept all of it from me because Bridge asked her to.

"Don't get mad at her, okay?" she says.

"I'm not mad."

"Are you going to bring it up?"

"Can I?"

"I can't stop you. But it would be better if you didn't. Not *here*. I mean, what difference would it make?"

"Probably none."

"So. Breakfast?"

"To be honest, I don't know if I want to puke or eat."

"Start with eating. Then we'll just roll with it."

I can tell this is something Bridge told herself during her treatments, a way of summoning the will to move on to the next task, the next meal, the next endurance of discomfort. I decide to use it the same way.

We start for the lodge. Now I smell the fire too. The cherrywood smoke from the lodge's chimney.

And in the next second, both of us see that the front door is open.

Had it been this way moments ago when we'd come out of the trail? Had it been this way all night, for anyone to enter, or had Mom or Franny opened it this morning for us once they got out of bed? It's a question I mean to ask but slips away when Bridge and I come around the corner of the foyer to find Franny loping at us. Sliding on the walkway's smooth wood in fluffy pink slippers that must have been included in her duffel bag.

"Morning, *Brigitte*," she announces, saying Bridge's name in a French accent that has always annoyed her but Franny has never seemed to notice. "Mom's in the kitchen and there's orange juice and Lucky Charms. You like Irish cereal?"

Bridge recognizes that Franny is trying to get rid of her, but she decides to be obliging. Once Bridge is around the corner and out of sight, Franny leans in close.

"Don't tell Mom," she says, looking at me in a way that makes it clear she's referring to last night. Two sisters, two requests to not bring up upsetting things with our already upset mother within the last two minutes. All of which is fine with me. We're Quinlans. We might be bad liars. But all of us are good at keeping secrets.

"You're sure she didn't hear you?" I ask.

"I'm sure. She took a double dose of her bye-bye pills and she was zonked," Franny says. "This morning she's all 'I slept like a baby! Must be the fresh air!' "

"I already talked to Bridge about it."

"That's fine. She won't say anything to Mom either."

"How're you so sure?"

"Because she wants to protect her the same way we did when we were her age."

Once more I'm surprised by how one of my sisters knows so much more about the dynamics of my family than I do.

"You okay, Aaron?"

"Yeah," I say, rubbing at the itchiness of my face and feeling the new growth of beard there. "How about you?"

"Could use some sleep. Which is a hell of a thing to say first thing in the morning."

"Nothing that coffee can't fix."

"You're in luck then. I made a pot. Strong enough—

"For a spoon to stand up in it."

It's a Dad line. One of the few jokes I can remember him making.

"This stuff? Forget the spoon. It would hold up a fucking knife," she says, and slips her arm around mine, guiding me along the walkway toward the smell of toast and Danishes being warmed in the oven. It's sweet enough and I'm hungry enough that it fills the cavernous space of the lodge with a passable simulation of home.

"Hey, I wanted to ask you something. What ever happened to your friend from high school?" she says. "The super-cute one with the dorky name?"

"Lorne?"

"That's it. Lorne Hetman."

"Huffman."

"Whatever. Where is he now?"

"I have no idea. We weren't exactly friends by the time we graduated. In fact, we never spoke to each other again after that party at the Chaplets' house."

"Why? What happened?"

"Seriously? You were *there*."

"That doesn't mean anything," she says, and stops. "Tell me."

Lorne was the only person I might have once described as a best friend. We were both jocks but discovered a shared love for old movies, particularly the drive-in monster flicks from a generation earlier. *The Blob*. *Creature from the Black Lagoon*. *Godzilla*. We'd work our way through the cheesiest corner of the classics section of Blockbuster, then start all over again, staying up until dawn for sleepovers at my house.

It gave us the chance to talk about girls, his parents splitting up, my mysterious dad. It also allowed Franny to "bump into" Lorne after she came out of the shower wrapped in a towel, or for Lorne to ask Franny to join us, patting the cushion on the sofa next to him, promising her that Vincent Price in *The Tingler* would forever change her mind about "that dumb horror crap."

I was aware they were flirting. But I took it as only the most harmless kind: training for Franny (she was two years younger, a tenth-grade kid) and time-killing for Lorne. That's why when that spring Franny came down the stairs into the Chaplets' crowded rec room, reeking of pot smoke and wearing a Led Zeppelin T-shirt and cutoffs, I was surprised when Lorne immediately got up to offer her a beer. He wasn't being nice. He was *acting* nice.

A few beers later, as I watched from across the room, I could see Franny turn from looking playful to looking like she was going to throw up. I figured Lorne would retreat. She was wasted. She was my kid sister. But when he whispered something in her ear and started down the hall toward one of the basement bedrooms, Franny followed.

I remind Franny of all this, and when I'm done, she says she can't remember any of it.

"Well, the party, maybe," she concedes. "The Chaplets' place. The smell of it. Like cinnamon apples or something. We were there a lot, weren't we? Like, did the parents even *exist*? But Lorne and me getting it on—no, not really."

"You weren't getting it on with him, Franny. You were almost unconscious. He was—you were being *assaulted*. Or about to be, anyway."

"How would you know?"

"Because I checked on you. You heard me come in and looked at me from a thousand miles away."

"What did you do?"

"I told Lorne to stop. He told me to mind my own business. 'This is private, man.' As if that made everything cool. As if I had to honor whatever he wanted to do because it was happening in a room with a door."

"Did you leave?"

"No, Franny. I didn't leave. I threw Lorne off you, and when he started to talk shit to me, I punched him in the ear."

She looks like she's about to cry. But she laughs instead. "Why the *ear*?"

"I was aiming for his nose. But he moved."

"He must've been pissed."

"Not as much as I was. I started whaling on him in the hallway and into the rec room with everybody cheering us on at first and then, when they saw how freaked I was—like Lorne's-teeth-on-the-shag-carpet freaked—they got as far away as they could. I nearly *killed* him."

"I knew you guys had a falling out. I figured it was over a girl," she says. "I just didn't think I was the girl."

She looks out the enormous windows at the trees. Each taking on their own personality as the morning light plays over them, mutant branches and patches where leaves failed to fill in their green coat. An audience we'd only become aware of in the last moment.

Franny loops her arm around mine and pulls herself close, still looking outside.

"You gotta admit. This place is beautiful," she says.

"It's kind of unbelievable, actually."

"You're going to think I'm crazy, but maybe it's good we're in this place. Maybe we can be together here in a way we never could back there."

It's what I've hoped too. And right now it feels like something approaching the possible.

"You're right," I say. "I *do* think you're crazy."

She pulls away the arm that was around mine and gives my shoulder a whack, which is Franny's way of saying you're all right. You might just stand a chance.

11

WHEN WE JOIN THE OTHERS IN THE KITCHEN, I ASSUME THE BACON DUTIES AS Bridge works at her bowl of marshmallows and Mom looks in all the drawers and cupboards, taking inventory. Franny hands me a mug of coffee as the strips of meat send up salty smoke from the pan.

"Why would he make us do this?"

This is Bridge. And she's asking it of Mom, who rises from where she'd been rummaging through a stack of Tupperware under the counter.

"I was only his wife, baby," she says. "You're asking the wrong person."

"Whoever he worked for, did he do good things or bad things?"

"I always assumed they were good. Now? To be honest, I'm not so certain there's *anything* good you could do where they'd pay you the kind of money to buy a spread like this."

"But you have an idea," I say, and Mom turns to me.

"An idea about what?"

"Why we're here. You've got a theory."

Eleanor Quinlan is a woman who can say a hundred different things with a sigh. Right now, it's one of gathered strength. The resolve required to say the thing she'd rather dance around forever.

"Your father didn't have a very good family life growing up," she says. "I didn't know the details, but his own father left when he was young. His brother turned out to be a criminal of some kind. And his mother was unwell. Her nerves. That's all he would say about it. 'She had a nervous condition.' So he had to take care of her instead of the other way around."

"So what?" Franny says.

"I think he wanted something better than that for his own family, even if he didn't have the first clue how to achieve it. He approached you three, his marriage, his estate too, as it turns out—he managed all of it like chemicals in a beaker. And now that he's gone, he's hoping that by mixing us all together we'll grow."

"My guess is it's a challenge," I say. "Like rats finding their way out of a maze."

"More like rats making a home out of the maze," Mom says, and sits next to Bridge, picking a marshmallow star off the edge of her bowl and popping it in her mouth.

I've learned more about my father's history in the last three minutes than the preceding three decades, and I can only guess it's the same for Franny and Bridge. None of us, however, ask Mom for more. Maybe because we're absorbing what's just been shared; maybe we figure that's all Mom knows. In any case, there're only the pops of the bacon frying until Franny starts out in a new direction of her own.

"I had a weird dream last night," she says.

"So we're definitely not talking about anything real," I say, worried she's forgotten about our agreement not to speak of what she thought she might have seen in the woods.

"A dream, like I said. But so real *seeming*, you know? Like here I am, awake, and I can still feel it clinging to me."

"What happened?" Bridge asks.

"There was water," Franny says, squinting as if pulling her subconscious into clearer focus. "Salt water. I could *taste* it. Can you taste in a dream? Doesn't that mean you're insane or something?"

"That's if you see colors," Bridge says.

"Is darkness a color? Because the water I was in was blacker than night. I *really* didn't want to go down into it—not just because I was afraid of drowning; I was afraid of the water itself. But I was tired. Like I'd been fighting to stay above the surface for hours before the dream even started. And then comes the weird part. From out of the silence, from out of the ocean—"

"There was music."

I finish Franny's sentence without being aware of it.

"That's not what I was going to call it. But yes," she says. "How the hell did you know that?"

"Because I had the same dream," I say. "A version of it, anyway."

"Me too," Bridge says.

All of us look at her.

"I could hear it when my head was above water, but it was a lot louder once I went under," Bridge goes on. "Like horns or something. A bunch of trumpets and tubas tuning up before playing a song. Except the tuning up *was* the song. It was so beautiful it almost stopped me from being scared. I was so tired of fighting that I just went down. Swallowed up by this sound so big it felt like I wasn't in water anymore. Just the sound."

I don't want to ask this next part. But now that Franny looks at me to do it, I see that it's up to me.

"What happened then?"

"Nothing," Bridge says.

"You mean you woke up?"

"I mean *nothing*. It just ended. What about you?"

The way Franny and I don't reply to this confirms what we already know. The dream ends with darkness. It ends with the end.

"Mom?" Franny eventually asks. "Any of this ring a bell with you?"

"I don't remember my dreams," she says, and while I note that this isn't precisely an answer, I don't pursue anything more. It's the smell of smoke that pulls my attention away. The bacon burning in the pan.

"Hope you like it well done," I say, happy for the diversion of scooping the hardened rashers out of the pool of spitting fat.

"It's bacon," Bridge says, holding her plate out. "How bad can it be?"

12

AFTER BREAKFAST I GO FOR A RUN. NOT THE PANIC-DRIVEN DASH OF LAST NIGHT, but still a near-full pace of the kind I used to be able to maintain for several hours. My hope is I can keep it up for maybe a quarter of that. A fact-finding mission to discover how truly out of shape I've let myself become.

I'm only a few minutes along the drive we came in on when I realize I haven't worn my watch or brought any water with me. I could go back, but I'm feeling strong, flushed with that bloom of optimism that runners in their first mile share with alcoholics downing their first drink.

The day is a classic Pacific Northwest game of bait and switch: the sun promising clear skies ahead before being obscured behind tectonic plates of clouds. Soon, the possibility of rain, implausible minutes ago, becomes a certainty with the first cold drops on my cheeks.

I like it. The air stretching the billows of my lungs, the rivulets of water dripping off my lip and into my mouth. And then, before I feel it coming, I'm bent over with my hands on my knees, wondering if I'm about to puke.

When I stand straight again, I realize two things at the same time. One, I'm dehydrated and farther out than I should be. Two, the estate's fence is visible a couple hundred yards ahead around the next bend.

I tell myself that, now that I'm here, I might as well walk the rest of the way to the gate while hoping the dizziness sloshing inside my skull eases away. By the time I get there, it's almost worked.

The fence is higher than I would have guessed. Eighteen feet, maybe more. And I don't recall the tight bundle of barbed wire at the top. A look along the fence's length, left and right, shows it going on as far as I can see.

The gate itself is a section the same width as the lane that, when opened, slides along a track in the ground. On the other side is the lockbox that Fogarty mentioned, the one that contains the satellite phone we can use to call for a ride.

To the right of the gate, above a small concrete pad, is what must be the food and supplies delivery system. It's basically a metal plate that rotates through the fence on this side and the other side. In the space of the opening between the two—a bit more than a square foot—there are wires that hang down like the rubber flaps you pass through in a car wash. In this case the wires are probably electrified. A discouragement against trying to crawl through the opening (even if there's no body other than a toddler's that would have a chance of fitting).

Something about being here at the limit of the property, contained within miles of woven steel, reminds me again of the figures Franny and I thought we saw last night. The idea that they are here as well. Inside.

Until now, I'd assumed the fence was meant to protect Belfountain from those who might try to get in. I'd read about people who would illegally clear-cut entire acres of redwoods up here. And that was before the riots and curfews. Now this place would offer more than free wood. It would offer a refuge.

But what if it is the other way around? What if the fence's height, the razor wire—what if it is meant to keep the ones in the forest inside?

I step closer to the fence. Careful not to touch it in case the whole thing is electrified. Fogarty said we were free to go any time we wanted. If that's true, how do we get out? There must be something here at the gate. A button or lock. But I can't find anything.

Nothing other than the gate itself.

To try to move it will require me putting my bare hands on it. I should know better—I'm a physician who's seen all the ways people can injure themselves by way of dumb decisions—but I tell myself that if I'm quick enough, I can test it with a glancing touch.

I uncurl my fingers held in a fist. Swipe them over the steel.

There's a jolt. But it's not electricity. It's the scratch of the metal's surface on my skin.

This time I throw both of my hands against the fence. Find the best grip I can through the holes. Pull hard to the right. The gate's frame shivers. So I yank it to the left. It moans before sliding a few inches out of position. With two more heaves I've opened it all the way.

It's only more forest on the far side. The same million dripping leaves as there are on this one. Yet there's a line between where I stand and the trees I stare at through the open gate that pulls them into sharper focus. *There* is more particular, more real, than *here*.

The instructions are clear.

Fogarty's voice returns to me so vividly I can imagine him speaking next to me, his polished shoes sinking into the rain-softened mud.

The perimeter of the estate marks the extent to which you may travel.

So here I am. I've finally achieved what I never could over all those marathons years ago. I've run all the way to the end of the world.

But I won't step off the edge.

It's not for the money. And I don't care what Dad wants us to learn. I'm here for Bridge. For her to discover whatever it is that makes her believe it's important to stay. For her to be safe.

I take in a full inhalation of air from the other side and hold it as if readying to dive underwater. Pull the gate closed. Walk back toward the lodge before ramping it into a cautious jog.

How far out *is* here? Other than being tired and thirsty and nauseated, there's no measure my mind can latch onto. The sun remains on sabbatical, so it's hard to say if it's still morning or if the grayness isn't the clouds but encroaching dusk.

The idea that I might pass out and not get up becomes more real with every stride. And if I go down, there's a good chance I'll lie here soaking wet through the night, a night that can drop twenty degrees between midnight and dawn.

I'd forgotten how, on long runs, thoughts at first multiply and compete for attention before filtering away to a single purpose.

Don't fall.

Everything reduced to this.

Just. Don't. Fall.

I figure I've got to be close when I hear something running up behind me. A rush of air, followed by the crunch of gravel.

Big. And faster than I am.

I could turn to look, but I know that would probably send me tumbling into the ditch. There's also the option of striking out into the woods and finding a place to hide. But if I can hear whatever it is, it's already seen me.

Don't stop. Don't fall.

All that's left is to do what I'm doing.

Except do it faster.

13

A BLAZE OF SOUND. SO LOUD IT TURNS MY MUSCLES RIGID, FORCING ME TO HOP TO the side of the road and close my eyes against contact.

Then my mind recognizes the sound for what it was. A car horn.

One limo and then another roll past. The same models, possibly the very same vehicles, that brought us here. I can't tell who the passengers are through the tinted windows, but there are the outlines of heads looking at me, the man in the ridiculous neon outfit who doesn't seem able to breathe properly.

The two cars pick up speed once I'm behind them and disappear around the curve ahead.

Heading toward the lodge. Toward Bridge.

It heaves me forward again. A sensation like a hive of ants released into my ears, carving their way inward.

Two more turns and I see that I was right: I was close. The limos are both parked out front of the lodge, but no one—not the drivers, not Bridge or Franny or Mom—stands outside. I weave toward the limo closest to me and stop when, at the same time, all of the vehicles' rear doors open.

Four passengers get out. Two from the first limo and two from the second. The former is a set of adult identical twins. Blandly good-looking, slightly overweight. Not dressed exactly the same but close enough to be confusing, their hair home-dyed the color of hay.

The latter are a man and a woman, both looking at me. The woman is dressed in a professional skirt and blouse, her hair an aura of dark curls around her head. The man is a couple inches shorter than me but wider. His body is as purposeful as the woman's but more muscled than graceful, a guy who spends his gym time grunting with the weights. Yet his face is boyish, open. A wholesome assembly of features that used to be called "all-American."

Because she happens to be closer, or because she's been brought up to be polite (or is required to be for the job that bought her the tasteful jacket and skirt she wears), the woman approaches me.

"Sorry we didn't stop to offer you a lift back there, but our driver—"

"What are you doing here?" I gasp, a string of spit lashing onto the ground before my hand can reach my lip.

"I'm here—we're *all* here—to satisfy the legal terms," she says.

"I don't understand."

"Mr. Fogarty explained everything to us."

"Fogarty? Explained *what*?"

"You know who Mr. Fogarty is, don't you? I mean, I'm assuming you're a member of the staff or a caretaker of some kind?"

"I'm not staff. I'm not the damn caretaker either."

Her polite smile loosens. She's found herself standing too close to someone who's not of his right mind, someone breathing hard and now lurching in a dizzy circle, and she takes a long step back. It makes room for Mr. All-American to step into the space she's left.

"Everything okay?" he asks.

"You're trespassing."

"Really?"

"Yes. So unless you can tell me what the—"

His hands come up. So fast I only realize he's holding me back from coming closer after I press my weight against his palms. A defense of the woman behind him that proves the connection between them.

"Easy now. I don't know who you are," he says without threat, his eyes twinkly with what may be amusement. "There's no problem here. We just have to sort this out, okay?"

The wooziness instantly worsens, graduating into head spins that jolt my vision left to right and back again, over and over. Yet I manage to ask the man what I should have asked at the beginning.

"Who are you?"

"Jerry Quinlan. Raymond Quinlan was my father. What about you?"

He doesn't push me. He doesn't have to. He just brings his hands down, and it's not only his face that's spinning, it's the well-dressed woman, the dyed-hair twins. Mom and Franny and Bridge rush out of the lodge, all of them shrinking into a pinhole of light I try to hold on to, but when they're gone, there's only darkness.

14

THEY'RE STANDING AROUND ME. NONE OF THEM CLOSE EXCEPT FOR BRIDGE, wringing out a cloth from a bowl of ice water and folding it onto my brow.

"Hey," I croak.

She offers me a coffee mug of orange juice. "You need some sugar."

I drink it down and within seconds I'm feeling halfway human again.

"Welcome back. You passed out," the guy who'd introduced himself as Jerry Quinlan says. He stands the farthest away, silhouetted against the great room's windows. "I carried you in."

I scan the faces of the others. There's the brown-eyed woman who's come to stand behind Bridge, the paunchy twins, along with Franny and Mom between the sofa and the raised dining area, standing close together as if for warmth.

"We haven't really talked about anything yet," the woman says. "I guess we were waiting for you to come around."

"That's very kind," I say, intending a bite of sarcasm; but it eludes me, so it comes out sounding prim instead. "Maybe I can start?"

"Sure."

"Who are you people?"

"My name is Lauren. That's my brother Jerry," she says, pointing at the man by the window, then switches to the twins. "And these are my other brothers, Ezra and Elias."

"You're related."

"That's how brothers and sisters work."

"But outside your brother Jerry told me his surname too."

"Quinlan."

"Quinlan," I say immediately after she does.

"That's right. We're Ray Quinlan's children. This was his property, and the directions of his will brought us here."

Mom pulls away from Franny and comes to sit on the edge of the sofa next to me, drawing Bridge protectively against her legs.

"Is your mother with you?" she asks Lauren.

"Our mother passed away two years ago."

"I see."

"And you? May I ask—"

"Eleanor."

"Eleanor," Lauren repeats, her face brightening as she makes a connection in her mind. "Yes! I think I get it now."

"I'm sorry?"

"My father's secretary. Eleanor. He mentioned you sometimes. You're here as part of the division of the estate as well?"

Lauren smiles at my mother with kindly certainty, the look of someone who's unknotted a shoelace for a child. But the smile doesn't last long. It's the twisting of my mother's face that does it. I'm sure it's heading in the direction of the wailing sobs I've been expecting since we first got here, but it comes out in wracking laughter instead.

"His *secretary*? *That's* what he called me?"

Jerry comes to stand directly over Mom, over the three of us on the sofa. Close enough for us to read the sympathetic setting of his face.

"Forgive me, Eleanor," he says. "But if you weren't his secretary, who *are* you?"

My mother assesses the man standing over her as if for the first time. The kind of nice, clean-cut boy she'd call a "nice, clean-cut boy" and chastise Franny for failing to have found. But instead of being charmed, she hardens. Not from anything she detects in him, but who he represents, the evidence of the deception she's been victim to that he asserts just by standing in front of her.

"I'm Eleanor Quinlan. Raymond Quinlan's wife."

Jerry pauses. Then, as if internally deciding on a program and waiting for the software to boot up inside him, he softens. Shows us his solid, milk-hardened teeth, and brings his hands together in a single clap.

"That is *something*!" He lets out a whoop. "That is most *definitely* something!"

"Hold on," one of the twins says. It's the first one Lauren pointed at, which would make him Ezra.

"You're his family?" the other twin, Elias, says.

"His second family, it appears. Or his first, and *you're* his second, depending where you start counting," Mom says, once more suppressing a fit of giggles that's more disturbing to me than anything else going on at the moment.

"So you and you and you," Ezra says, pointing at Bridge, then me, then Franny. "You're our half sisters and half brother?"

"It would follow," Mom says.

This appears to be all the twins need to know for now, the two of them retreating to murmur between themselves. I can't hear what they say but I lip-read it as numbers. Calculating what our existence means to their diminished cut of the pie.

Franny comes to sit on the arm of the sofa as if to complete the arrangement of the four of us for a family portrait.

"Lauren? Do you mind if I ask you a question?" she asks. "Do you have any children?"

Lauren is momentarily startled by the question, and it's not what I was expecting Franny to say either.

"No, I don't. You?"

"Yes. A boy. But he died."

"I'm sorry to hear that—"

"Franny."

"I'm very sorry, Franny."

"You're a therapist or social worker. Something like that, right?"

"A psychologist. That a guess?"

"I'm an addict. Been all over the rehab map. I can tell the professional listeners from civilians right away."

"You're good."

"Nah. I'm bad, actually," Franny says, and while it's meant as a self-deprecating joke, it comes out so crushingly sad all of us are struck by it, even the twins, who stop their murmuring.

"My name is Brigit, but I like Bridge," Bridge says after a quick suck of air.

"Okay, Bridge," Lauren says.

"Can I ask you something else?"

"I think we've all got a lot of questions, so fire away."

"Are you related to me? Like, genetically?"

"I understand," Lauren hedges, and now I can see the psychologist in her now too. "You're asking because we look different."

"Yes."

"Different from my brothers. From you. You're asking because I'm black."

"I guess."

"Fair enough. I'm adopted. Me and you? No genetic relation. But your dad is *our* dad," she says. "So for better or worse, I'm a Quinlan from the ground up."

Bridge nods at this, and so does Lauren. We all do.

"I'd like to know who you *are*," Mom says finally with the willed composure of a hostess attempting to recover a dinner party conversation from difficult terrain. "Not just your names."

"We'll go first," Ezra and Elias say at the same time, not seeming to notice their shared words and mirrored facial expressions, the consistent oddness of their twinship.

They don't wear the exact same color clothes, but the same style, same brand. Preppily rumpled shirts with frayed collars, the galloping horses and mallet-waving jockeys faded and curled over their hearts. They look like golfers. Like men who never resist the opportunity to tell jokes to dental hygienists and flight attendants.

As it turns out, they're actors. Mostly commercials now, some guest spots on police procedurals ("Every show eventually has twins that murder their parents"), though it's been rough the past few years. While their identical appearance was their main selling feature, it put them in competition with the three other sets of twins of the same age in LA up for the same parts—parts that now mostly went to the Ludmarks, a pair of broad-shouldered brothers from Nebraska who sold themselves as "decent Mormon types," but were in fact "coke-snorting dicks."

They've tried getting out of the business. They almost made a go selling real estate, investing in ads on bus stop benches that played up the twin angle (*Most Agents Can't Be in Two Places at Once . . . But the Quinlans Can!*). The phone rang for a time. But they soon discovered that while they were good at *acting* like real estate agents, they were terrible at actually selling real estate. And to live in LA was to be constantly reminded that they were semi-famous once. Ezra and Elias were on the cast of *Better Together*, a family sitcom that ran for two seasons in the '80s.

"I don't remember that show," Franny says.

"We get that a lot," Ezra says.

"I remember. You two played the same part," Mom says. "I read an article about it ages ago. You weren't twins on the show; you traded in and out playing the same child."

"There are laws about on-screen time for kids," Ezra explains, pleased to be recognized. "So they'd hire twins to put one on set in case the other one was sleeping or had to get his diapers changed."

"Yes, that's right," my mom says, tapping the side of her chin. "You were the youngest. They gave you all the best lines."

"'Ah poop,'" Ezra quotes.

"That's it. 'Ah poop.' You were the cute one."

"We were adorable," Elias confirms dismally.

Lauren is next. A private practice in Spokane. Trauma recovery. Victims of violence, soldiers returned from service, survivors. She chooses to take only the ones she can assist in making measurable improvements, instead of the "midlife crisis cases and suburban melancholics" that bring home the bacon for the majority of her colleagues.

"You got any openings?" Franny asks, in her joking-but-not-joking way.

"Are you a survivor?"

"I was actually thinking about my brother."

"Franny. Don't—"

"What? Aaron is a doctor. But definitely a physician who won't heal thy self. Because despite the stoic exterior, he's a shitshow on the inside. Not that it's his fault. He went over to Africa, see, to do the savior act *there* instead of *here*, but he—"

"*Don't.*"

"Got caught up in more than he signed up for. An ambush. The real shit. And the good doctor couldn't do anything to—"

"*Stop* it, Franny!"

Overseas.

I close my eyes against seeing it, but see it just the same.

The rust- and blood-speckled blades of machetes thudding into bodies. The dying at my feet, writhing and choking. So many of them it appeared as if the earth itself was fighting for air.

"Aaron?"

Bridge's voice brings me back. Not entirely, but enough to nod as if I'm fine.

Lauren looks between the two of us. When it's clear we aren't going to offer anything more, Franny starts to tell us who she is. Which is, for her, the telling of how she lost Nate.

She speaks matter-of-factly, so that the story of how she was a crackhead who left her four-year-old with a group of other addicts she was squatting with in Rainier Beach one night is conveyed with the same evenness as an account of how she forgot her purse after heading out for groceries.

While she went out to score, Nate suffered an asthma attack. His mostly comatose caretakers later claimed they didn't notice the boy clutching his throat in the room they were sitting in, "But they were all liars, so they probably closed their eyes so they wouldn't have to get up off the floor." What's known is that none of them went to find the boy's inhaler. By the time Franny returned, it was too late.

"I found my rock," she says, "but I lost everything."

It would be a difficult, if not impossible, story for anyone to follow. But Jerry does a remarkable thing. Wearing a look of empathetic loss, he comes over to place his hand atop Franny's shoulder. A simple gesture, one that might otherwise risk the appearance of insincerity. Not from him. There's a directness about Jerry that marks him as the only one in the room who seems able to fully register the horror that Franny has just confessed to.

"I'm a gym teacher in Portland," he announces after withdrawing his hand, as if there were no other imaginable outcome to his life.

After a football scholarship to Wisconsin that ended with a thwarted attempt at a career in the pros ("Got dinged going up for a catch one time too many," he says, tapping his skull to lightheartedly indicate repeated concussions), he pursued the next best thing. Teaching.

"Those who can, do," he says. "Those who can't, join a union."

He laughs at his own expense, good-natured and mildly heartbroken.

Over to me.

I swiftly hit the bullet points of my medical training, the surgery post at Swedish First Hill Hospital in Seattle. The truth is I love what I do: repairing bodies, taking out the bad parts, fusing and cleaning their interiors. So much simpler to fix people than understand them.

I don't talk about *overseas*.

But a quick glance at Lauren makes me feel certain that she knows. Not the details. The damage it left me with.

None of us, aside from Franny, mention children. None of us speak of a spouse, boyfriend, or girlfriend. It may be that they don't rate as figures of sufficient importance. It may be that, as Quinlans, we've all been similarly injured in ways that have conspired to see us live alone.

When we're finished going around the circle, Elias addresses us all.

"Excuse me for pointing out the pregnant elephant in the room, but does anyone else think this is fucked up?"

"I do," his twin brother answers.

The fact that no one else speaks to this suggests unanimous agreement.

"This may seem weird to ask at a time like this, so please don't think I'm too much of a jerk," Jerry says, addressing us with a bashful apology that I can sense Mom and Franny responding to. Me too. Perhaps it's impossible to respond any other way. He's my brother. There's some of me in him, and at the same time I recognize I want him to see something of value, something of himself, in me.

"Is there anything to eat?" he asks.

15

A FULL-ON FRIDGE RAIDING. THE SAME EMOTIONAL HUNGER TRANSLATING TO THE physical appears to be as true for the second Quinlans as much as the first, judging by the way they divide up what's left of the roast chicken and zap a pair of frozen pizzas in the microwave. Still feeling weak from my run, I make grilled cheeses for Bridge and myself. All of us carry our plates to the banquet dining table and take seats—accidentally or otherwise—alternating a member of the first Quinlans with a member of the second. There's a moment when all of us look across at one another, acknowledging the way we would appear as one family, not two.

"Did you guys say grace before dinner in your house?" Jerry asks me.

"No. You?"

"Not even at Christmas."

"Have at it then."

Me, Mom, Franny, and Bridge watch as the others destroy what's on their plates. It makes me tentative at first when I pick up my sandwich, but after the first mouthful my body responds, and I eat as ravenously as they do.

When we're done, we look up at one another and are plunged into a deeper awkwardness. The twins reddening. Lauren can't stop shaking her head. Franny, I can tell, is on the verge of telling one of her pitch-dark tales from her years in the gutter. As for Mom, she casts her eyes over the four newcomers and squeezes her lips tight.

Eventually Jerry pushes his chair back and pulls a silver flask from the inside pocket of his jacket.

"Those limo assholes took my phone," he says. "But they didn't take this."

He unscrews the flask's top and takes a drink. Then he offers it to Mom, who surprises all of us, or certainly the first Quinlans, by accepting it. She swallows a dainty sip before passing the flask to Lauren.

It goes around to all of us wordlessly, Bridge and Franny passing it on without drinking each time. Yet they too seem to be warming to the liquor's effects, the animosity and shock gradually giving way to an acknowledgment of the absurdity we've found ourselves sharing.

When the flask returns to him for the third time, Jerry frowns, shakes it, proving it's empty before returning it to his pocket.

"Well, what do you all think?" he says. "You figure we could talk for real now?"

We take it in small steps. The whisky helps. Chatter about where we grew up, the possibility that we'd unknowingly crossed paths at Mariners games or during childhood trips up the Space Needle. It's as if we're people who've found instant camaraderie with another group waiting to board a flight, and now we were working to discover the extent of the shared ground between us, plotting out the dots of coincidence between our lives.

The second Quinlans lived in Kirkland, while we, the first Quinlans, lived on Mercer Island. Similar suburbs on different compass points from downtown and far enough apart that we attended different high schools, dated boys and girls whose names we don't recognize, never played on a team that met the other in an all-city tournament. Yet there must have been close calls. So many, in fact, it's stranger that we aren't able to find a direct hit between us than if we did.

Our conversation is buoyed by full stomachs and Ballantine's and the mutual experience of the peculiar. Confronting one another and the secret that's now been exposed could have gone one of two ways, the traumatic or the humorous, and for now at least we've opted for the latter. We relate anecdotes of our father's behavior. Funny stories about how he never remembered our birthdays or would present random gifts bought exclusively at airport souvenir gifts shops, handing invisible ink pens to toddlers or electric razors to Jerry and me five years before puberty. Also hilarious were the times he would assure us that he'd join us on a holiday only to invariably bail at the last minute, waving at us as we reversed the station wagon out of the drive on our way to a golf resort (nobody played except him) or drive north to Canada only to be quizzed by customs agents suspicious about a mother, husbandless, driving her children over the border.

Mom is the only one who doesn't join us in the performance of One Big Happy Dysfunctional Family. She listens and pretends to recall the details as bittersweetly as we do, but it's obvious there's something she can't shift her mind from.

"How did they meet?" she says finally. "Your mother and Raymond."

Mom's curiosity leaves her so vulnerable all of us lean toward her to participate in it, a communal attempt to bear some of her pain so that she won't be crushed, as she appears she may be.

"It's a little bizarre, actually. But Mother thought it was romantic," Lauren says gently. "She was a nurse and Dad was one of her patients."

"Go on," Mom says.

"'He had a way of talking.' That's what she'd say when I asked how an older man in a hospital bed could charm a young woman into being his wife. 'He had a way with words.' She said it like it was a spell that had been put on her. Like she'd been fooled."

"Pleurisy," Mom says.

"Yes," Lauren says. "That's what he was in for. Lung infection."

"We were married then," Mom says. "I was pregnant with Aaron, but there wasn't a day I didn't visit him. I must have spoken with your mother. To think I was witness to it! My ill husband falling in love with one of his nurses right before my eyes while I was carrying his child."

It's not me or Franny who reaches out to Mom. It's Jerry. Cupping her hand under his as if to warm it.

"What was she like?" Mom says, looking to Jerry.

"She was a good mom," he answers. "Kind, a little fragile. A good cook, in a tuna casserole sort of way. She looked after us fine, but mostly her job was covering for Dad. 'He'd like to be here for your game, but work called him in.' 'Don't be angry at him, he's doing important work for the good of the country.' She was really good at deflecting blame. But she blamed him the whole time, like she was the only one who was allowed to."

He squeezes Mom's hand under his.

"She was probably a lot like you," he says.

Mom hasn't had much experience with honesty from men. Now that she's hearing it from Jerry, she sits up straighter to absorb it, weigh it. Eventually she draws her hand away and rises, leaving the table and going down the steps into the great room to stand at the windows with her hands on her hips, a homemaker's pose, as if discouraged at all the work ahead of her in raking up six hundred acres of leaves.

Bridge is about to go after her, but I shake my head, signaling Mom's need to be alone, but as soon as I've done this, I wonder if I'm right. I've been brought up to manage hurt by retreating, and to manage others' hurt by standing back from it, just as I kept away from Franny when she cried out watching them lower Nate into the ground and said nothing more than *It's over now* when Mom called to say Dad was gone.

"So other than doing the dishes—" Ezra starts.

"What happens now?" Elias finishes.

"Well, that depends on us," Jerry says. "It looks like we've got to make some decisions."

He pushes his chair back from the table, and I notice again how this man conveys physical strength built for practical purposes yet remains so boyish, almost cherubic. He's athletic, but he's only playing tough. This is what his rounded cheeks and over-long eyelashes say. The muscles and willfully deepened voice parts of an unsuccessful effort to disguise his prettiness.

"Before we get to that, tell me about the lawyer," I say.

"Fogarty?"

"That's the one."

"Lauren? You want to field that? I'm going to scare up some coffee."

"There's some in the kitchen," Mom calls at us, automatically shifting back into hospitality mode and then, hearing herself, returning her gaze out the window.

It leaves Lauren to explain how the four second Quinlans were awakened early this morning by drivers who told them they were to be taken to a meeting. The drivers could say nothing more about it, other than it concerned the administration of their father's estate. They were given no time to pack, and once they were in the cars, they had to surrender their phones. Fogarty addressed them over the limos' speakers on their drive to Belfountain, telling them their father had a considerable fortune, the primary piece of which was a property in the forest. The will instructed him, as executor, to distribute the assets among all the surviving members of his immediate family upon the satisfaction of a condition.

"To stay here for a month," Franny says.

"Without leaving," Ezra says.

"Or TV," Elias adds bitterly.

"All of which was twisted enough," Lauren goes on. "But then we arrive and find you."

"What about this place?" I glance over at Bridge, then back at Jerry. "Did he—did Dad—ever mention it?"

"Not directly," he answers, squinting. "But there were the stories."

"Stories?"

"The ones he'd tell us when we were kids," Lauren explains. "All about this magical place called Belfountain. I never liked them much myself. Made me think of that one about the witch and Hansel and Gretel."

"Well, here you are," I say, sweeping my arm around. "Welcome to the gingerbread house."

Jerry sits in the empty chair next to me. Takes a delicate sip of his coffee.

"Seems we're the eldest of our clans now," he says. "What do you think of that?"

"I think Ray Quinlan was one messed up son of a bitch."

"I'm figuring we've got a majority vote on that."

"And I think you're right. Each of us has to make a decision."

"About what exactly?"

"Whether we stay or go."

Jerry puts the coffee down. "This is a lot to take in. A lot of confusion. A lot of hurt. But I agree with Aaron. We have to put that aside as best we can to think about the core issue here."

"You're talking about money," Franny says, sniffing.

He turns to her. "Sure. Yes, I am. Because it's what's owed to us, what we deserve. Think of it as just money if you want. Me? I'm inclined to think of it as a second chance. I mean, if you do the math on—"

"Math? I thought you taught gym."

Jerry grins as if Franny is trying to flirt with him, even though it's fairly clear he represents something she can't stand. One of those outwardly flawless guys she never knew how to start with, the kind she saw the world handing over everything to just for showing up.

"I think even I can sort it out," he says, sustaining the grin. "Thirty days here to claim one-eighth of what? Thirty million? Forty? It's a weird ask, no doubt about it. But still, not much of a decision if you ask me." He looks from me to Lauren before landing on the twins. "What do you say?"

"If it means not having to say 'Ah poop!' a hundred times while getting our picture taken at a fan convention in Des Moines, I'm in," Ezra says, and Elias winces his agreement.

"Lauren?"

"I'm a psychologist," she says. "I'm in it for the research paper."

"There you have it," Jerry says. "The Quinlans of Kirkland are all signed up. How about the Mercer Islanders? Any of you looking to thumb a ride home?"

I look to Bridge.

"I'm not going anywhere," she says, and squeezes my hand three times. *It's just me and you.*

"Franny?"

"Thirty days? Shit. I've done half a dozen rehabs longer than that."

I consider shouting out to Mom to ask how she'd like to vote, but considering what she's already said on the matter, I don't see the need.

"We're in," I say.

"There it is! A full ship!"

Jerry grins his football-hero grin at me, an invitation to friendship. It decides something for me.

I want our side to win.

16

IT'S THE TWINS' IDEA TO HAVE A "CAMPFIRE" OUTSIDE TO MARK THE SECOND Quinlans' arrival at Belfountain. Jerry seconds the motion so fast I don't have time to suggest otherwise. It's not that I'm concerned about the things we may or may not have seen in the woods. After all, Franny and I had stood unarmed, and they hadn't approached, let alone threatened us. And that's assuming there was anyone there in the first place.

My hesitation has to do with letting ourselves see our time here as *fun*. Mom sent all of us to summer camp growing up, and while I loved the swimming and hiking, I preferred the quieter, solitary activities over the stories told around bonfires that ended with collective screams when the guy with a hook for a hand showed up. It cheapened the experience somehow. Things that weren't funny that we were all expected to laugh our heads off at.

I help Jerry and the twins carry out some of the firewood from next to the hearth and foldout chairs Lauren finds in the front hall closet along with those jigsaw puzzles Fogarty had mentioned. Soon we're sitting around a blaze in the circular driveway out front, sending our laughter out into the dark, sparks rising like fireflies to tame the night.

The twins in particular are the stars of the show. Their give-and-take is practiced, yet it doesn't come across that way. A series of comic routines that culminate in an epic tale about swapping dates in the middle of their prom without the girls being able to tell the difference between them.

"Until, you know, the big reveal," Ezra says with a lewd smirk.

"Or, in your case, the little peep show," Elias replies.

"We're identical twins!"

"Not *that* identical."

"I don't know if I'm comfortable with this."

We turn to Lauren, who in fact looks a little queasy.

"You've heard these gags a thousand times," Jerry says. "You always thought they were funny."

"There's just a lot for me to wrap my head around." She looks at me and Franny and Mom and Bridge. "We all had our problems with Dad. But he's *gone*. It's why we're here."

"That may not be totally accurate for some of us," Franny says, not unkindly. "We're here because the will forced us to be."

"He's not forcing us," Lauren says, her voice shriveling.

"None of this was our idea. It was *him*, it—"

"He was my father!"

Lauren gets up and heads off into the lodge. I consider going after her, but she's not my sister, and I wait for Jerry or one of the twins to fulfill their role. But none of them move.

"We all have different takes on Dad," Jerry explains, shifting to squint at us through the licks of flame. "It's probably the same with you guys."

"Yes," Bridge answers.

"Well, in our case, Lauren is the soft touch," Jerry says. "The benefit-of-the-doubter."

"She has a point," Elias says.

"Maybe we should think of Dad in ways we can—" Ezra says, searching his mind. "What's the word?"

"Memorialize."

"Yeah. Maybe we should *memorialize* him."

"Okay," Franny says, clapping her hands together. "I've got one."

I didn't expect there to be as many Dad stories as we come up with. Through it all the tone remains light, almost affectionate. The edge of hostility, lurking beneath every anecdote, only increases the deliciousness.

"There was nobody worse at carving a turkey," Ezra announces.

"Nobody in the turkey-carving world," Elias agrees.

"To be fair, that's because he always got called away before he could finish the job," Mom says, automatically defending him before she can prevent herself.

"Remember the Thanksgiving when he had a cast on his arm?" Jerry says. "He was fighting with that big old bird, hacking at it with one hand. When I offered to help he said, 'Why would I need any help, Gerald?' and kept whacking at it until the carving board looked like a crime scene."

"Wait, I remember the year he had that cast on too," Franny says. "He chopped up our turkey the same way. But if Dad was at your house for Thanksgiving dinner, how could he be at our house too?"

"Maybe it was a different night," Elias says.

"We always had holiday dinner on Thursday," Bridge says.

"Us too," Jerry says.

"It's because he was at both houses," I say. "He started at yours and got a call. Then he came to ours, got another call—"

"And he was gone," Jerry says.

The fire makes a sound like snapped fingers.

"All those years, those times we thought he was ours," Mom says, "he was yours too."

In the quiet, there's a sound all of us hear. Somewhere a great distance away, well beyond the estate's fence, comes the repeated boom of a shotgun. It's followed by a gun of a different kind. A tat-tat-tattling of an automatic. Then it stops too. We've grown used to these noises over the past months. They happen, and we move on, pretending they hadn't.

"It's getting bad out there," Bridge says.

"It was always bad out there," Ezra says.

"He's right. We only caught glimpses of it before," Franny says. "Now all the ugliness is breaking through."

Franny's words make me think of hands punching up from the soil of freshly covered graves, of shark fins rising out of the water, of spiders skittering and spreading from nested holes in the ground. Buried things finding a way to the air.

"We better put this baby to bed," Jerry says, meaning the fire.

The whisky has left us dry-mouthed and headachy. We throw handfuls of dirt onto the fire until it's a sputtering mound of embers. Before going back inside, we pause to listen for gunfire again but there's nothing. It makes me wonder if we ever heard it at all.

17

FAMILIES TEACH US WHO WE ARE. THAT'S WHAT THE KIDS' MOVIES I WATCHED growing up and the sappy commercials they air over the holidays tell us. Family binds us. It's the download for our politics and faith software. The way to see yourself more truly than any mirror.

And maybe it is all that. But I would define it as something else.

A family is a group of people who have different versions of the same experience.

What I remember of our years in the Mercer Island Cape Cod with a red-brick chimney and the Stars and Stripes hanging limp from a pole out front isn't what Franny remembers, and is probably further still from what Bridge took from living under the same roof.

Not that it was *bad*. There was a station wagon that puttered us to practices and birthday parties, a rec room where we played the music loud, a living room where we'd prop a fresh-cut spruce in the corner and hang strings of popcorn from its branches once a year. But there was something distinct about our house compared to the homes of our friends. It was like we were acting at being a family instead of living as one.

I may be alone in this.

Or maybe I'm not.

Sometimes I think something happened to me growing up. A harm of the suppressed kind. I've wondered, if I went to one of those therapists who puts you under and takes you to the place you least want to return to, what I might find way back there. Would I know it was real if such a moment came to mind? How is a story distinguishable from history?

Chances are there's nothing there. What I am only reflects my particular scars from growing up as Ray and Eleanor Quinlan's son.

But they did nothing wrong.

They did nothing.

Once the fire is quieted, the second Quinlans collect the duffel bags the limo drivers had dropped outside and go off to find their quarters. It's decided that the twins will take the Red cabin, Jerry the Green, and Lauren the Yellow while me and Bridge remain in Orange and Franny and Mom in the lodge. I leave Bridge with Mom and offer to accompany Lauren along the trail to her cabin, throwing her bag over my shoulder and immediately regretting it, my legs still wobbly.

"I can manage," she says at the trailhead, pulling the bag off my shoulder. "But I appreciate the company."

"Are you a runner?" I ask as we start off into the trees.

"I try to get out a few times a week. Why do you ask?"

"I can just tell. Skiers know skiers, hunters know hunters. Or so I'm told."

"So runners know runners."

"That's it."

The trail narrows, forcing Lauren to proceed a step ahead. There's only the sound of our breathing, the dull clumping of our feet, the swinging light of our headlamps.

"It's bizarre, isn't it, to think about Dad making the drive up and down the I-405 between our two houses," I say, "and none of us having a clue about it until today."

"There's a lot none of us had a clue about until today."

"I can't stop imagining him in his car, heading a few miles north from dinner at our place so he could tuck you in for bed. What could he have been thinking?"

"I couldn't say. But I'm pretty sure he wasn't worried about getting caught."

"Why not?"

"Because someone who would keep two separate families, with two wives, two homes—those kind of men never are."

The trail takes an abrupt turn to the right and starts a switchback down a slope much steeper than the one that leads to the Orange cabin. It takes us a while to work our way left and right and back again, tackling the degree of descent in small servings. Once the trail levels out again, there's still no sign of any clearing or cabin ahead. The darkness is thicker here. Seamless.

"Did you get along? You and Dad?" I ask Lauren, genuinely curious. What if Dad loved her and Jerry and the twins more than us? What if *we* were the real second Quinlans and they the first?

"We didn't fight, if that's what you mean," she says. "I don't think he cared enough to get involved like that."

"That's not exactly what I meant."

"He was benign. As in *not there*. But when you're in my field, you know that that can leave its own kind of scars."

"Do you think it was harder for you being adopted?"

Lauren stops to look at me, and I wonder if I've offended her and then realize all the ways she'd have a right to be.

"I'm sorry," I say. "That was an incredibly stupid thing to—"

She raises her hand, the index finger up to show my apology isn't necessary.

"We're all adopted, if you think about it. At least it's how *I* think about it," she says. "None of us choose our family. We just *arrive*, one way or another."

"And make the best of it."

"Or the worst."

She starts on again and it takes a moment to catch up.

"So what's your theory?"

"Theory?"

"On Dad," I say. "What he did for a living. Who he really was."

"Well," she says, and comes to a stop again, turning to scan the endless green around us. "It certainly paid well."

"And was classified."

"He didn't tell my mother, as far as I know. And he certainly never told me. So maybe secrecy was required of him. Or maybe it was something he chose. Either way, he practiced it to perfection."

"Franny and I have wondered if he was maybe involved in espionage in some way."

"No chance."

"Why?"

"He was too interested in his own project, whatever it was, to work for some institutional bureaucracy."

"Something on the corporate side then."

"Could be. Likely a branch of the sciences or engineering. If you've discovered something useful, there's somebody who'll pay you enough to buy your own national park."

"It must have been good."

"I'd say bad, more likely. Think about it. If he parented his children and conducted his marriages the way he did, what do you think he was capable of in his professional life?"

"You think it was illegal?"

"I'm not saying that. But it's a professional hazard of mine to profile people, even the ones closest to me," she says, and grimaces, what I take to be a hint at the failed relationships in her past. "I see Dad as a more extreme case than my brothers do."

"An obsessive."

"A sociopath."

"Which would mean he didn't ask us here to hold hands around the campfire and promise to get together at Thanksgiving."

"I don't see that, no."

"So what do you see?"

"This? This is a humiliation," Lauren says, bitterness sharpening an edge to her words. "He couldn't feel, but he was interested in managing how other people felt. So here we are."

I'm not sure I agree with her but it's clear that her anger is not something to be tested. I also see now that it wasn't love for Dad that made her storm away from the fire earlier. It was her finding it wrong to be acting normal when none of this is normal. When Dad wasn't normal.

Lauren carries on ahead. I've got my foot raised to follow after her when my body goes still.

The sensation of being watched.

When I turn to look, I see that I'm right.

A tree that's not a tree at the top of the slope we've just made our way down. A quarter of the height of those around it and unnaturally shaped, its limbs hanging downward, a bulbous squirrel nest at the top. And moving. Weaving side to side in a way that has nothing to do with the direction of the wind.

These are the tricks the brain tries to play to prevent me from seeing what it knows is there.

The Tall Man Franny saw last night. Now revealed in more detail. Each announcing its unforgettability in the instant I notice it.

The mouth hanging open like his jaw's been broken. Arms at his sides. His hands lost inside what appear to be a pair of construction gloves that are too big for him, fattened and leathery. The look of something that's lost and has been that way for a long while. Unreachable.

Even though we'd covered a hundred yards of trail from where he is now, only a quarter of that distance separates us in a line up or down the slope.

As if reading my thoughts, he starts forward.

Not on the trail, but coming straight at us. Plowing through the brush, a controlled fall that his legs are able to negotiate, he is advancing at a seemingly impossible pace.

Trying not to trigger him into an outright run by seeing me do the same, I speed-walk up to Lauren.

"Don't stop. Don't turn around, okay?"

"Why?"

"Just drop your duffel bag and keep going."

"What are you—"

"Do it now."

She drops the bag.

Then she does what I asked her not to and turns around.

"Jesus Christ," she whispers, her fear lowering her voice into the tenor of an actual prayer.

The Tall Man breaks through the last of the brush to emerge onto the trail at the base of the hill. Unobscured by the forest, in the electric flash of our lights, he shows more of himself now—glaring and gut flipping and real—so that it's difficult to stitch all of him together. He can't be taken in as whole but only as a loose collection of particulars you see and move your eyes from only to see something else, something worse than the thing before.

A patchwork of a man. One who's no longer a man. An undead scarecrow who leapt from his post.

Clothes so stained—by dirt, by blood—they cling to him like plastic wrap.

A boot on one foot, the other uncovered, the skin swollen to the point of rupture.

The mouth. A black oval ready to bellow an announcement or bite or suck in all the air of the forest for himself.

"My God, my *God*," Lauren whispers in her prayer voice again.

She is spellbound by her terror, just as I was by mine. But watching her take in the Tall Man pulls me out of it.

"We have to run," I say, and the sound of the word offers a counterspell of its own. *Run*.

With his bare, torn-up foot the Tall Man shouldn't be able to match our pace. I try to listen for him—his step on an unearthed tree root, his wet breath, whatever words he might want us to hear—but there's only the tidal rush of panic in my ears.

A moment later another sound joins it. Hissing. When it stops, I realize it was a scream that failed to make it out of Lauren's throat. She gasps and swallows a new breath.

She's looked back. Just as I do now. Sees that he's faster than us.

The cabin comes into view.

Lauren bolts ahead of me. I try to make up the ground between us and realize I can't. My legs, already burning from the run this morning, harden into planks. No matter what I do I can't manage more than a toe-dragging shuffle.

It's not far to the cabin door. If it's unlocked and Lauren opens it, I should be able to throw myself inside right after her.

Her fingers are around the handle. Is it turning? Or is it only her hand sliding over the brass? A second later I see it's neither. She's looked back and seen the Tall Man behind me.

"Open it!"

I don't sound like myself. I sound like a child. A little boy witnessing his house burn down with his family inside.

"Don't look at him! Open the *door*!"

I don't see her do it, but she must turn the handle—or lean her weight into the already opened door—because one second she's there and the next she's swallowed into the cabin's interior darkness. Then I'm there too. Slamming into the door and crashing into the murk.

Lauren is on the floor. I almost come down on her but skid on one foot instead, holding an unlikely balance.

I watch as the door swings hard against the wall and starts its return. But slower than when it opened. Long enough to see the Tall Man launch himself forward.

I do the same.

Elbows, thumb, cheeks, teeth—random parts of me landing against the wood and propelling it closed. I don't lock it. I can't. Not from where I am after I slide down to the floor.

I wait for him to make contact. But there's nothing.

I bring myself up onto my knees, searching for the handle. When my fingers find it, I click it locked.

"Is he there?" Lauren whispers.

"Yes."

"Why isn't he trying to get in?"

"I don't know."

"Oh shit. *Shit—*"

Scratching.

A slow stroking over the outside of the door from the hinges to the handle. Growing louder as it goes. Harder.

His gloves. The ones so big his hands must be glued into them. Now dragging over the outside of the door, side to side.

"What do we do?" Lauren asks, though it's unclear whether it's a question addressed to me or herself.

"Find something to fight with."

"Like what?"

"The kitchen. Maybe there's something we could—"

"Stop."

I listen for what Lauren has heard. It takes a moment to realize there's nothing to hear.

"He's still out there," she says.

"How do you know?"

"I can feel it."

Time itself can be painful. There is nothing other than time that touches us as we wait on the cabin's floor for the Tall Man to find a way in. Time burning against our skin, inside and out.

"He's gone," Lauren says finally.

How does she know? It would be impossible to hear him leave. It can only be wishful thinking on her part. And yet, as soon as she says it, I join her in the same wish.

"You sure?"

"No," she says. "I just—"

"You feel it."

"Yeah."

I start to crawl over toward the sofa set against the wall under the nearest window facing out front.

"What are you doing?"

"Taking a look."

The Tall Man can look in at me more easily than I can look up at him, given the way I have to climb up onto the cushions and nudge the curtains apart with my nose before I can cast my light through the glass.

"Is he there?" Lauren asks.

"Not that I can see."

I walk back from the window, stepping over where Lauren still lies on the floor, into the kitchen. Pull a cheese knife with a decoratively curled point from the drawer. Come back into the living room and grip my hand on the locked handle.

"What are you *doing*?"

"Testing those feelings of yours," I say, and pull the door open wide.

18

IT'S STUNNING.

For the first time since coming to Belfountain, the rain forest—now, in the night interrupted only by my headlamp's bulbs—presents itself not as an enclosure but as a beautiful garden, magnificent and wild. The trees reaching out to each other, swaying to an undetectable music.

"He's not out here," I say.

Lauren comes to stand behind me. Scans what can be seen from over my shoulder.

"Okay," she says. "What're our choices?"

"Stay or go."

"You think we should wait until morning?"

"No," I say, thinking only of Bridge. Of the Tall Man making his way to the lodge. "We should go back."

"Now?"

"Now."

"Let me get a knife first."

"Take mine."

Lauren grips the cheese knife and frowns at its stubby length, the tip curved up like an elf's slipper. "Really?"

"It's the best there is."

"Aren't you bringing one?"

"This will come down to running, not fighting," I say, and it sounds like something imported from the outside, a logic that may not be applicable in this world. Here, it may be that running takes you where you least want to go.

We don't see the Tall Man on the hike back to the lodge. More than this, it's as if the return from the cabin peels away the memory of him, diluting his reality, so that when we step out of the trees and approach the front door, we're both clearing our throats with embarrassment. What will we say?

A skinny, homeless-looking man followed us in the woods.

So what? There were two of you, one of him.

He didn't seem right.

Did he say anything?

No.

So how do you know he wasn't right?

It's reassuring. But then we come inside and I see Bridge and Franny and Mom huddled together on the sofa as if clinging to a raft adrift in the great room, and the fear returns. The idea of them seeing what we've already seen.

We tell them what happened. I try not to dwell on the Tall Man's physical details, but they keep asking about him, and my hesitation ends up making him sound even worse. What did he want? This is what they demand to know next, but it's the one thing we can't answer. He came at us. He stroked his gloved hand against the door. But he didn't touch us, didn't attempt to force his way in.

"Was it him?" Franny asks me.

"I'm guessing it was, yeah."

"Was it *who*?"

This is Bridge. When I'm done telling her the full story of what Franny says she saw in the woods the night before, Bridge weighs the options in her head. It doesn't take her long. She decides to forgive me.

"We said no more secrets," she says.

"I know. But I told you I saw something."

"You didn't tell me *everything*."

"Full disclosure from now on. I promise," I say, and though the four of them are all present to hear it, it's one I make to Bridge alone.

Mom takes the report of the Tall Man the hardest. There aren't the nervous tears or blank-faced shock that would be consistent with her repertoire, only coldness. She removes herself to a corner of the room. Her lips moving noiselessly, as if teasing out a set of possibilities.

"You okay?" Franny asks, putting her arm around Mom's shoulder and pulling her close.

"I just thought, after today, there couldn't be anything new under the sun," she says with one of her feeble laughs. She looks at me. "What do you propose, Aaron?"

I'd hoped it would be enough to disclose, to share our disturbing experience with others and have them say it's over, we're all awake, there's nothing to be afraid of. But now I see it doesn't stop with that. It's not a dream that concludes with its telling.

Lauren asks if we should go warn Jerry and the twins. All of us look at the solid darkness outside the windows.

"First of all, there's probably nothing they need to be warned about," I say, sounding calm, which goes some way to actually calming me. "We should wait until morning. At first light, I'll head out to the Green cabin where Jerry is. Come up with a plan. How's that sound?"

Vague. Improvised. But nobody suggests anything else.

I offer to sleep on one of the sofas; Lauren will take the unoccupied room, Franny another, and Bridge will huddle in with Mom. These are the decisions we make out loud. But none of us move. In the end we stay where we are, sleeping in chairs with Mom and Bridge on a sofa. I tell them I'll keep watch through the night, that nothing will get in without me stopping it. This time it's a promise I make to all of them.

19

THERE ARE ASPECTS OF IT THAT REMIND ME OF A SLUMBER PARTY. THE DISCOMFORT of sitting tense and alert, for instance. The unfamiliar sounds and smells of a night spent in a strange house, the snoring bodies all around and me the only one awake.

Except this isn't some Mercer Island high school kid's birthday party.

Except the man wandering around outside, his face a portrait of emptiness, is the opposite of the bogeyman we told stories about and pulled the sheets up to our chins to protect ourselves against. Because we knew those monsters weren't real. And I know the Tall Man is.

I make myself some toast, and by the time I return to the great room, the rest of them are stretching and asking what time it is.

"Early," I say.

"You want me to come with you?" Lauren asks when she sees the chef's knife, an upgrade from the cheese thingy, in my hand.

"No, I'm good. Stay here. Someone will send word."

I'm hoping for something from Mom, an emboldening gesture for the walk ahead. But she only looks my way with a combination of pity and dread, as if an aura of disaster surrounds me and she doesn't want to come close enough to enter it.

Bridge follows me to the door.

"You're going to be okay," she says. But as I step outside, she locks the door behind me before I can reply.

Was it a better idea to do this in daylight?

I walk across the parking area toward the Green trailhead feeling exposed, even if the relative brightness reveals nothing waiting for me. But how would I know? Judging from the way the Tall Man had come down the hill, ignoring the course of the switchbacking trail, he knows how to travel through the forest, how to hide and track and survive in it. This is his element, not mine.

I make a point of not pausing before starting down the path to avoid running back and banging on the door to be let in. If I'm not capable of genuine courage, then the appearance of courage will have to do. Maybe this is all there is anyway. The soldiers storming out of their foxholes, the child promising her mom that today she'll find a friend at her new school. All of them finding bravery by faking it.

You pretend to not be afraid for this step, then the next. In time, you come to the Green cabin's door.

I'm about to knock but Jerry's voice sounds through the wood first.

"What are you doing out here?"

"We've got to talk."

"Why are you holding a knife?"

"That's what we've got to talk about."

He's not going to let me in. The doorknob doesn't turn, there's no call of *Just gimme a sec*. There's nothing.

"Jerry. This is serious. Open the goddamn—"

The door is pulled open a third of the way so I have to edge in sideways before it's shut again.

"Was it you?"

It takes a moment for me to find Jerry in the gloom. Standing off to my right and also holding a chef's blade in his hand, though his appears rustier than mine.

"Was it me *what*?"

"Walking around outside last night."

"No."

"But you know who was."

"A man I've never seen before. He followed Lauren and me on our way to her cabin."

Jerry lowers his knife, and I realize mine has also been held out in front of me, so I do the same.

"She okay?" he asks.

"She's fine. She's at the lodge."

"What do you mean he followed you?"

"One minute he wasn't there, and then he was."

"Could he have just been an employee? A maintenance guy or something?"

"I don't think so."

"Why not?"

Because he looked like the most lost thing I've ever seen.

"Because he wasn't," I say.

Jerry's eyes dance between the cabin's front window and the door, and back to me.

"Okay," he says. "So. What did he look like?"

"Tall. Dressed like he dug his way out of his own grave. His *face*. Mouth open like a shotgun wound. This stunned expression, as if he were searching for something but he didn't know what it was." I hear myself say this last part and it comes at me fresh, as if it were somebody else's thought altogether.

Jerry takes a step back and bumps his legs into the sofa. Instead of moving away from it, he lets himself fall back into its cushions.

"What's going on here, Aaron?"

"I don't know. He could have tried to break into the cabin, but he didn't. He could've hung around until we came out, but didn't do that either."

"You think it's all a game? Something Dad put together?"

"I guess it's possible. Being made to stay out here for a month—it's a game in itself, right? And then—surprise!—a second family he didn't tell any of us about. Why not throw another curveball into the mix?"

I don't know what I'm expecting. Some more pondering, probably. But without anything more to say, Jerry is up.

"You coming with me?" he says as he passes me and opens the door without checking to see if there's anyone on the other side.

"Where are we going?"

"To find this guy."

Unlike mine, Jerry's bravery performance is convincing. It's possible that, for him, it isn't a performance at all.

Jerry heads out and I follow him. My hand grips the knife so tight my fingers lose all feeling, and somewhere along the trail, it falls to the ground without my noticing.

20

JERRY HAS THE AIR OF A HUNTER ABOUT HIM. AN AUTHORITY AS HE PAUSES TO STUDY a print in the mud or a bent branch that suggests he knows more about searching for a predator in the woods than I ever will. Then again, given the twins' vocation, acting could run in his family in a way it doesn't in ours. It could be that Jerry is nothing more than a gym teacher who's used to ordering teenaged boys around and applies this confidence to every aspect of his life.

We work our way closer to the lodge at a tiptoed pace for fifteen minutes or so before Jerry detects a side trail I hadn't noticed on the way in. At first it doesn't look like much of anything. But twenty feet or so deeper, there's an evident pattern of pushed aside branches and indented grass underfoot that indicates a repeated course of travel for a large animal or man.

"There's another game Dad might have wanted us to play," Jerry says out of nowhere, as if we'd been conversing about the same topic without interruption since leaving the cabin.

"What's that?"

"Family Feud."

"Sorry?"

"Us against you. The two Quinlan teams. Only the strongest and smartest make it to the end and win the prize."

"You're not being serious," I say, even though it's pretty much what I was thinking.

"Look at us. This is some pretty crazy shit. And no offense or anything, but I don't even *know* you."

"Sure you do. I'm your long-lost half brother."

I try to keep my tone light. What Jerry is saying could be suspicious, or he could simply be explaining how unnatural this is. It's impossible to tell which is his intention, as he maintains a tone as half-jokey as mine.

He turns to face me. Smiling apologetically, but standing with his feet wide apart, rooted to the ground.

"How can I be sure of that, Aaron? How can I really know who you are?"

"You can't. We can either trust each other or not. Do you think I'm lying?"

"No. I don't."

"So I say we work together. We're family. It's an advantage we have."

"I agree. Believe me, I'm not accusing you of anything," he says with a sigh. "I'm trying to sort this out, that's all. I'm thinking how Dad might have thought."

"And how's that?"

"What?"

"I'm curious how you understand Dad's way of thinking."

It's a harmless query. But because we're out in the woods, possibly being watched—because we're invoking the presence of Raymond Quinlan—it comes out sounding loaded.

"If he's had a hand in this, it's going to be a jack-in-the-box," he says eventually. "We keep turning the handle until something pops out."

"That's an interesting way of looking at him."

"Is there another way?"

"Well, your sister's the shrink, not me. But seeing Dad as wanting each of us to open him up—I don't know, it speaks to a certain kind of experience."

Jerry cocks his head. Shakes an apparent stiffness from his legs. "You seem to be aiming at something here."

"We were both his sons, Jerry. Odds are, whatever contact you had with Dad was of the same kind I had with him," I start. "I just think, now that he's gone, we might compare notes. Maybe help each other see stuff that maybe we'd rather not see."

"I think I know where you're going here. And I'm going to ask you to stop."

"Don't you ever think about how Dad is kind of *blocked* from us? If something happened to me, maybe to all—"

"I'm asking you to shut your mouth."

Jerry looks more wounded than angry.

"I'm sorry. This is difficult for me to even bring up. And I didn't mean to—"

He holds his hand up. I figure it's to cut this conversation off, but then both of us hear something in the trees off to the right. At least, that's the direction I turn, though Jerry looks in the opposite direction.

He doesn't say anything. Not *Stay here* or *Get down* or *Circle back around*. He just bends low and starts into the bush to the left.

If he's wrong about the direction, whatever made the dull whump on the forest floor is closer to me than it is to Jerry. But he sure as hell seems certain. If I've learned anything over the last forty-eight hours, it's that noises can bounce around in the forest in a way that makes it hard to figure their distance or position. He may be going straight at the Tall Man. He may be leaving me behind.

I move in the same manner he did—crouching low and striking into the bush—except to the right. Hoping I'm wrong. Looking for a place to find cover and wait.

There's lots of potential camouflage out here if you happen to be wearing any shade of green. But if, like me, you're dressed in blue jeans and a blue Seahawks T-shirt and matching windbreaker (Dad getting all our favorites right in his duffel bag clothing purchases), there isn't anything but tree trunks to use as shields. None of them quite wide enough to be sure something on the other side couldn't spot you.

I keep moving as quietly as I can. Not looking for anything in particular now, not even a place to disappear, only advancing into the forest because the idea of waiting to be found is worse than the slow chicken walk I'm doing now.

When I look up after a minute or so, I find that the underbrush has thinned around me, the thistle and ferns only recently reclaiming the cleared soil. I wonder if it's an old burn site, maybe a lightning strike, a bald anomaly in the otherwise ceaseless thicket. But a few steps on and the growth only thins more and more before opening into a broader clearing.

That's not what stops me.

It's not much of anything now, but I recognize what it was. A single L-shaped wood structure the length of two tractor trailers fused together. Here and there on the flat ground around it are wood platforms that once acted as the foundation for wall tents. A circle of stones bordering a black mound of cinders. The two iron spikes of a horseshoe pit.

A summer camp.

It's not a place I've ever been to before. In fact, it's hard to imagine any parent sending their kid here, even when it was in good repair. The space of the site slightly too small, as if the effort of cutting its grounds out of the forest proved too difficult and what resulted was a cramped compromise. Hard to find even if you were looking for it.

Abandoned places are always a little sad, especially ones where children once played, sang songs by the fire, ran laughing. Yet this place feels more ghostly than sad. Maybe it's because I can't imagine what laughter would sound like here, what music would be allowed.

I think of turning back but convince myself there's a reason I'm here, push away the immediate counterquestions—*Why? Who says there's anything here for you?*—and start toward the sagging building I'm guessing was once the dining hall. Looking for something. A piece of my father. Something to convince myself that he'd intended I be the one to find it.

The windows along the walls and in the main entrance doors are boarded up, but carelessly so, leaving gaps at the corners and between the two-by-fours. On the ground, there are stray tent pegs and opened tins of food, the labels melted away on most but only faded on a couple others. Baked beans. Beefaroni.

There's a sign over the door I hadn't noticed when I first entered the clearing. Letters gouged into a slab of tree trunk and nailed into the pine so that, as all of it succumbed to the sun and mold, the words looked like they were becoming something else. A retraction.

BELFOUNTAIN

For as many times as I'd heard my father say the name, this may be the first time I've seen it written out. Pretty to hear and to speak, but it looks different to me now, the obese *B* followed by a jumble of letters. Over-voweled, inviting misreadings. *Elf* and *bell* and *mountain*.

Inside, I'm met by long-past odors: fried margarine and boiled bones for the making of soup. But these are only phantom smells. There couldn't be any of that left in the air after the years of neglect that have passed in this place. The watery strands of light that seep through the cracks of the windows show a row of tables and benches, award plaques high on the walls with the names of past orientation and archery champions engraved on brass plates. There are squares paler than the rest of the wall where photos probably hung, but they must have been taken away when the place was left, apparently the only things that were.

I should go because Jerry might wonder where I am. Because there's nothing here. Because I'm afraid that there is.

One of the swinging doors to the kitchen has been ripped away, and the fact that I won't have to touch the other one to step inside brings me closer. I float forward, reading the painted sentences on the exposed roof beams as I go.

MY LITTLE CHILDREN, LET US NOT LOVE IN WORD,
NEITHER IN TONGUE; BUT IN DEED AND IN TRUTH.

On the floor, boot prints in the seedlings and dust. Comings and goings along the same aisle I walk down. Likely from years ago. Though they could be more recent than that.

THE MEMORY OF THE RIGHTEOUS IS A BLESSING,
BUT THE NAME OF THE WICKED WILL ROT.

Lines of Scripture. *Little children*. Stern, magical, ambiguous. Is all of the Bible like this? Or is it only me not wanting to be here yet having to be, like many of the campers who would have read these same lines as they looked up from their hamburgers and oatmeal.

THE WICKED WILL ROT.

There's something on the floor. I can feel it before I see it, a series of cuts carved into the planks, the simple outline of a map. Then

I look down and see it's more like a compass—but no, that's not it either.

I recognize it from the movies we'd rent for those teenage slumber parties where I could never sleep. Something bad.

A pentagram. The circle with a star made of triangles inside it. Wider than the aisle, so that it reaches under the tables. I bend down to fit a finger into one of the grooves and it comes back blackened with soot. The lines not drawn. Burnt.

When I stand straight, I notice similarly made, smaller lines in the tables and on the walls. Messages. Summonings. A crude language in competition with the biblical quotations overhead.

SATAN HEAR OUR VOICE

The sort of thing stoned vandals leave behind, kids who've got their hands on those paperbacks about rituals and "true" accounts of devil worship, sacrifice, possession. Hard to find a picnic table in a park or wall of a public toilet without some version of it.

Knowing this doesn't make me any less afraid.

WE SING FOR YOU

I step out of the pentagram's circle in the floor. Before entering the kitchen, I cast my eyes up at the ceiling and catch the last line of scripture on the rafters, sounding through my head as something close to a threat.

UNLESS ONE IS BORN AGAIN, HE CANNOT
SEE THE KINGDOM OF GOD.

In the kitchen's leaden light, the stainless steel counters shine greenish as a snake's skin. Some of the larger cooking pots are still here, sitting on the stove top, the lids on. I don't pull them off to see if there's anything inside.

It's the walk-in freezer that's captured my attention. The padlock hanging open through the latch.

The handle pulls back with a guttural *clunk*, and from there the door eases wide without my having to do a thing, as if wanting to show me its insides, wanting to breathe. It reminds me that I haven't taken a breath myself for a while. When I do, the sound I make is that of a child startled after being struck.

There hasn't been power here for a long time, which makes it even more unsettling to walk into the freezer's warm tomb. The insulation within the stained steel walls holds the airless humidity inside, as it would any sound or voice that might try to get out. There's more space than I was expecting. The shelving has been completely removed, leaving only rust-weeping holes in the walls. Room that had to be made for the trapdoor in the floor.

It's also made of steel except it's new, a square plate of dimpled silver the size of a compact pickup's flatbed. A handle on the left to lift it open. It would be heavy if I tried.

I try.

It sends a warning flare of pain up my back, from my hips to the back of my skull. But I manage it. Once I have it past the halfway point, I let it go and it rests against the wall with a single *nick*, like the touching of nails to a blackboard.

Stairs. Each step made of smooth cement, heading into the ground beyond the range of what I can see.

Why do I do it? I ask myself this as I start down, ducking my head and reaching my hands out blind. It may be raw curiosity, but if it is, I don't experience it as *wanting* to know what may be down here. If anything, it's the opposite. I wish only to be protected from discoveries, from any new layer of Belfountain's possibilities. It's like the patients I have who demand surgery instead of the alternative therapies or pharmaceuticals or waiting and seeing, things they could do to avoid it. They don't want to be opened up, but if they submit to it, they hope they can put the entire matter of illness behind them.

The stairs are steeply sloped but remain straight so that once I get used to it, just enough daylight filters in to see shapes and outlines by. The equidistant seams in the ceiling. The irregularities in the cement's cratered face.

The steel wall.

There's no way around it. The stairs come to an end and there it is, no space to stand.

A moment of inspection shows it isn't a wall, but a door. One with no handle, no markings. I smooth my hand over its cold surface, drawing lines through the condensation, and feel nothing interrupt its gray surface but a single keyhole built into the metal.

I press my shoulder against it. It feels more than locked. Sealed tight.

As an object, as an incongruent *thing*, it makes no sense. And the longer I lean into it, feeling for a vibration or voice from within, its possible meanings flee from my grasp. The door has a purpose and history distinct from the forest, from the Christian kids' camp built on the ground fifteen feet above my head. Beyond that there isn't a single guess I could make.

But I do know this: the door is special. My knowledge of it even more so.

Which means I can't stay here.

For the first few steps I don't turn, backstepping my ascent and keeping my eyes on the door as if in readiness for it to be pulled open. Then the darkness reclaims it and not being able to see it frightens me more than imagining the thing that might open it, and I spin around, jumping the last few steps up into the walk-in freezer's airless space.

I don't drop the trapdoor closed. Don't touch the freezer's door. I just get out.

WE SING FOR YOU

Through the dining hall, dancing over the lines of the pentagram in the floor, keeping my pace to a walk as if to do anything else would confirm how terrified I am, I bring out the childish moan I can feel swelling up my throat.

Only once the light makes visible the stones around the charred circle and the overgrown horseshoe pit, a verifiable place in the world where things not only happened but are happening now, do I feel like I'm being watched.

A sudden wind picks up, blowing fast against my face. That's what my mind interprets it as before it discovers my body has taken charge. Moving my legs. Throwing me forward.

Running.

21

I HAVE A SENSE OF THE WAY I'D COME AND WHERE THE MAIN TRAIL IS BUT I CAN'T find any sign of either. I'm relying on the logic that if the trail is reasonably straight I'll meet up with it if I don't get turned around.

The sight of Jerry standing a hundred yards ahead proves it's a good guess.

He doesn't see me approach, but he hears me, judging by the way he searches the horizon of brush surrounding him. It gives me the strange feeling of being the Tall Man myself. Semi-visible, deciding what action I will take next.

"Hey!"

I call out to him as I step back onto the main trail and he approaches with deliberate steps.

"Where'd you go?" he asks.

"Back that way."

"See anything?"

"Nothing. You?"

"Not a goddamn thing."

He keeps his eyes on me.

"You look spooked," he says.

"It's a spooky place."

He studies me a moment longer. Measuring the hazards I could potentially pose. It's only after he starts back along the trail that I realize I'd been doing the same thing looking at him.

When we return to the lodge, Ezra and Elias are in the middle of reprising their roles in a recent Delta Airlines commercial. A tearjerker involving twins separated at birth reuniting at JFK Arrivals after a lifetime apart.

"You haven't changed a bit!" they both declare at the end, chins trembling with emotion, before throwing their arms around each other.

Mom, Bridge, Franny, and Lauren, seated on one of the great room's enormous sectional sofas, applaud in the restrained manner of a golf gallery.

"A single day's work," Ezra says.

"Paid the mortgage for two years," Elias says.

"Do you two live together?" I ask, and all of them swing around, startled to find me and Jerry standing there.

"No," Elias answers.

"That would be *weird*," Ezra adds.

Lauren is the first to get up. "Hold on," she says. "How'd you get in?"

"The door was open," Jerry says. "I'm assuming that the boys didn't lock it after they came in looking for breakfast?"

The twins look first accusingly, then guiltily, at each other.

"Sorry," they say at the same time.

"Did you find anything?" Lauren addresses this to me.

"No."

"So what's next?"

"Maybe your brothers could do a live performance of the first season of *Better Together* for us?"

It's meant as a tension reliever, but it comes out as unkind. Everyone hears it, none more acutely than the twins themselves, who take seats on opposite sides of the rug from each other, turtling their shoulders forward against further injury.

"I didn't mean—" I'm on my way to apologizing, but Jerry steps ahead of me to stand directly in front of Lauren.

"This man that Aaron saw," he says. "You saw him too?"

"Yes."

"You're certain?"

"*Jesus*, Jerry. *Yes*. I'm certain."

Jerry paces once between Lauren and the twins before stopping to look down at Mom, Franny, and Bridge on the sofa—one, then two, then three—counting them off in his head as if taking a head count.

"I say we all stay here until we can sort this out," he announces.

Franny snorts. "It's so funny," she says.

"What part?"

"You. Automatically assuming that you get to make the decisions."

"I'm offering my opinion, that's all."

"Please! *Look* at you. Standing in the center of the room with your arms crossed and all of us waiting to hear what the great leader is going to say. We're out here and there're no cops, no laws, and you see an opening. Grabbing power."

"First of all, what's going on here—this isn't *political*. And second—"

"You voted for *him*, didn't you?"

"What? Hold—"

"Thought it was time to build some walls, go back to the good old days when nobody *bothered* people like you."

Jerry pauses. "How do you think you know who I vote for?"

"When's the last time you looked in a mirror?"

I wonder if Jerry is going to hit her. Not that he looks like he will. Not a violent man in the compulsive sense, but one distilled in the culture of weight rooms and off-campus keggers and sports bars who proves his masculinity through the giving and taking of shots to the jaw. As a pretty boy, he's probably had to prove it more than most.

But Jerry doesn't hit Franny. He grins at her. As warm and genuine an expression as I've seen him or any of us make.

"Okay, you got me, Francine," he says. "Of *course* I voted for him."

"Bingo!"

"Here to help."

Fear doesn't always take the form you assume it will. It can be a scream into the darkness, paralysis, a hopeless sobbing. But it can also come out in a guffaw, hearty and loud, as it does now from my own throat. I'm not the only one either. The twins rouse from their sulk to giggle like a pair of school kids. And Bridge, uncertain at first, is soon laughing along with the rest of us.

It's a release. But soon it distorts in our ears, the hysteria rising up through the hilarity, twisting our voices into those that come from behind the closed doors of an asylum.

"We should leave."

Without any of us noticing, Mom has gotten up and watches us from the farthest edge of the room. She doesn't speak loudly but we hear her clearly all the same. One by one, the laughter dies and returns to ice in our chests.

"We should leave," she says again. "Now."

"Why do you say that, Eleanor?" Jerry asks, ready to be convinced.

"It's not safe."

"Well, with respect, we don't know that. If you consider the facts—the likelihood that it's just a vagrant that Aaron and Lauren saw. Some tent-city guy who hitched a ride up here and can't find his way out again."

"That's not what's happening."

Nobody denies this. Not even Jerry, who, whether out of deference to Mom's seniorhood or to avoid hearing the sharpness that may come out in his voice, shrugs and sits on the arm of the sofa.

"We're all free to go," Lauren says, moving closer to Mom. "It's just a matter of the will—"

"I *hate* that word!"

Because I'm still standing at the top of the steps down to the great room, I can see how all of us jolt back at the force of Mom's shout.

"It was *his* will that was the only important thing all his life, and it's still him telling us what to do," Mom goes on. "What about us? What about *our* will?"

"I understand what you're saying, I truly do," Lauren says. "But it seems you're making a more practical suggestion. Am I right?"

Mom calms herself before speaking. Whatever she's about to attempt to convince us of, this may be her only chance.

"If we all leave, we can be safe," she says. "If any of you are concerned about the estate, we can contest it. Legally. What's going on, what he's asked—it's not normal. I can't imagine it standing up in a court of law, especially not if it's all of us together."

"I dunno. That Fogarty guy seemed pretty legit," Ezra counters.

"And we can't get legal advice without a phone," Elias adds. "To walk out now—that's a hell of a risk to hope some judge sees it our way."

"Bridge?" I say, and it takes a moment for her to blink her eyes clear. "What do you think?"

"We're all here," she says. "There's a reason for that."

There's nothing in her delivery to suggest if she thinks this reason will work for us or against us. But her posture is firm. She's not going anywhere.

Mom looks to Franny. The most likely vote to go her way, under the circumstances. But Franny only sighs.

"It's millions of dollars, Mom," she says. "There's so much that could be done—so much good. So much change."

"It *is* a lot of change," Elias agrees.

"A good chunk of change," Ezra nods.

"Just because nothing awful has happened doesn't—"

Mom lets this sentence hang there, as if speaking aloud the words we know to logically follow would risk triggering some magic of fate.

"Shall we take a vote?"

I'm the one who asks this, and so it's me who my mother looks at with despair.

"Don't trouble yourselves. I know the count," she says, and starts away toward the kitchen with first Bridge, then Franny following after to console her. I consider doing the same, but Jerry is coming at me to deliver a clap to my shoulder.

"What do you say we fortify the castle, doc?" he says.

22

TURNS OUT THERE'S NOT MUCH WE CAN DO. ONCE WE CONFIRM THE BEDROOM AND bathroom windows are locked, we search the lodge for any other possible points of entry. There's the front door, the glass door built into the giant windows along the length of the great hall that Franny had used to slip out for her smoke, and a third one off the kitchen that leads to the garbage bins with metal lids to discourage animals and bears. All locked.

Which still leaves the giant windows. Jerry guesses they're more solid than the walls; the reinforced glass is of the kind used in skyscrapers. Yet as the afternoon fades and the dusk grows, what's worrying is what we might see outside as much as how it might find a way in.

Over dinner, there's a discussion about the threat the Tall Man poses that eases our minds somewhat. His appearance suggested mental illness of one kind or another, and as Lauren points out, the mentally ill are statistically no more inclined to violence than anyone else. Our best guess is that he found his way inside Belfountain's fence somehow and is trying to survive.

There's also some talk about ways we could get our hands on the satellite phone in the metal box on the other side of the gate. But the rules Fogarty laid out would disqualify whoever went to fetch it from participating in the will's proceeds. How would anyone know if someone did? Maybe they wouldn't. Then again, maybe there're cameras recording our movements all along the perimeter.

None of us volunteers to try. Partly this is because we actually don't need the phone. It's also partly because nobody wants to be the one eliminated from the will and have to trust the rest of us to voluntarily make up for their lost cut. I wouldn't say this latter thought indicates any deep distrust between the two Quinlan families. It's simply a consideration that all of us judge best left unspoken.

After we've eaten, Bridge, Mom, and Franny retire to their rooms, leaving Jerry, Lauren, me, and the twins to determine two-hour shifts for each of us to keep watch while the others doze in the leather chairs. I take the middle of the night. Two to four. An island of nervous wakefulness between two seas of insomnia.

Yet there must be some sleep for me before the morning, because when I wake, I remember the dream I had. The same one from the first night at Belfountain that I shared with Franny and Bridge.

Jerry is up already, as he isn't in the chair he slept in. Judging from the restless snorts and coughs from the twins, they're having nightmares too.

When they both open their eyes, I ask if they can remember their dreams.

"Not usually," Ezra says. "But the one just now was a doozy."

"Got that right," Elias says. "Like *nas*-ty."

"What were they about?"

"Water," Elias says.

"Dark water. *Salt* water," Ezra adds.

"And this weird music. Like singing."

“Alien singing.”

Elias turns to his twin brother. “You were there,” he says. “In the dream.”

“You too.”

“Treading water.”

“Not a pool or pond or lake, nothing with a shore. The water all the way to the horizon.”

“Except you couldn’t even see the horizon.”

“Or the bottom below us.”

“Like it was deeper than the ocean.”

“Like space.”

“Yeah. Empty as outer space.”

Lauren sits upright in the chair she slept in.

“I had the same dream. I had it the first night I was here too,” she says.

“Me too,” I say. “Except last night it was different from before.”

“Different?” Elias asks.

“Different how?” Ezra adds.

“My sisters were in it. And so were you.”

23

ONE OR TWO OF US WERE MISSING IN SOME OF THE RETELLINGS. OTHERS HAD A small detail to add that the others lacked. But unless some of us were outright lying, everyone who slept in Belfountain's castle last night dreamed the same dream.

Everyone except Mom.

She doesn't say she didn't, just avoids the topic when she shuffles into the great room in her slippers and purple velour tracksuit that must have come in her duffel bag. She listens to us talk about the dark water, the fear of what lived beneath our kicking feet, the cosmic singing. When Franny asks her directly about it, she shakes her head—what could be a *yes* or *no* or *I can't think about this now* sort of gesture—and heads off to the kitchen to get started on mixing pancake batter.

"You're the shrink," Franny says to Lauren. "What the hell is happening to us?"

"I've heard of shared dreams within families before, but nothing this extensive," she says. "There are theories of how telepathy can be explained—you know, how people claim to have jumped out of bed at the exact same time a relative died miles away. This is different. Psychology proceeds from an individual clinical basis, not a group. We work on the assumption that while we influence one another, our minds process these interactions in distinct ways."

"So, bottom line, you have no idea and you're as freaked as the rest of us."

"It sounds like you're after my job, Franny."

"To be the shrink to *this* crew? I don't want it."

After an assessment of the dwindling supplies that remain in the freezer and fridge, it's decided we ought to send someone out to the gate and see if any food has been left for us. On the basis that I'm the only one to have made the journey there and back, all eyes turn to me.

Before I go, I wait for an opportunity to speak with Bridge.

Ever since I returned from the forest after discovering the camp, I've hesitated in sharing it. Even with all the strangeness of this place, the tunnel leading down through the hole in the walk-in freezer radiated something different. A thing not meant to be seen.

The best course would be to keep it to myself. An underground staircase, a solid steel barrier—none of it is going to attack us all on its own. If we never come upon it again, whatever it may contain will stay below.

I wouldn't disclose it to anyone if it wasn't for the promise I made to Bridge.

Later that morning, as Lauren and the twins busy themselves making a couple trays of lasagna, Franny and Mom whisper to each other in a corner of the great room, and Jerry walks through the place checking on everyone and giving pats on the back and little pep talks like the high school coach he is, I pull Bridge aside. We close the door to the bedroom Mom and Franny are using, and I tell her about the camp.

I'm expecting her to voice the same questions troubling my own mind—Who built it? Why way out there?—but she makes a statement instead.

"Daddy took me there."

"Where?"

"To that old summer camp. The door at the bottom of the stairs," she says, nodding as she works to summon the details. "He didn't call it a door though. He just said, 'There's something I want you to see.' "

"What did he show you once you got there?"

"Nothing. We were walking through the trees for what felt like a long time, and then it was there. A couple old buildings, a swing set. We went into one place, into the kitchen. Inside the freezer there were stairs going down. When we got to the bottom, he seemed about to say something but then changed his mind, and we turned back."

"Did he have a key? Did he open it?"

"I don't remember a key. And like I said, I don't remember it as a door. It was just the *end*, y'know?"

The sound of footsteps creak over the floorboards in the hallway outside. There's a pause as whoever it is notes the closed bedroom door before turning and heading away again.

"What do you think it is?" Bridge whispers.

"My guess is a gate of some kind."

"Like the fence we drove through? A gate *inside* a gate?"

"Something like that."

I start for the door, seeing this as an opportunity to return to the others without rousing suspicion, but Bridge stops me.

"Why me, Aaron? Why would Dad bring me there?"

"I don't know. Maybe he had to show someone, and he thought you'd have the best chance of understanding."

"That might make sense if he told me. But he didn't."

She flinches. A blade within her twists with the effort of trying to grasp our father's intentions. That I know how these attempts will invariably prove useless only doubles my sympathy. She needs a theory to cling to, a narrative that indicates he was human. It's not about making excuses for him. It's about seeing a way of not being the child of a man who meant to break you.

"Secrets—the big ones—are hard to let go of," I say. "Even when you want to, even when they're too much to bear. It's like they hang on to you by a power of their own."

Bridge nods again.

"We should get out of here before someone asks what we're talking about," I say, pulling the door open.

"We're not telling anybody else about this?"

"I don't think so."

"Because if they knew, they might try to find the camp."

"They might."

"And that would be bad."

"I'm not sure it would be good."

Judging from the way Bridge walks past me without another word, she agrees.

24

AT THE LAST MINUTE BEFORE I SET OUT, LAUREN ANNOUNCES SHE'LL COME WITH me. It's a decision Jerry doesn't look too thrilled about but doesn't attempt to prevent.

We start out walking the bike but soon guess it will take us the better part of what remains of the morning to reach the gate at this pace. That's when I suggest Lauren ride in the wagon attached to the back.

"This is ridiculous," she says, correctly, as she curls herself up in the plywood box.

"You'd rather do the pedaling?"

"Are you kidding? I just hope nobody sees us."

It felt like we were about to break into laughter a moment ago, but the idea of the two of us being observed by something out here, out in the woods, chokes it off.

After I get us up to a speed I can maintain, I'm impressed by how well the contraption rolls along, the momentum of our weight combined with my pride in showing Lauren I can handle the physical challenge of getting us to the gate in what feels like not much more than forty-five minutes or so.

When I dismount, she's out of the trailer and heading straight toward the food-delivery opening in the fence.

"Looks like we got a drop-off," she says.

Two cardboard boxes sit on the half of the metal circle on the outside of the fence. There's no sign of a vehicle or anyone waiting to ensure the delivery gets into our hands. I squint to see if there are tire tracks in the road and there may be—snaking lines that could be tire treads—or all I'm seeing is the dried retreat of rain.

"So this thing just turns around, like this?" Lauren says, spinning the plate around and plucking the boxes off.

"Okay," I say. "Let's get out of here."

"Hold on. How do you think this works?"

She's looking at the dangling wires over the hole in the fence the boxes passed through.

"I'm guessing it's part of the security features."

"You think they're electrified?"

"I haven't touched them to find out. But I—"

She pinches one of the wires with her thumb and forefinger before I can stop her.

"Nope," she says.

I watch as she stacks the boxes in the bike's trailer and rips one of them open. Pulls out a loaf of bread and a jar of peanut butter.

"Picnic?" she says, holding them both in the air.

"If you can find some jam in there, I'm in," I say, happy to be with someone brave for a change, instead of pretending to be brave myself.

Lauren puts her hand into the box and brings out a jar of raspberry jelly without looking.

"Where there's the *pb*, there's got to be the *j*," she says, settling into a level circle of tall grass at the edge of the trees a dozen feet behind us.

It's mostly shady, but the light finds its way through the overhead branches in irregular shapes so that as I sit next to her, she is visible in blocks of gray and dazzling yellow. We open the jars and each roll up a slice of bread, dipping it into the peanut butter and then the jelly with each new bite.

"You're not afraid, being out here?" I ask her.

"I'm not afraid of you."

"I wasn't talking about me."

"I know what you're talking about. The *unknown*," she says, and takes another sticky bite.

"Yeah. I guess I am."

"Well, I try not to worry about that too much," she says once she's swallowed. "As a matter of fact, I go out of my way to face it down. It's helped me."

"I suppose your patients are like that. People just imagining things."

"*My* patients? No. *My* patients have been through the most real shit ever. They have no need to imagine anything except maybe a day of feeling close to normal or a good night's sleep. It's why I've never understood people who go to horror movies or read novels about dragons or demons or whatnot. Why go looking for scary stuff when there's plenty of that available all around us?"

"Unless you've been protected from it."

"Safe," she says, and pauses, as if the word was the name of a fabled island. "Safety is a privilege."

"But it's one you had, right? We both did. I mean, we're Quinlans."

I intend this as a kind of joke, an acknowledgment of how, despite our upper-middle-class circumstances, our upbringings were fundamentally less than picture perfect. Instead, it nudges Lauren into a cloud of thoughts that make her lower what's left of her bread onto her knee.

"I've never told anyone this," she says, "but I think I know what it is to be a Quinlan better than anyone."

Lauren looks up into the branches and the new angle of her face makes her look different. Sadder, angrier, less controlled. More beautiful too.

"After she had the twins, my mom wanted another child, but their birth was hard on her—she couldn't carry children on her own after that," she says, lowering her eyes to me again. "Adoption. She liked the idea of rescuing a kid from the wrong side of the tracks, someone she could use the Quinlan sandpaper on to smooth away the rough edges. Dad seemed okay with all of it. If anything, he paid more attention to me than my brothers. It was like he felt more comfortable with someone who wasn't biologically his than the ones who were. It's funny, but sometimes I got the impression that he saw himself as an outsider just like I was, someone dropped into this reality who had to bluff their way through it, find a way to fit in. As if we were both adopted. Know what I mean?"

"Maybe he never liked himself," I say, and hear the subtext so clearly I worry I actually said it aloud. *Maybe he never liked me*.

"Did he *like* himself? That would've been a question he'd see as beside the point," Lauren says. "He simply *was* himself. A narcissist so self-involved he couldn't even be bothered to look in the mirror."

"You really did understand him in a way none of the rest of us did. How did that make you feel?"

She blinks at me. "*How did that make you feel?* Really, Aaron? Who's the therapist here, anyway?"

"That was dumb. All I—"

"No, it's okay. Nobody's ever asked me that before. Not about Dad." She moves her hand through the grass but I can't see it. I imagine it as a snake slithering between us. "I was five when I was adopted, which is fairly old as those things go. So when I became a Quinlan, I had a chance at having a real father for the first time. I just wanted to love him and for him to love me too. But he couldn't do that. The best he could do was remind me that I would always be on my own. It started me on this journey toward seeing how everybody could be reduced to a profile, a set of tics and prejudices and fetishes. Everybody is a fake. That was his message. A fake like him. Like me. But because we came from outside, we had an advantage. We *knew* we were fakes."

"But you're not."

"How are you so sure?"

"You just told me that. And because you're trying to get to the bottom of who you are because you believe there's something real there. It's why we decided to stay here, isn't it?"

"It might have had something to do with the money."

"Not for us. Not for you."

I hear the sound like a snake in the grass but this time I don't see her hand move.

"No, not for me," she says.

We screw the lids onto the jars and stuff them along with the bread back into the box. I offer Lauren a ride back to the lodge and she pantomimes a curtsy before getting into the trailer.

"Why'd you come out here with me, anyway?" I ask after a time, pedaling up a slope and taking a break as we roll down the other side.

"I told you. I don't like letting myself be afraid." I think she's done, but then she adds something I'm not expecting. "I realize things are kind of tense between our families. I mean, how could they not be? But I want you to know that I think you're okay, Aaron. In fact, I kind of wish you'd been a big brother of mine."

"I'm touched," I say without irony.

"You know what I hope?"

"What?"

"I hope there's hot sauce at the bottom of one of these boxes."

"And a bottle of whisky."

"I wouldn't get your hopes up."

Lauren's right. In addition to the rules that won't allow us to leave, the absence of outside news or entertainment lends a monastic quality to Belfountain. It's something I took at first to be a denial of pleasure, part of the sacrifice that must be made to earn the prize Dad has dangled before us. But now I wonder if, like the monks who devote themselves to their enlightenment, it's more about staying focused.

"What if we're wrong?" I ask, thinking about the camp but not willing to share this yet.

"Wrong about what?"

"What if this isn't personal? Not about Dad messing with our heads one last time, but bigger than that."

"Bigger?"

"His work."

"What was his work?"

"Exactly. Whatever it was, like you said, it was enormously lucrative."

"Assuming he made his money from his work. He might have inherited it."

"From an ancestral line of Quinlans none of us ever knew?"

"I hear you," she says. "It doesn't fit."

"None of it does. But if you're right about Dad being a sociopath of some stripe, why would he go to all this trouble in the service of feelings? Your theory is he didn't really have any of those, right?"

Her silence communicates her agreement.

"Where are you going with this?" she asks finally.

"What if Belfountain isn't the fruit of his work, but his workplace?"

"Doubt it. There's no offices or desks. No computers. There isn't even a phone line. Nothing."

I'm about to say something about how the lodge may not be that kind of office when the old woman appears in the middle of the road.

She's dressed as she was when I saw her our first night here. The bare feet, the threadbare robe and exposed chest, the hair standing high and stiff with filth.

What's different is this time she moves. Spreads one arm wide from her side as if beckoning me into her embrace. The other arm slides behind her back. To hold her straight. Or grab hold of something.

We're still rolling down the hill, the fastest speed we've reached. The wind huffing in my ears.

I could try the brakes—the old-fashioned backpedaling kind—but I doubt they'd make much difference. And I don't want to stop. I want to hit the old woman, feel the impact of her body. Prove she's real.

Lauren doesn't see the woman because she's facing backward. The next moment will come at us whether two of us witness it or only one.

When the old woman is ten feet away, it's clear she's not going to get out of the way.

My arms twist the handlebars by reflex. The bike jolting to the right.

Behind me, Lauren's weight is thrown from one side of the trailer to the other but she stays inside it. Not that I look. All of my attention is on the old woman. Eyes milky with glaucoma. Tar-covered gums. The spiky whiskers of a beard.

Followed by the feel of her.

The burn of her fingernails that scratch my face as we pass.

"Aaron!"

I'm pedaling now. The slope has evened out and the bike's speed relaxes into the same steady pace as before. Could the old woman catch us if she ran? I look back, half expecting to see her flying over the road, a witch with her robe flapping behind her like rotted wings. But we're taking a curve and the trees obscure where she stood from view.

"What *happened*?"

Lauren is pulling herself up onto her knees.

"I thought I saw something," I say.

"Was it him?"

"No."

"So—"

"I don't know what it was."

I touch my hand to my face. It comes back thinly glazed with blood.

"You're bleeding," Lauren says.

"Must have got hit with a branch back there."

"It looks too neat for that. There's, like, three lines on your cheek."

"Hold on," I say, and stand up on the pedals, driving us faster and faster until the leaves become a solid tunnel of green.

25

ONCE WE'VE TAKEN THE BOXES INSIDE AND LOCKED THE LODGE'S DOOR, LAUREN busies herself restocking the fridge and pantry shelves, hoping these tasks will transport her back to the everyday world. I know because I try the same thing myself. Shave. Take a shower. Put a Band-Aid over the worst of the slices on my cheek and repeat my story about an errant branch to the others.

None of it works.

I decide to tell everyone at dinner. Not only about the encounter with the old woman, but about how I've changed my vote. Mom was right. We have to go. The will can be contested, and our case will either hold up in court or it won't. But we were wrong to see this as an eccentric's amusement park. Dad told us the stories about Belfountain not as flights of fancy, but as the truth. Possibly even a warning.

I never get the chance to say any of this.

We're sitting at the dining room table, the twins' lasagna steaming on plates in front of us, when there's a banging at the front door.

If Jerry hadn't jumped out of his seat and broken into a sprint toward the foyer, we might have waited to see how long it went on for. But watching Jerry respond the way he does prompts all of us to rush after him.

When we make it to the door, Jerry is peeking through the three-inch-wide windows set on either side of the entrance.

"What's out there?" Elias and Ezra ask at almost the same time.

"I can't see—"

Bang! Bang! BANG!

Not against the door this time. The great room's windows.

It only takes a few seconds to turn and rush to see what's there. But by the time we look across the living area there's nothing to see outside. Only the glass still visibly vibrating in its frame.

"There's two of them," Jerry says.

I'm ready to talk about what we ought to do. But there's no talk. There's only Jerry unlocking the front door and stepping out into the night.

"What the *hell* are you *doing*?" Lauren shouts after him.

"Oh shit, oh shit, oh *shit*," Elias moans.

I lock the door.

"Why'd you do that?" Ezra asks.

"I'm keeping us safe."

"Jerry's out there."

"That was his decision."

The twins shift their weight from foot to foot in the way of drunks readying to throw the first punch.

"What's going *on*?" Franny asks.

"They're out there," Lauren answers.

"Who?"

"The ones who live in the woods."

The ones. The choice of words, along with the way she says it, suggests Lauren believes there is not only more than one, but more than two.

"Let's sit down," I say.

"And do what?" Ezra says, now coming up close to me along with his twin.

"Talk about our childhoods?" Elias says.

"We need to work this out together. And we need to stay controlled. Whatever is happening—"

As if in response to a whistle sounding at a pitch none of the rest of us can hear, the twins stalk off down the hall at the same time.

"Aaron?" Bridge pulls away from Mom's hold to stand next to me. "We should find a smaller room. And tools. Sharp things. Anything to fight with."

"Those are good ideas," I say, but remain where I am.

"Aaron?"

"Yeah?"

"We should do it now."

We start to. All of us heading toward the kitchen, when Elias and Ezra return holding serrated, wood-handled steak knives.

There's a helpless moment when I think they're going to attack us. I push Bridge behind me, shielding her. But the twins pass by and unlock the door.

"Don't do this!" Lauren pleads, but only Ezra faces her.

"That's our brother out there," he says, an actor at his most convincing because he doesn't appear to be acting. Then he too walks out into the darkness.

"Close the door," Mom says.

When we're locked inside again, there's nothing to do but put Bridge's plan into action. Go through the kitchen drawers and find what may be useful as a weapon (even harder than before, as the larger knives have already disappeared). Then we cram ourselves into Mom's room only to discover that none of the bedrooms' doors lock.

It's still better than standing in the middle of the great room. Here at least we can conceal ourselves and, if found, mount a focused defense against anything that tries to come in.

"I'll be back in a second," I tell them. "Don't open the door for anyone until I get back. I need to check that all the entry points are still locked."

"You think someone left a way in?" Lauren asks, a note of defensiveness in her voice.

"I just think it's worth checking."

I circle the lodge's interior to confirm all the windows and doors are secure. When I'm at the great room's wall of glass, I squint outside. It's too dark to see much of anything, so I flick on the floodlights.

They're powerful but don't penetrate the forest, only pull it claustrophobically closer. Yet turning on the lights triggers something to be heard, not seen. What may be a voice from outside. A possibly human cry from not too far off.

"Turn off the lights," Lauren says behind me.

"I heard something."

"Me too. That's why we should turn them off."

26

"WE NEED TO BARRICADE OURSELVES IN," FRANNY SAYS AFTER LAUREN AND I return to the bedroom and tell the others we heard something outside.

I bend down to grasp the end of the bed frame. "Someone help me with this."

"That won't work," Bridge says. "It's too big."

"How about this?" Lauren asks, pulling a wooden chair away from the desk against the wall. "We could jam it under the door handle like they do on TV."

"Does that even *work*?"

"Hell if I know."

"Okay," I say. "We'll do the chair thing. Then push the desk in tight behind it."

We're trying to figure out how to get the back of the chair in tight under the handle when there's a new round of slams at the front door.

Boom! Boom! BOOM!

Vibrating through the log bones of the structure and up our legs through the floor.

Bridge comes to me. Her face held up to communicate something that words, even if she were to attempt to speak them, couldn't capture. She looks so young. Like the day on the floating dock after playing Peter Pan. Her fear expressed as a need to reach me, for someone she trusts to share in it, to not be alone with the sudden fact of death.

"Help! *Help* us!"

A voice from outside. Shouting through the front door.

"We need a doctor! Aaron! *Please*!"

It's one of the twins.

"I have to go," I say to Bridge. "Stay quiet. Hide in the closet, under the bed. Nobody knows you're here."

On the way to the front foyer, I try to tell myself there's some measure of safety in where I've left Bridge, but of course the truth is if anyone gets past me, it will be a matter of minutes or less for her and the others to be found.

So why do I go?

Because this is what doctors do.

What I've done on transatlantic flights, after coming upon car accidents at the side of the highway, at a Mariners game when a man fell sideways out of his seat from a coronary. Why I went overseas. They call for a doctor and, even when I'd rather be as useless as everyone else—the head-shakers watching the clips of faraway disasters on TV or the rubberneckers rolling past the wreck—I go.

It's not bravery. Not goodness. It's like being the eldest child, the only son. It's an expectation.

"Move back from the door," I shout through the wood.

"Hurry. We need—"

"Move away!"

There's what may be a shuffling retreat from the other side. Then I unlock the door and pull it open.

It's Ezra. Standing at the bottom of the steps down to the gravel parking area, shaking so violently it's like I've caught him midway through the performance of an experimental dance.

"He's over here," he says.

27

I FOLLOW HIM BUT HANG BACK JUST OUT OF REACH. THERE'S NOTHING TO INDICATE this is a betrayal and yet the better part of my instincts believes it is. If not set by Ezra himself, then by the thing in the woods that has trapped us both.

Ezra stops at the corner of the lodge and looks around it to where I can't see. Perhaps the Tall Man stands there, making him do this. Or they've been working together from the beginning, an elaborate performance now coming to its end. The twins are actors, after all. Maybe all the second Quinlans are.

These thoughts don't stop me from joining him and looking around the corner.

There's no Tall Man. Only Elias on the ground. Lying on his back, a dark stain seeping through his shirt, widening from the place where the polished silver handle of a hatchet sticks out from his belly.

He looks like a clockwork toy.

My first thought. It's the smooth, glinting metal of the handle coming out of him. Maybe two feet long, the right size and color for the winding key you'd twist to make him come to life.

No, that's not part of him. Somebody put that there.

The blood has spread even within the couple seconds I've stood looking down at him. His eyes roll around before fixing on me. His breathing a series of oddly coquettish gasps of surprise.

"What happened?"

"We got separated," Ezra says. "There was a voice—Elias thought it might have been a woman, but I couldn't tell—and he went after it."

"Was it—"

"I don't *know* what it was! I just heard him struggling with something. When I found him—" Ezra shakes his head, freeing himself from everything that doesn't matter now. "Can you help him?"

I get down on my knees next to Elias, roll the shirtsleeves halfway up my arms.

And do nothing.

A man is bleeding out from a wound to his abdomen. That's all I know, all I see. I try to summon a chapter from a medical textbook that covers the treatment in a case like this, but nothing comes.

I should remove the hatchet. Or is that exactly the wrong thing to do?

I don't *want* to do it. That probably means I should. In moments like these, the things you don't want to do are the things you have to.

The silver handle is jittering as Elias's breathing becomes more labored. This makes it even more difficult for my hands to find the handle, grip hard. The little pulses of waning life traveling through the blade within him and into me.

I should warn him. Reassure him. *This might hurt a little. I'm going to sort this out, okay?* But there's no sentence that seems remotely utterable, remotely true, and so before I succumb to the dizziness prickling around my face like a cloud of gnats, I pull a snort of air through my nose and lift the handle up and away.

He makes a sound. Not one that comes from his voice, but his body, an exclamation from the momentarily open space the blade once occupied.

I drop the hatchet on the ground. The top half of me weaving over Elias, fatigue draining me so abruptly I'm worried I'm going to drape myself over him and not be able to roll off.

"Okay, okay," Ezra is saying somewhere off to the side of me. "Now the next thing."

The next thing? What could that possibly be?

Apply pressure.

It's not specialized knowledge. Just something recalled from movies and TV shows. But how is pressure applied? Where? What is *pressure* in a situation like this?

I try.

Kneel closer and place one palm over the wound, then lay my second hand over the first. Push down hard.

Elias screams. His body spasming inward then falling back again. The heat of his blood pushing up through my fingers.

"That's *wrong*! That's *wrong*!" Ezra is shouting inches away from me.

This isn't applying pressure. This is an amateur version of CPR. And that's for heart attacks, isn't it?

I pull away from Elias and his eyes follow me, pleading. A second later Ezra's fist meets my shoulder.

"Do something!"

"I don't—"

"For fuck's sake. He's *dying*—"

"I don't know what to do!"

Ezra looks at me and sees that it's true. He doesn't argue anymore, only bends closer to his brother and whispers looping phrases of comfort—"It's okay. I'm here. Don't be afraid."—until Elias's breathing becomes a half dozen shallow hiccups before stopping altogether.

I've never seen them as twins as much as now. Before this, I took them as a comical adaptation of a single man, one who carried a mirror with him wherever he went and mimicked his own accent. They were one in a way none of the rest of us were. But now they are divided.

Ezra rises. His hands held out from his sides as if he's a tightrope walker finding his balance. Then he walks, toe to heel, toward the lodge's door.

28

THE DOOR IS LOCKED.

Nobody comes when I knock. I wonder if Ezra and I will have to survive the night out here. Behind me, the forest feels alive with new movement. Some of it animal, some of it unimaginable.

I knock on the door again, pounding with both fists this time.

When it opens, it's Jerry standing there.

"You left them? Hiding in here *alone*?" he shouts at me. When he sees his brother's face, my bloodied hands, his anger drains instantly away. "Where's Elias?"

"He didn't make it," I say.

"Didn't make it from what?"

"He's dead, Jerry. He was murdered."

The words themselves taste strange in my mouth. *Dead. Murdered.*

"That was him—that was his voice in the woods," Jerry says.

"We heard it too."

"I thought it was Lauren or one of your sisters. A woman. That's why I came back here."

I believe him. If I hadn't known Mom, Bridge, Franny, and Lauren were all inside the lodge when I heard the cry through the great room's windows, I would've guessed it was a female voice too.

"Jerry?"

Both of us turn to Ezra as if surprised to find him still here.

"Yeah?"

"Is this happening?"

"Yes."

Ezra grimaces, as if he had one last attempt at making all the badness go away and it failed, as expected.

But then his brother is there. His other brother, one half of all the family he has left, pulling him close in an embrace that gives them both permission to weep.

Lauren takes the news even harder than Ezra. As she's held by her brothers at one end of the sofa, at the other end Mom and Franny and I console Bridge, whose fear has finally overwhelmed her. It's overwhelmed all of us, but lending support to the youngest lets us hide the worst of it from view.

When we've partway recovered, the first thing Ezra demands we talk about is me. How I failed to help Elias.

"I honestly don't know. I don't," I say. "I just—nothing came to me in the moment. I'm so sorry."

"You must have been in shock," Mom offers.

"I guess. But it didn't feel like that."

Lauren studies me, the psychologist within her performing an assessment. "I'm sure there wasn't anything you could have done. Not without equipment or facilities."

"Maybe if we were in a hospital, it all would've clicked in," I say. "But I'm—I'm not sure—"

"You're a fucking doctor!" Jerry is suddenly close to me, shouting. "You were supposed to *help* him!"

"I *tried*!" I look over at Ezra. "You were there."

Do they see that I'm telling the truth? Whether it's that or the recognition that this debate won't solve anything, everyone now turns to Ezra.

"What about the body?" he says.

"What do you mean?" Lauren asks.

"I mean do we bury him now? Or do we do it in the morning?"

"Hold on a sec. I'm not sure anybody should go out there to dig a *grave*," Franny says, as gently as she can, though her ingrained sarcasm can't be wholly veiled.

"Not until the morning, anyway," Lauren offers.

"In the morning we're getting out of here. I'm assuming we're all agreed on that," Franny says. "Once we're back, we can send people to get Elias."

"No. Nope. No," Ezra says, shaking his head. "We can't leave him out there."

"I'm sorry for your loss, I really am," Franny says. "But why not?"

"He'll get cold."

I send Franny a hard look, silently telling her not to point out that Elias is going to be cold no matter where we put him, and she lets it pass.

"This must be unbelievably hard for you," I say. "You lost your brother tonight. But we can't forget how he was lost. How we're all in danger now and we'll only make it worse if we don't make smart decisions."

Ezra faces me. Dry-eyed. His head still.

"I'm not leaving him out there," he says, and rises.

"I'll go with you," Jerry says, and looks to me. "We're going to need some help carrying him."

• • •

I'm almost surprised he's still there.

I imagined the Tall Man dragging him off. Doing something worse. Yet, other than the whole of his shirt now discolored by blood, nothing has changed from how he was left.

Except I'm wrong about that.

"Where is it?" Ezra says.

"Where's what?"

"The ax thing. The hatchet."

We both look around the body, kick at the grass with our shoes. It's not where I dropped it after pulling it out. It's nowhere.

"Somebody took it," Ezra says.

Somebody took it back.

I can see Jerry understand this at the same time I do.

"You two get the arms," he says. "I'll take the legs. Let's do this fast."

Elias is even heavier than he looks. It slows us to shuffled half steps through the high grass.

"What was that?" Ezra asks. I didn't hear anything, and can't decide if I want to stop to listen for whatever it was or keep going.

"Nothing," Jerry answers, opting for the latter.

When Lauren opens the door for us and we lay Elias down on the foyer floor, the violence of the attack becomes more vivid in the full light. We can see it in the breadth of the wound, but also in his frozen expression. The terror not from death, but the way it came.

"Cover him," Ezra says, and walks away as if, now that his brother is inside, the duties to the other part of himself have been forever satisfied.

29

WE START OUT FOR THE GATE AT DAWN.

Jerry managed to convince Ezra to give up on the idea of burying Elias before we left, which still left the awfulness of all of us having to walk around his body on the floor, the white bedsheet we laid over him soaked through over the course of the night.

There's some discussion about whether we should take the bike or not. Jerry doesn't see the point, but I argue that one of us might need a rest along the way, and they could sit in the wagon and I could pedal for a time. In the end he doesn't stop me from squeaking along behind the rest of the party.

We don't talk much. Once in a while someone will ask how much farther it is, and it's left to me to provide an estimate. The route doesn't have many landmarks, only the curves around boulders and berms that look like the other curves around boulders and berms, the endless undulations of wooded ground on either side. It both stretches time and shrinks it so that just when I think the fence will be there over the next rise, it isn't, and its not being there makes me think it's still miles off.

"Not far," I keep saying until they stop asking.

It's good that we brought the bike. After what feels like a half hour or more of trooping along like a defeated platoon, Mom starts to hang back farther and farther. When I invite her to ride in the wagon, she refuses at first, repeating what may as well be the motto of her life. *I don't want to be a bother*. But eventually even she acknowledges her weakness and climbs in.

This time, it really isn't far.

The fence comes into view as a gray lattice. As we move closer its height, the sharpness of the razor wire laid atop it, its purpose to repel and contain, becomes clearer.

"That's where they keep the phone?" Jerry asks, spotting the metal box next to the road on the other side.

"That's what the lawyer said."

"Okay. We're all decided then? We leave together, all of us, right now. Agreed?"

We show our votes of assent through small nods and kicks at the stones by our feet.

"Good," Jerry says. "How do we open it?"

He poses this question to himself as he inspects the outline of the gate just as I had done when I first encountered it.

That's when I notice the humming.

An ambient resonance, constant and low, as if the product of the air itself. An electric lullaby.

"Don't!"

Jerry looks around at me, puzzled, at the same time he grips his hand to the metal edge of the gate.

His body stiffens. As in a game of Simon Says, his posture, his facial expression, the way his back heel is lifted in midstep off the ground—all of it is frozen. You could think it was a brilliantly deadpan joke if it wasn't for the reddening flesh of his hand. The wisp of smoke that seems to push its way out through the skin.

Jerry is flying.

There is no visible effort on his part, no kicking away or rolling of arms, and he looks like a plastic action figure that's been arranged into an inhuman contortion and then tossed by a giant's invisible hand.

He hits the ground next to Bridge, and she kneels next to him, putting her hand to his cheek, asking if he's okay.

"Don't touch it," Jerry manages, locking eyes with Bridge. "Nobody touch it."

Ezra hurls himself to the ground next to his brother on the opposite side from Bridge. Mom releases one of her sob-laughs.

"You're kidding me," Franny says. "It's electrified?"

"Locked too, I'd guess," I say.

"All of it?"

"Unless there's another gate somewhere along the perimeter, I'd say yes."

No one says aloud what this means. No one needs to. The only one of us who speaks is Lauren, who is saying the same thing over and over. "Oh my God oh my God oh my God."

Eventually, she's quiet too.

From out of the forest, something howls.

LEGACY

30

EZRA GUESSES COYOTES. FRANNY THINKS IT TENDS MORE TO THE MOURNFULNESS of a hound. I don't say it out loud, but to me the howling could only be wolves.

It doesn't carry on for long. Distant, but not unreachably so. As likely coming from a source within the fence as outside of it.

When the sound stops, we don't speculate on what it was or where it came from any further than we already have. Every thought in our heads is a threat. Every turn from that thought only confronts us with another.

"We have to go back," Bridge says.

Jerry rides in the wagon. He's conscious and not outwardly injured aside from the burn on his hand, but his balance is shot. That means the trip back takes a while. Jerry's extra pounds force me and Ezra to push the bike along by the handlebars every time we come to a hill. But what really deadens our legs is the recognition that everything has changed. Even more now than after Elias's death. The cold fact is that was the end for him but not necessarily for us. Now we slouch back into the heart of the woods, the air pressing down on us with the weight of our error.

Here's what we know. What each of us is working to order in our minds according to our own fears or outrage or calculations of survival:

The stay on Dad's estate wasn't intended to be a get-to-know-one-another therapy session. It wasn't a game. The gate may be opened after another twenty-seven days, or it may not. It won't take nearly that long to determine how this turns out. Belfountain was never a fairy-tale kingdom. It's a prison.

Once we return to the lodge, we're reluctant to go inside. All of us seem to remember Elias's body in the foyer at the same time.

"It's going to take shovels," I say.

The equipment shed. The only chance we have to find not just what we need to dig a grave with, but tools to barricade the lodge's doors and smaller windows. There may even be something we can use to fortify the great room's wall of glass, if not cover it altogether.

The problem is the padlock on the shed's door. We talk about taking a rock to it or even heating it to a temperature where it would melt off (Franny vaguely remembers her high school science teacher saying such a thing was possible). As the rest of us carry on the brainstorming, Ezra walks away. We watch him head into the lodge. A moment later he emerges carrying the poker from the fireplace, long and heavy as a knight's sword.

The loop of the padlock is just large enough for the first third of the poker to slip through. Ezra positions it flat against the shed, grips the handle tightly with both hands, hikes one foot against the door. He puffs his lungs full like a squatting weight lifter. Heaves back on the poker.

The lock snaps and falls to the ground.

"Leverage," he says.

We all go in at the same time, including Jerry, who rises from the trailer and shambles into the shed's gloom. I'm the first to spot the pair of spades leaning against the wall, but there are other items of interest we pull off shelves or discover lying under oil cloths on the floor. Eight or nine two-by-fours spotted green with mold. A Folger's can of finishing nails.

The things we can use right away we haul out, and the rest—mostly just gardening tools, a battery-powered weed whacker, a box of mouse-traps—we leave in the shed. For some reason I slip a pair of pruning shears into the pocket of my windbreaker. A butter knife would probably make a better weapon. But I like the weight of them bumping against me, another heartbeat held close as I walk.

"I'd help but—" Jerry offers once we're all outside again, indicating his dizziness with the same tapping to his head he used to show the effects of his football concussions.

"We got this," Ezra says, picking up one of the shovels and handing the other to me. "Don't we?"

"This would be a good spot for him," I say, pointing over to a shady patch next to a clutch of buckthorn saplings between the Orange and Green trailheads. "What do you think?"

Ezra nods his approval. Steps close to me and grips my elbow with his free hand.

"Okay," he says. "Let's do this."

It takes the rest of the day to dig a hole, carry Elias's body swinging between us like a roll of wet carpet, and drop him in.

For the first hour of shoveling, I blink through the sweat and stop to look around the lodge's cleared drive, expecting to see the Tall Man step out of the trees. Ezra must be plagued by similar thoughts, as he proposes taking shifts with one of us digging while the other stands watch.

Plunge the spade's edge down. Separate the soil from the ground. Launch it to the loose pile beside the hole.

Stab, divide, heave. Stab, divide, heave . . .

It dulls the urgency of wondering what we ought to do next. It also quiets my guilt over watching Elias die.

Stab, divide, heave.

When we return inside, Jerry shows us how he's hammered some of the two-by-fours over the bedroom and kitchen windows, and done the same to reinforce the door next to the pantry. The nails he had to use are too short to make them very secure. And as for the great room's windows, there's nothing to be done. Yet he seems as grateful for the tasks he was able to complete as Ezra and I are.

"Just have to keep an eye on it," Jerry says, as if all of us aren't doing that already, looking for the monster to step out of Belfountain's snarled mass of life.

31

I COME OUT OF THE BATHROOM AFTER A SHOWER AND FRANNY IS THERE TO CORNER me in the hallway.

"You were in there awhile," she says, and with these words she's a teenager again, complaining about me hogging the hot water.

"I had a lot to scrub off."

"That must have been rough. Having to drag—"

"I'd rather not go through a play-by-play, if that's okay with you."

She grimaces in apology. "I'm scared, Aaron."

"Me too."

"Not just about what's happening out there. But in here."

She looks at me as if expecting her meaning to be clear. I assume she's talking about suspicions she has about members of the second Quinlans. In the next second, another possibility arrives. The *in here* refers not to the lodge, but our heads.

"Help me out," I say.

"Do you ever have the feeling you're losing your memory?"

"Little bits here and there. Names, some words. That's what getting older is all about, right?"

"I'm talking about since coming here."

"It's hard to keep a grip on the outside world in this place."

"That's *not* what I mean." She squeezes her eyes shut. When she opens them, they're shining with tears. "It's like I never had a past to begin with."

Had a past.

That this is something close to the feeling I've had my whole life takes me by surprise, as I've always assumed Franny was shaped by more objective injuries. What's different is that she feels that coming to Belfountain has triggered it. Unlike me, who's felt this way for as long as I can recall.

What's important is that Franny is telling me this. Reliably unreliable Franny. What she's experiencing is a symptom of withdrawal, most likely. A warped perception of time triggered by the anxiety of being here. All of it bringing her back to the loss that pulled the ground out from under her.

"This is about Nate, isn't it?" I say. "Trauma like this—it can strand you from what you know, what you love. It's like losing yourself. But he'll always be with you."

"That's just it. All I *have* is my love for him."

"And once we're out of here, what you carry of him inside—"

"You don't understand, Aaron," she says, and steadies herself, pushes aside her frustration for one last try. "I love Nate. But the boy that love was for, the games we'd play together, his first words, the shape of his face—all the things a mother never lets go of—aren't where they should be."

There are at least two deaths that result from dying. I've seen it a thousand times. The first is the failure of the body. The second is the failure of the living to remember. I'd always assumed the impact of the latter was buffered by its gradual retreat, the pulling of images out of the mind's photo album, one by one. But maybe for some—for Franny—it can come faster than that. Maybe it can come all at once.

Never had a past to begin with.

"I meant to tell you this, was waiting for the right time—but you know how it is with right times."

"They never come."

"I didn't want to hurt you more than you already were. Maybe I was chickenshit, and just ran away," I say, and pull in a ragged breath. "No, it was that. Might as well admit it."

Franny looks up at me about as soberly as a person could. "Is this about Nate?"

"Yeah. After he died."

"Tell me."

So I do.

I tell her about coming back to my condo a few days after the funeral, looking around at the collection of furniture and unread magazines and unhealthy plants that made up my life, and deciding to clean the place. Top to bottom, floors, corners, the whole deal. I'd been doing it a lot after I'd come home from overseas. My therapist called it "mental cleansing."

What was different this time was that it wasn't the attack I was thinking of as I dusted and scrubbed. It was Nate. And as if these thoughts of him brought part of him back, I was moving the sofa to reach the vacuum behind it and found a balloon. Green. Still fully inflated, with streamers and fireworks stenciled on it. A leftover from the little birthday party I had for Nate a few weeks earlier.

"It felt light in my hands but warmer than it should have, as if a pair of other hands had been holding it before passing it to me," I tell Franny, and she watches me as I speak, her chin trembling. "I don't know why I did it, but I untied the knot and let the air out. Just stood there feeling it pass like a warm breeze over my face. Except it *wasn't* a breeze. It was the air from Nate's lungs. He was the one who blew up the balloon. And I'd helped him do it, holding it as he huffed and puffed, and then tying the end when he was done. It was *him*. This thing I could *feel*. This voice I could almost hear."

"What did it say?"

"Something like, 'This is me. I was here. I was alive, Uncle Aaron.' But not in words. Just breath."

Franny is crying, but her body is more still and solid than it's been the last twenty-four hours.

"Thank you for bringing him back," she says, and gets up on tiptoes to give my cheek a cold kiss.

For dinner, Mom pulls out the lasagna leftovers, but when Ezra spots the aluminum trays, it's as if he sees a portrait of his lost twin in the baked cheese and noodles they made together, and we all silently agree to return it to the fridge.

"Ham sandwiches?" Mom offers with the same brittleness as when she would sell us a menu for school lunches on a Monday morning.

As we eat, to avoid complete silence, I ask the others what gifts Dad left for them. In addition to a compass for Bridge and the neon running gear for me, Lauren found a magnetic chess set in the bottom of her duffel bag.

She tells us it was the only thing she and Dad ever did together, just the two of them. He never let her win. Something she appreciated, actually. It meant he took her seriously. His intent was to teach her to look three, four, five moves ahead. What she came to learn was that you saw the way the game would play out not by tactics alone, but by thinking the way your opponent thought.

"It was psychology. Getting past the rules and strategizing in order to reach into the motivations of the person across the board from you," she says, before putting her sandwich down on her plate. "Once I understood that, we never played again."

Ezra and Elias were meant to share their gift. Dad's watch. The vintage Bulova they were always asking to wear.

"I don't remember that watch," Lauren says. "Do you have it on now?"

Ezra pulls back his sleeve to show us his bare forearm. "I left it with Elias," he says, and we all involuntarily glance at the wall as if we have the X-ray vision to see the freshly covered grave thirty feet on the other side.

This wasn't where I wanted the conversation to go. I ask Franny what was left for her, and as soon as I do, I realize this was an even bigger mistake.

A baby rattle. She found it in a drawer in the bedroom she and Mom are staying in. A really beautiful one, hand painted with colorful birds flying over a lake with snowcapped mountains in the background. Japanese, she guesses. Something Dad brought back from one of his trips for Nate, his only grandchild.

When she finishes, Franny glances over at me, and I can tell she doesn't recall the rattle. It's something else that's been lost to the years of junk put in her veins or, if she's to be believed, stolen by Belfountain itself in the time she's been here.

"What about you, Jerry?" Lauren asks.

"Me?"

"You're the only one left. What souvenir did the old man leave for you from the great beyond?"

Jerry digs into his pocket and pulls something out. Brings his hand to his mouth and blows.

Tw-eeeeee-t!

So shrill it jolts all of us in our chairs. When he's done, Jerry drops the referee's whistle onto the table.

"What do you make of that?" he asks nobody in particular.

"You're a coach," Lauren says, reassuring. "It's what you do."

"I know! I *know* that! Wouldn't he also know I've already *got* a damned whistle?"

You don't have to be a psychologist to see it. Jerry hasn't yet let go of being a player, the guy on the field that people watch from the bleachers. He's a teacher now, but one still young enough, fit enough, to think he could get back into the game someday. The whistle tells him something different. It says there's only the sidelines left for him.

"Don't look at me like that," he says to Lauren.

"Like what?"

"Like you're assessing one of your clients."

"I'm actually on your side here, Jerry."

"My side? What does that mean, exactly?"

Lauren takes a steadying breath. The kind I imagine a therapist must make before venturing into a topic she'd prefer to avoid.

"It means we're family," she says.

Jerry stares at her, and I almost expect him to ask her to repeat what she's just said because he hadn't heard it.

"That's one of those things that depends on how you look at it, am I right? Family," he says. "Consider us, for instance. Consider you. The twins had each other from birth. I had Mom to hold up. And you, Lauren? The special little gift who arrived late in the game? You were the observer. Watching us like you were the director of the psych ward. And this was when you were eight years old! You found your calling early, I'll give you that."

All of Lauren remains still except for the pooling tears in her eyes, thickening but not yet falling. She won't let them.

"That's not fair, Jerry."

"Maybe not. But it's true."

He rises with his plate in his hand.

"Thanks for the sandwich, Eleanor," Jerry says, and with his free hand picks up the whistle, weighs it in his palm, the plastic marble rolling around inside, then stuffs it back into his pocket.

There's more howling that night.

It comes through the wall of glass and reaches me in the chair I've almost fallen asleep in, which makes it hard to guess its distance, though I'd say it's closer to the lodge than it was when we were at the gate.

Not coyotes. A single animal. Throaty and hoarse.

I can't tell if Ezra or Jerry, the ones who've chosen the sofa and other chair, hear it too. They don't move. They don't ask in a whisper if anyone else is awake.

Which probably means they are.

32

WE DON'T ASK IF WE ALL HAD THE DREAM AGAIN. WE JUST START TO TALK ABOUT the ways last night's was different. The new details that, as Bridge puts it, make it like one of those invisible spy papers kids play with where the message is only revealed after shading with a pencil until the whole page is covered.

"So you go first," I say to Bridge in the kitchen as I spread peanut butter on her half of the bagel we're sharing. "What's your spy message?"

"My page isn't totally filled in yet," she corrects me. "But last night there was a boat."

The activity in the kitchen—Franny pouring Lucky Charms into her bowl, Jerry pulling hash browns from the toaster oven, Ezra cutting an apple, Mom frying up a storm—comes to a stop.

"It was sinking," Ezra says.

"Yes."

"The tallest part, where the captain steers, it went down last," Franny says.

"Yes."

"And then the outer space singing again," Jerry says.

"But it wasn't coming from space."

"It was coming from the water," I say.

That's not all that was different. This time, Bridge was in it too. Floating next to me but struggling, too tired to keep treading water, her arms slapping at the surface before she started going under.

I woke up then. Even in my dreams I can't tolerate the idea of anything bad happening to her.

"If we're all thinking what each other is thinking," Jerry says, "then you know what I think we ought to do this morning."

"Hypnosis therapy?" Franny suggests.

"No. How about you, Aaron? Take a guess."

"See if there's another way out through the fence."

"That'd be it."

"I'll go," Ezra says, popping the last of the apple in his mouth.

I would volunteer but I don't want to leave Bridge here on her own, not again. Jerry reads my hesitation, seems to understand it and approve as he looks my way with the smallest shake of his head.

"It's the two of us then, Ez," he says, and starts to pack his breakfast up in the plastic bag the bagels came in.

None of us can estimate how long it will take to hike around the entire perimeter of the estate. The terrain may be variable in the corners of the property we haven't seen. Whether the brush has been cleared away from the fence or allowed to grow thick against it will be a factor too.

What we're dancing around but not addressing directly is the thought that Jerry and Ezra may have to spend the night out there.

"What if there's another gate and it's wide open?" Franny asks before they go. "You won't just skip on out, right? You'll come back and let us know?"

"I will," Ezra says.

"We *both* will," Jerry says, and follows his brother out the door. "We're family, right? Leave no Quinlan behind."

33

FOR THE REMAINDER OF THE MORNING, MOM, FRANNY, AND LAUREN TAKE STOCK OF what's left in the kitchen so that we can ration it into portions if we have to. There's still enough to get us through the next couple days. More if we're careful. And there's no reason we can't expect further deliveries will be made to the main gate. Still, with the electrification of the fence and with it the removal of the option to leave, our dependence on supplies worries me almost as much as the Tall Man.

I'm sitting on the enormous slate slab that juts out from the base of the fireplace, a modernist plank of stone floating a foot off the floor, when Bridge joins me. She sits next to me, and I can feel the undercurrent of sorrow coming off her like heat from someone who's just finished a run, though she hides it with playfulness.

"You know what day it is?" she says.

"No idea."

"Tuesday. If we were back home, we'd be having one of our dinners tonight."

"God. You're right."

She looks up at me. "Tell me about them."

"Don't you remember?"

"Of course. I just want to hear you tell me."

"Well, we'd talk. I usually didn't have much to report, but you always had news."

"What was the news of my life?"

She's looking for a way out of this place. So I do my best to give her one.

When she was six and I first started taking her to a Chuck E. Cheese or a steakhouse (we took turns choosing), Bridge was still in the tail end of the Princess Era. This was a time when she'd happily spend an hour wearing the plastic tiara or white elbow-length gloves I'd buy for her, retelling the plotline from *Sleeping Beauty* or *The Little Mermaid*, which always ended with her eyes closed, imagining the scenes in her head.

Eight was the Age of Dance. Modern, ballet, hip-hop—her twice-a-week teacher singling Bridge out as her most promising student. Dance was the first career pursuit she ever declared, and based on my impressions when I attended her recitals, she actually had a shot. I was disappointed when she quit (a twisted ankle, then displacement as the teacher's favorite at the hands of a rival). But forever after I could detect the trace of sophistication she brought to the simplest movements as she returned a jar of pickles to the top shelf of the fridge, or waved goodbye and ran to the front door after exiting the taxi when I brought her home.

At ten came boys. Crushes. Jealous conflicts with classmates over the cute new kid (or the kid who everyone had ignored for years who'd returned from spring break with a haircut that elevated him to cuteness). Longing. Its reach swinging between the innocent to the worrying borderlands of grown-up desire.

During those dinners, what Bridge wanted to know about me above anything else was when I had my first date, first girlfriend, first kiss. The precise dates of these events were of crucial importance. She kept a literal calendar of when, based on my responses, she could expect these milestones to happen to her, and she would pelt me with questions when they didn't.

Our most recent meetings, from the age of twelve to the present, carried over many of the issues of romance but combined them in a newly curdled pubescent mixture of unpredictable moods, bodily alterations, ruthless girl politics. Bridge no longer looked to me for answers on any of these matters. What I offered was a dumping ground, a place to disgorge the self-contradictions I couldn't offer a prescription for even if I tried.

Tuesday dinners with Bridge are, by a wide margin, the event I look forward to most. They're not just a way of connecting with her, but with time. I told her this when we last got together. How following the stages of her life meant more to me than my own.

"That's because you haven't *had* stages, Aaron," she replied matter-of-factly. "You've always just been you."

Is this true? Did I enter the world feeling obligated and angry and alone?

"How're you doing?" I ask her now.

"I'm okay. We're getting out of here. I keep telling myself that. Seems to help."

"I was asking about you."

"I don't feel the cancer coming back, if that's what you mean."

"It's not," I say, though in truth it more or less was. "Just checking in."

Bridge gets to her feet, pats the top of my head. "Next Tuesday?"

"Wouldn't miss it."

34

I DON'T SLEEP THAT NIGHT. WANDERING THROUGH THE LODGE LIKE A GHOST LOOKING for other ghosts.

Everyone else is in their rooms at the end of the hall in the direction I think of as north even if there's no way of saying for sure, the direction of the sun these past days pursuing a random course through the clouds. The moon too. An angled crescent false as a clown's smile.

I'm trying to find the light of it through the trees, moving from the great room's glass to the small windows on either side of the front door, when I see it.

Not the moon. A figure standing outside. Watching.

There's not enough light to confirm it's the Tall Man. Whether it is or not isn't the right question anyway. It's about saving lives now. About Bridge. Is the best way to do that waiting to make sure a monster stands outside? If he moves back into the trees, this could be a lost opportunity. If he finds a way in, it could be a danger I won't have a chance of heading off.

"Aaron?"

Franny is in the foyer. One look at my face and she can see there's something outside.

"Lock the door behind me," I say.

I'm outside before Franny can demand I come back. Not that she does. There's only the *clunk* of the bolt sliding shut.

I hold a hammer in my hand. The one that Jerry used to nail the two-by-fours over the smaller windows. It felt heavy and decisive a moment ago. Now, in the cool night air, it shrinks to the size of a fork at the end of my arm.

The figure doesn't shift. Fifty feet away, maybe less. A distance that if crossed at a walk would give him the chance to square into position. But at a run, there might not be time for that.

I'm sprinting forward. The hammer raised over my head.

Feeling the weight of it, what it can do if I bring it down hard enough, takes me to a different moment. A different place. Something I'd forgotten from *overseas*.

The men emerging from the trees. Coming into the village with the machetes held at the level of their waists, swinging and slashing. And me doing the same thing. My hand gripped to a blade of my own. One that finds the arms and hips and throats of the men from the forest. Attacking the attackers. Cutting them down.

Stop!

It sounds like me. The part that wishes this wasn't happening, that would rather be running away from the bad thing than at it.

Aaron! Don't!

Hearing my own name is the first correction that brings me back to this forest, this night.

The second is seeing that it's not the Tall Man I'm about to bring the hammer down on, but Ezra.

He has his hands held up in front of him, and once I'm still, he brings them down to show how frightened he is. Not just by me about to attack him, but by whatever he's gone through, whatever he's seen.

"I'm sorry," I say.

"It's okay."

"I thought you—"

"I get it. But could you put that thing down?"

He means the hammer. It takes a moment to lower it, as if the metal and wood have interests of their own.

"How're we doing here?" Jerry asks, approaching with caution.

"We're good," I say. "Bridge, Franny, Mom, Lauren. Everybody's safe. What about you? You find anything?"

"Maybe we could talk about it inside," Jerry says. "I'm about done with this walking-around-all-night shit."

Jerry had told Ezra to wait out front while he walked around the lodge, making sure there were no signs of break-in before knocking at the door. By the time he returned, I was charging at his brother with a hammer.

"I wasn't going to wait for someone to get in," I explain in a whisper, the three of us along with Franny standing in the front foyer.

"It was a good plan," Jerry says.

"He nearly cracked my head open," Ezra says.

"But the *plan* was good."

"What about you two?" Franny asks. "You make it all the way around?"

"Every damn foot," Jerry says.

"Find anything?"

"There was an old lady," Ezra says. "We both saw her."

"What did she do?"

"Nothing. Just watch us."

"Did you try to get closer?"

"We figured she might be looking for us to do just that," Jerry answers. "And if that's what she wanted, it may not have been a good idea."

"You think the Tall Man was with her?" This is me, whispering again, not wanting Bridge to come around the corner to hear whatever the answer is.

"Is that what you're calling him?" Jerry says.

"You got a better name? Slim, maybe? Frederick?"

"The Tall Man it is. And no, we didn't see him."

"Anything else?" I ask.

"Three things," Ezra says. "There's nothing on the other side. No power lines, no roads, no buildings. Two, we took one of the shovels with us and tried to dig under the fence by the gate. Didn't work. It goes down *deep*. And the metal underground is charged just the same as aboveground."

"The third thing?"

"There's no way out."

"What about a ladder?" Franny asks.

"We don't have a ladder," Jerry answers.

"Maybe we could make one? With the tools in the shed?"

"It would need to be twenty-five feet high at least. To build that without lumber? Using a can of finishing nails? Not gonna happen."

Even though the four of us knew all of this, we were holding on to threads to the outside world. Now they've been cut once and for all.

"Not through the fence. Not over it either," I say, spinning a new thread. "But there might be another way. We'll just have to get a little lucky."

35

THE PLAN I PITCH AT THE FRONT DOOR IS SIMPLE: STAND BY THE FENCE'S GATE AND wait for whoever delivers the supplies to return. When they do, have them open the gate, and if they can't, ask them to call an ambulance to treat one of us at the lodge for emergency medical assistance.

"Why tell a story?" Jerry asks. "Why not just say we've been kidnapped or whatever is actually happening to us?"

"The truth could be something they already know about and have been instructed how to handle," I say. "But if we tell them there's a *problem*, it could push them off their game. Get them to act spontaneously."

This will either strike all of us as a good idea or we'll be too tired and shaken to come up with anything better. Franny and Ezra wait for Jerry's response.

"So who's going?" he asks.

I'm not planning to volunteer. But Jerry holds his gaze on me after asking his question, and it's clear he's not about to head out there again after walking around the entire estate in the night.

"Guess it's my turn," I say.

Jerry gives me a damn-right-it-is nod, but I don't read it as bitter. We're a team now and I've been tapped to take a shift.

"When're you heading out?" he asks.

"Now."

"In the dark?"

"Nobody said the deliveries would come during daylight."

Jerry pulls his headlamp off and hands it to me.

"Take some batteries with you," he says. "Believe me. You don't want this thing to go out."

I pull together a plastic bag of food, one of the steak knives from the drawer, the batteries Jerry suggested, an empty pickle jar of water. Tie the arms of a sweatshirt over my shoulders. When I'm back in the foyer after making Franny promise to keep Bridge safe until I return, Lauren is standing there.

"Ezra filled me in," she says.

"He woke you up just to give you bad news?"

"You think I was asleep? That's really funny."

She raises her arm to show me a plastic bag of her own.

"I'm coming too," she says.

"You don't have to."

"No. But if you go alone and we have to wait a long time for you to come back, it makes sense to have a messenger."

"You didn't mention how I might not come back at all."

"I didn't think I needed to mention that," she says, and clicks her headlamp on, blinding me.

• • •

It's still dark when we arrive at the gate. After a sip from the water in the pickle jar, we nestle down in the grass at the edge of the road. Lauren faces to the left and I to the right. We don't pull the steak knives out. It's as if doing so will risk materializing the danger that, for now, remains waiting just beyond the range of our headlamps.

Should we speak? Would that make sitting here, slapping mosquitos from our necks, any better? The dark decides it for me. There's too much of it to not attempt to push it back with conversation.

"Lauren?"

"Yeah?"

"I've got something I'd like to ask you."

"That makes two of us. You go first."

"How did Dad die?"

She pauses. Not upset by the nature of the question, only working to retrieve the answer.

"A cardiac event. That's what the lawyer said. Or did someone else say it? Jerry or one of the twins? I definitely remember that word, anyway. *Event*. Like it was an opera or wedding reception."

"Did you ask for any details?"

"I suppose I didn't need any. You?"

"Same."

"A man Dad's age—it happens."

"It's not how he died I'm stuck on. It's how little we know about it."

"He's a man of mystery."

"Yeah, but this time the mystery isn't him. It's us."

Around us, within the space of seconds, the plants, the trickling stream at the bottom of the ditch, the road's gravel, all of it gains a muted color. The dawn painting the forest.

"My turn," Lauren says, pulling her legs up and wrapping her arms around her knees.

"Okay."

"What was that about you forgetting how to be a doctor? After Elias was—after what happened?"

"That's not exactly how I'd put it. Forgetting. But I'm not lying, Lauren."

"I'm sorry. That sounded like an accusation. I was just laying out the logical problem—"

"I know what the logical problem is. And I don't have the answer to it."

"Then what do you have?"

A feeling of helplessness. Being an alien to myself. Angry without knowing who to be angry at.

These are all the things I consider saying but don't. They don't get at the larger thought I've been having, something I haven't arrived at fully in my own mind, so I take a run at it now.

"I wish I could have done something for Elias," I say. "But since coming here—there's been a change. That's the only way I can describe it. Which makes me wonder if you feel the same."

She doesn't answer this right away.

"Being here—" Lauren stops with a tiny gasp. "Let's just say it's made me question who I am."

The morning continues to color itself into existence. But instead of the different shades of the forest's green making it less formidable, it reveals its capacity for deception, to hide in plain view.

"I was thinking about our families," Lauren announces.

"What about them?"

"Don't you find it interesting that none of us have romantic relationships to speak of? That none of us, other than Franny, ever had kids?"

"I blamed Dad for that. It's kind of automatic for me now. You got trouble making friends? *Dad.* No girlfriend? *Dad.* Feel like only half a person most of the time? *Dad.*"

"I came to the same conclusion myself for a long time," she says. "But now that I see all of us here together, the absences we share in our lives, the same dream we have at night—they're conditions I recognize from my practice."

"Trauma. That's your specialty, right?"

"So I'm wondering if we've all been through something. I'm wondering if that's why I was drawn to this area of therapy in the first place."

If Lauren is right, why don't any of us remember? She'd probably say this is precisely the way trauma works—it conceals its own scars; it masks, obliterates. But wouldn't *something* come through?

It's my powerlessness to grasp what might have been done to us that brings the outrage. If I knew what my trauma was—the one before what happened *overseas*, the one that feels like it might have involved Dad somehow—maybe I could have shielded Bridge from it. I could have stood up to whatever wanted to take part of our identities away (*Let's just say it's made me question who I am*) instead of filling the space with work or dope or whatever each of us put at the top of the daily to-do list that we pretended was a life.

"Shhh."

Lauren hears something. Then she sees it. Her eyes widening before she wills herself into composure, stands up, and walks toward the fence.

36

A WHITE PANEL VAN. NO WRITING ON THE SIDES, NO WINDOWS IN THE REAR, AS nondescript a vehicle as there exists. It seems to slow its approach when it spots us so that it rolls up to within twenty feet of the gate at a walking pace, the individual stones grinding and popping under the tires.

It stops. The engine cuts off. The audible ratchet of the emergency brake being set.

Nobody gets out.

It hadn't occurred to me that the driver would be under orders to have no contact with those on the other side, that he might turn around and no van, this one or any other, would ever come back. How do we appear to whoever considers us through the windshield that mirrors the patch of sky overhead so that we can't see who sits behind the wheel? A man and a woman. Respectable, intelligent sorts under normal conditions, but desperate now. People to avoid.

Lauren doesn't speak. I can only assume she fears what may happen if she does. The sound of our voices, calling for assistance, will be the end of it. It would be so easy to not help. Any additional nudge from us might decide the matter.

The door opens. The driver, a man, gets out. Slow as someone trying not to antagonize a bad back, though this may only be what suspicion looks like.

"Well, well," he says, louder than necessary as he comes a few steps closer but leaves the van's door open. The seat belt warning bell tolling from inside, but he doesn't go back to close the door. "Good day to you!"

The delivery man is middle-aged, portly, his bald head covered by a wool cap set at a comical angle atop his head. The fleshiness of his face welcoming in the way of a contented husband and father, a lover of simple pleasures: extra gravy on his potatoes and telling stories to the grandkids who climb onto his knees. A man who would not only provide you with directions if you asked, but offer to drive you where you're going.

"Can you help us?"

I ask this as plainly as possible. A reasonable man asking another reasonable man a question; there's no need to see it as anything but what it is. And while the delivery man mostly appears to hear it this way, his round face droops a little. His natural friendliness, the muscles used to hold his grin up loosening at the indication of something not quite right.

"You two don't work in there, do you?" he says.

"No, we don't."

"Then who are you?"

"My name is Aaron Quinlan, and this is my half sister, Lauren. We're being held prisoner. One of us—a child back at the main building—has been seriously injured—"

"Hold on now, *hold* on—"

"Needs medical attention. Could you open the gate?"

By the look on his face he hears this last part as if it was something to take offense at. An insult directed at his wife. His country.

"Open the gate?" he repeats.

"Let us out. Or if that's something you're not able to do, could you get on your phone and call for an ambulance?"

He scrutinizes me through the woven metal. Takes his time. The friendliness incrementally vacates from every aspect of him.

"Wait, wait, *wait*," he says finally, as if a number of options have cohered in his mind all at once. "Y'all refugees or something?"

"What?"

"The fence. All the hush-hush. This one of those detainment facilities?"

"No. It's not that—"

"You must be pretty special if you've got the whole place to yourselves," he says, too pleased by his internal detective work to pay any attention to me. "Most camps I've seen on TV are a lot more filled up with illegals than this here. How many *are* you, anyway? Half dozen? Dozen? Man, you've got to be bad news. You've got to be *spies*."

Lauren quiets me with a little back wave of her hand. This isn't working and now it's her turn.

"I understand what you're thinking, but we're not refugees or spies or anything like that," she says, her tone confiding, respectful. "We're the victims of a crime. Kidnapping. If you don't believe us, that's fine, just tell the police we're here. It won't be on your hands."

"But it *will*, lady. I've got instructions. 'Don't tell anybody what's going on up there.' Good thing is, I don't even know. *Boom!* Done."

"You're making a mistake. We're—"

"No. Uh-uh," he says, shaking his head so hard his jowls shudder. "*You* made a mistake. If you're in there? *You* made a big mistake, and I promise you, it's not touching *me*."

The delivery man starts toward the van.

"We'll die in here!"

Lauren's cry stops him. He looks back at her, then at me. He appeared so likable and open a moment ago. Now the hatred alters his features even as we watch, transforming him. He looks through the fence and doesn't see a man and woman. He sees the cause of every problem he's ever had. *Why me? Why hasn't it been easier? Why haven't I gotten all I wanted?* And the answer is us.

"I'm not helping you," he says. "I quit. What's more, I'm not *telling* them I'm quitting. And I'm the only one who drives these boxes up."

"Please. Don't—"

"Shut up! *Please, please, please*. That all you people do? Beg for handouts?"

He regards us with the same exasperation he would a pair of stray dogs who keep coming around scratching the paint off his door. It firms up the decision he'd only tried out seconds ago.

"Well, you can starve in there. Understand?" he says. "Because I sacrificed for my country. My family was *born* here. So it's what you deserve, far as I'm concerned."

A handful of sentences run through my mind, appeals I might voice aloud.

I can give you millions of dollars.

Do you have any children? You do? Because my little sister, my fourteen-year-old sister, is in here too.

I'm trying to decide between them when the delivery man hops up into the van and pulls the door shut.

It's the engine throat-clearing to life that starts us shouting for him to come back. There's no argument anymore, no attempt to reach his emotions or loyalties. Lauren and I wordlessly holler and wave the same as anyone standing on the wrong side of a fence.

The van reverses and goes forward twice, making sure not to slide into the ditch. When he's got himself straightened out, he rolls off down the road, the brake lights winking as he goes.

37

WE TRY TO TELL OURSELVES SOMEONE MAY STILL COME FOR US. THE DELIVERY man will have a change of heart. Even if he carries through with not bringing us the supplies he's supposed to, his employers will figure it out and replace him. There must be a system in charge of this operation, some kind of oversight.

The more Lauren and I work to buttress these arguments, the less convincing they sound. The forest itself seems to mock our attempts at hope. When we finally give up, the willow leaves applaud in a breeze too high up for us to feel.

When we make it back to the lodge, Franny is standing at the door. I assume she's waiting for us. But she's not looking our way, her gaze seemingly fixed on the mound where Elias is buried.

"Franny!"

She swings her head around and clasps her hands to the doorframe as if steadying herself on the deck of a rolling ship.

"She's gone, Aaron! She's *gone*!"

• • •

It's true that life can flash before your eyes.

It's also true that life may not be your own.

As I rush to the lodge's door, Franny's tear-puffed face coming into detail with each stride, I measure my existence through the Tuesday dinners I've had with Bridge. The "cocktails" with Shirley Temples (for her) and lager (for me). The comic books created on napkins to kill the time as we wait for our orders to arrive. The permission we'd give each other to be goofy, a pair of bratty kids out on the town.

Bridge is gone and she's taken both of us with her.

"Where'd she go?" I demand of Franny when I reach her, grabbing her hard by the knobs of her shoulders. "What *happened*?"

"She didn't say she was going. She didn't—"

"I told you to *stay* with her!"

"No, no, no," Franny says, stepping out of my grasp. "Not Bridge. *Mom*."

And she's there. My little sister approaching from behind Franny and squeezing into the space between us. Looking up at me.

"Mom left us," she says.

"Why?"

I'm not expecting an answer from her. But she offers one anyway.

"I'm not sure. But I think she went to look for Dad."

38

NOBODY SAW HER LEAVE. THE OTHERS WERE KEEPING TO THEMSELVES, WAITING for Lauren and me to return, and then Franny noticed the front door was unlocked and Mom was nowhere to be found inside. Jerry offered to go out and look for her but Franny begged him not to. There were forces trying to pull them apart—something the Tall Man and the old woman were part of, but more powerful than the two of them put together—and they had to resist.

"We have to find her!" Bridge shouts at me when I lean against the foyer's wall to avoid slumping to the floor.

"I know. I—"

"Aaron!"

"Just give me a second. Just—"

"*Please*! It's our *mother*—"

"Stop it!"

Franny's shout quiets both of us.

"It's scary that Mom's not here, Bridge," she goes on once all of us are looking at her. "I'm fucking scared too. But now is the time to work through things. Be smart. Wouldn't Mom want that? For you to do the right thing not just for her but for everybody?"

This reaches Bridge the same as it reaches me.

"Yes," she says.

Bridge sits cross-legged on the floor. A student who's made a presentation and now it's someone else's turn.

Jerry and Ezra take the opportunity to ask me and Lauren questions. When we're finished relating the exchange we had with the delivery man, Jerry speaks for us all.

"Nobody's coming for us."

Lauren attempts to reason how there must be people who know we're here, that they wouldn't just leave us like this.

"Nobody's coming," he says again. "Fogarty said thirty days. Maybe they'll open the gate, maybe not. But we're on our own until then."

Now that we hear someone say it all other possibilities dissolve.

We talk about whether or not we should look for Mom. Without referencing Franny's earlier mention of "forces" or what happened to Elias, it's decided it's too dangerous to just fan out into the woods calling her name like we're searching for a lost dog. We'll wait until late afternoon to see if she comes back on her own. If not, we'll consider our alternatives.

All I want is to rest. Talk with Bridge about anything other than what's happening so that the fear I can see in the way she's now breathing through her mouth instead of her nose might be quieted. But Franny won't let me. She pulls me into her room and closes the door.

"I saw him, Aaron."

She means Dad. I'm so sure of this I can see him too, waving at us through the great room's windows, laughing in the superior way he did when we'd tell him the bedtime stories he told were too scary, as if the only humor he responded to was seeing how unstoppably the seeds of irrationality could grow in inferior minds.

Which means Dad isn't dead.

Which means this really is only a game. Soon Elias will walk in wiping the dirt of his grave off his face. Fogarty will show himself too, ask if he can keep the silk Princeton tie as a souvenir. The limo drivers will arrive to return our phones and laugh as they pull corks from champagne bottles. It's over. We can go home, wherever that might be or how it might be changed after Belfountain.

Then again, it could be another kind of game altogether. One that was never intended for anyone to win.

"He was there, just outside the window. While you were gone," Franny goes on. "It was *him*. It was Nate."

Who's that? I almost say. A second of forgetting followed by a burning shame.

"You're under a lot of stress," I hear myself say, my voice as empty as the words it speaks.

"This wasn't stress. This was my son. This was Nate. He was there. Looking through the glass like a kid at the zoo. He was cold. He was *shivering*, Aaron."

"He wasn't there, Franny."

"Because he's dead."

"Yes."

"It doesn't feel that way."

"That's grief. That's denial."

"You're telling me about denial? About grief?"

"I was only—"

"I'm not arguing. I need you to understand."

"Understand what?"

Franny takes a moment to line up the words in her head.

"I'm not sure what dead or alive mean anymore," she manages finally, slow as someone reading a book aloud by candlelight. "This side of the fence or the other. All those lines, those boundaries. They're not what we thought they were."

"What are they then?"

"They're stories."

Franny doesn't look well. If anything, she's gained weight since coming here, but it's been added to parts of her that needed it least. Her jawline, her hands. She appears swollen instead of well nourished.

"Ghosts aren't real," I say.

"But in stories they can be. When Dad talked about this place, they were."

I'm back to where I've always found myself with Franny. Even during her good stretches, we'd come to the point where she revealed herself to be less strong than she proclaimed, less changed for the better. The circle always returned to the essential Franny: making empty assurances or spinning ridiculous narratives of conspiracy and victimhood. The only thing different about this time from all the others is that even as I see her as having lost her hold on reality, I don't entirely disagree with her.

"I miss him too, Franny," I say. "I miss Nate too."

They're magic words that achieve two things. The first is how they bring Franny to hold me close. The second is how they show me how much I do miss him, that my sister's not the only one who's been broken by the way her son was taken from the world.

39

I MUST HAVE FALLEN ASLEEP ON FRANNY'S BED. WHEN MY EYES OPEN, BRIDGE IS there, sitting in a chair in the corner of the room.

"Hey there," I say.

"Hey."

"How're you doing?"

"Take a wild guess."

"Worried about Mom. About everything."

"Aren't you?"

I'm worried about you.

"Of course," I say.

Only then do I notice the box resting on Bridge's lap.

"Whatcha got there?"

"That's what I want to show you."

She pulls her chair closer into the circle of light from the lamp on the table. I look at her to continue, but she says nothing, only glancing down at the box.

"What's in it?" I ask.

"That part's interesting. But so is the box."

"How?"

"Look again."

So I do. As if new particulars have been added to it as we spoke, I see it for what it is. A tackle box. The same one I opened to pull out the silver X-Acto blade I used to cut a hole in Bridge's throat.

"How did you bring that in?"

"I didn't. I found it."

"Where?"

"In the shed. Yesterday, when the rest of you were looking for shovels and tools. I saw it right away and brought it inside."

She sets it on the bed. Its reality deepens without my touching it. An enhanced, hyperrealism to the bulbous handle, the scratches in its paint that show the steel beneath.

"How'd it get here?" I ask.

"Dad must have brought it."

"Why? There're no rivers or lakes I've seen to do any fishing."

"He wasn't using it to fish."

I'm supposed to open it. I think of those potato chip cans with springs inside that look like snakes that leap out when you pull off the lid. Then I think of worse things.

The lid is cold to the touch, as if Bridge had hidden it in the freezer. It requires one hand to grip the box and another to wrench the lid up, which comes away with grinding complaint.

I have to lean directly over its dark insides to see what's there.

A key. Different from any car or house key I've seen. The neck rounded and long, the jagged end cut more deeply and numerously, so that it looks like the mouth of a miniature creature, grinning.

"Was there anything else in here?"

"Nope."

"Does anyone know about this? Even Franny or Mom?"

"Just you." She's not looking at the key. She's looking at me. "You know what it opens, don't you?"

"I have an idea."

Bridge has aged in the last two days. I have a similar initial impression every Tuesday when we meet. She's growing up. But this is only what it is to be fourteen years old. Going around shocking the people who know you with all the ways you're not how they remember you or how they would prefer to hold you in time.

"It's not the fence we have to get over, Aaron," she says. "It's something else we have to find."

I've read a study about how married couples can read each other's minds. Not just anticipate the other's decisions and actions based on precedent, but complex webs of reasoning dictated almost word for word, picked up from the other like a radio signal. It's also true between brothers and sisters at least some of the time.

"Okay," I say. "I'll go."

"You're not leaving me behind again," she says, and slams the tackle box's lid closed so hard I'm worried someone will hear it all the way down the hall.

"It's not *safe*, Bridge. And I—"

"Why are you always *doing* that?"

"Doing what?"

"Pretending you're the brave big brother even when you're scared shitless. It's not an *act*, Aaron. Being the Good Guy isn't the same thing as being good. Being you."

She almost yells this, and what's far more alarming than any concern she's been heard outside the room is how acute her frustration is.

"You're right. I've got that mixed up my whole life," I say. "But here's the deal. I care about you. Mom and Franny too. My patients. I want everyone to be okay and I'll put on the Good Guy costume—no matter how bad it fits me, no matter how itchy it feels—if it helps make that happen."

"You *are* good, Aaron. But that doesn't mean you have to be alone."

This hits me harder than her raised voice of a moment ago. It's the simple truth of it that's so striking.

"Okay," I say. "Come with me."

She doesn't need to hear where I might take her. We're together in this now, no more leaving her hiding under beds pretending it will make a difference. I won't go without her, and she's prepared to wait for the next step.

"Take it," she says, and I pull the key out, half expecting it to be sharp enough to cut me.

"What about the box?"

Bridge has it under her arm as she goes to the door.

"This?" she says. "This doesn't mean anything to anyone but us."

We start a fire in the great room's hearth because it's something to do. Soon the heat from the blaze has all of us sweating, keeping as far back as the room allows, waiting for the flames to die down.

"Maybe Mom will smell the smoke and follow it back," Franny offers.

Nobody replies to this. I don't think any of us can picture Mom pushing through the underbrush, led home by her sniffing nose. And then there's the consideration of what else might be drawn out of the forest.

Once the fire has calmed, Jerry smothers it in ash, and it hisses and pops with demonic threats.

"There's about two hours of daylight left," he says when he turns to us. "Either we go out there now and try to find your mom, or we let her go it alone all night."

"She's not strong enough," Franny says to me, and I take her not to mean Mom's chances of surviving a meeting with the Tall Man, but the night itself. I can't say I disagree. The thought of our mother poking around somewhere out in Belfountain's hundreds of acres isn't sustainable for long before it collapses, dissolving like a sugar cube in a warm rain.

"So we do a search," I say. "Two groups, with somebody staying behind to man the fort."

Bridge comes to stand next to me, indicating her intentions. Lauren raises her hand.

"Could you use a third?" she asks.

I look to Bridge, who nods. "Sure. Jerry and Ezra, you good?"

"Good to go," Jerry says.

All of us separate to collect headlamps and water, but I stay where I am to speak to Franny.

"You okay with this?"

"What do I have to do? Not open the door? Yeah, I think I can handle that."

"It means you're going to be here on your own."

Franny slips her hand into the front pouch of the hoodie she wears. Pulls out the gift Dad left for her. Nate's baby rattle.

"I won't be alone," she says.

"Let's go! I want us back by dark," Jerry calls out, and I leave Franny where she stands, swaying from side to side as if rocking an infant to sleep.

40

BRIDGE STARTS FOR THE GREEN TRAILHEAD BEFORE ANYONE ELSE DECIDES which way they'll go. Lauren and I follow after her. Once the trees have obscured the lodge from view behind us and we're well out of earshot, I ask Bridge why we're going this way.

"This is where you found the way to the camp, right?"

"Yeah. But I'm not sure I can remember the exact direction I took."

Bridge turns to face us. Pulls her compass out. "You find the side trail that took you there. I'll take care of the coordinates."

"Hold up," Lauren interjects. "What camp? What's happening here?"

I look to Bridge. "Can I tell her?"

Bridge comes back to take Lauren's hand. "Lauren should know *everything*," she says. "But let's keep moving while you talk. We don't have a lot of time."

"So we're not looking for your mom anymore?" Lauren asks.

"We're looking for her," Bridge says. "We're *also* looking for a way out."

Bridge pulls on Lauren's hand, and the three of us march up the trail's steady grade, the forest's air heavy in our throats.

The born-again Christian camp. The underground gate. The key.

I bring Lauren up to speed as swiftly as I can, in part because I'm also keeping an eye out for the side trail, in part because it all sounds less unsettling with some of the details edited out. The claustrophobic darkness of the stairwell under the walk-in freezer. The sense that some living thing breathed on the other side of the door.

When I'm finished, she doesn't say anything, and I wonder if it was a mistake sharing any of it with her. Bridge and I have a history, a trust that goes without question. The two of us like Lauren, and based on that we brought her in, but we've overlooked that she belongs to a different family from ours. She's obliged to tell Jerry and Ezra about all this just as I was to tell Bridge, and now she'll turn and start back.

But that's not what she does.

"I'm assuming you don't want my brothers in on this?" she asks finally.

"This puts you in a difficult situation, and I'm sorry about—"

"Just tell me, Aaron."

"No. We'd like it kept between ourselves for now."

"Fine. I think that's the best way to go too," she says, putting her hand on Bridge's shoulder. "Let's see if that key works."

Just when I start to think there's no way I'm going to find the path I started off on before coming upon the camp, I stop at a divot in the soft ground off to the right. My shoe print. Already partly overgrown in a weaving of grass and clover.

"This way," I say.

"Wait," Bridge says, pulling a small notebook out. She scribbles down the readings, the estimated distance we've traveled from the lodge, the side trail's direction. When she's done, she signals for me to carry on and the two of them fall in line behind me.

I'm worried there won't be time to find the camp, discover we were wrong about the key opening the door, and get back before nightfall. I'm worried even more about what we'll find if the door can be opened. But I believe Bridge is right. The only possibility of escape isn't over the fence, or through it, but deeper into the ground beneath our feet. It makes me think of Elias. His body being dropped into the hole. How where he is now, in the cool soil, is closer to the outside than we are.

Wasn't that what Bridge had remembered Dad said to her when he brought her here as a child? The crucial decision on the direction we ought to take.

Where does the path lead after it ends?

He must have meant something more than encouraging his daughter to be courageous. It was about having to go so far in whatever you set out to do that you encountered a border. And once you did, what was important was to forge your own passage through it.

Lauren finds the camp before I do.

"There," she says, and goes forward into the clearing without pausing.

I take mental note of everything as if there were some chance that it had been folded up and taken away since I was here. The horseshoe pit, the shabby dining hall. And just as Bridge noted but that I hadn't seen last time, a swing set in the forest's lengthening shadow, lopsided and seatless, the chains swinging slightly as if someone had given them a push before disappearing into the trees.

Bridge leads us into the dining hall. She doesn't look up to read the Belfountain sign over the door, but Lauren does, glancing back at me. It feels essential that we make as little sound as possible, so I merely mouth the words *Just wait* and follow her inside.

I watch as Lauren takes in the scripture written on the rafters, along with the demonic messages on the tables and walls. *Satan hear our Voice.*

None of it slows her advance toward the kitchen. *WE Sing for YOU.* And then she finds herself standing in the center of the pentagram burned into the floor. It holds her in place like a magnet, pulling her earthward.

"What is this?" she says, raising her arms out to her sides, and for a moment, she actually appears to be sinking, her legs dissolving into darkness.

"Just kids, probably," I say.

"*What* kids?"

"I don't know."

"What kind of people would—I mean, Aaron, this is—"

"In here."

Bridge stands waiting for us at the kitchen entrance.

"It's in here," she repeats, and slips inside.

41

THE WALK-IN FREEZER'S DOOR IS OPEN. HAD I LEFT IT THAT WAY? OR DID BRIDGE pull it free herself, in silence, before Lauren and I joined her where she stands at its pitch-black threshold? I want to ask, but the words are too heavy to be spoken, their uselessness announced in advance.

We will enter the freezer no matter what. It's our fate. Our father's will.

Bridge flicks on her headlamp, and Lauren and I do the same. Gather around the open trapdoor leading into the ground, the three of us like mourners at a funeral.

"This isn't right," Lauren says. It isn't clear what she's referring to at first, but then I hear it as meaning everything. The hole. The camp. Us. We're not right to be doing any of this.

"I'll go first," I say, and step down into the stairwell.

The air is cooler beneath the surface, yet my skin feels hotter, an oily sweat that glues my shirt to the tops of my shoulders. The dark pushes back at the bluish spray of LED light, diluting it.

"Hey, Aaron?" Lauren says from what sounds like a hundred feet above and behind me. "Maybe we shouldn't be here?"

All of us hear the tremor in her voice. The fear of being the first to come into contact with whatever we might release. Whatever might already by waiting for us.

I don't answer her.

It's so much narrower than I remember from my first trip down, the walls almost bulging inward like an inflamed throat. At the bottom, the steel door holds me back at the deepest point. The moisture shining and nippled on the smooth surface.

"Here," I say, pushing my back against the wall so Bridge and Lauren can see it.

"Looks serious," Bridge says.

"Not a vault or anything like that," Lauren agrees. "Custom-built. And it would've been hell cutting and squaring it into the ground like that."

Nobody has to ask me to try the key but I hesitate as if it's a required step. When I pull the key out and come close to the door, I hear Bridge and Lauren move away. I wonder, if it opens, if whatever awaits on the other side will be slowed enough by what it will do with me that they will have time to make it out.

The key slides in and clicks into place.

It takes a little effort to turn it. There's an internal *thump*, a single, amplified heartbeat, when the key is rotated as far as it can go. I'm expecting I'll have to push or pull the door free, but it slides to the left, a smooth grating of metal against metal until it stops with a muffled crash.

The smell comes first.

Mold, primarily. Followed by the antiseptic sourness of a hospital waste bin, ammonia and soiled bandages, bodily discharges in paper bundles. Maybe something else. Something no longer alive.

A short hallway. I lean back again and let Lauren and Bridge look down the ten feet to its end.

"Another door," Bridge says.

This one is different from the sliding steel one. There's no keyhole for one thing, only a numerical pad on the wall next to it. For another, there's a porthole window, small and high, no more than a foot in diameter.

"We go back now, right?" Lauren says.

Bridge doesn't reply, just passes by me.

I hesitate, trying to think of a way to secure the steel door so that it doesn't slide shut on its own somehow—or can't be pulled shut by someone who waits behind us in the walk-in freezer—but there's nothing that will hold something so heavy as the door if it started to move. The thought of being closed in here almost hijacks my body completely, the urge to bolt overcome only by the idea of Bridge being trapped on the other side and me not able to get to her.

We approach the second door without asking what it might mean. It's the porthole window. The promise of the glass, the world within.

Bridge is there first, but because of the window's height she can't see through other than the glimpses she catches as she jumps up and down. The slap of her shoes on the cement floor resounding like smacks to exposed flesh.

"Let me," Lauren says.

She rises up on her toes. The reflected glare of her headlamp dazzles her, so she turns it off. She circles her face with her hands to shield the glow of our lights from her eyes.

"It's hard to see anything."

"Is there electricity?" I ask. "Lights?"

"There must have been at one time, but not now. The only light is coming from these—I don't know—these tubes on the ground here and there. Hold on. I can see a little better now."

"Is it a room?"

"A hallway. Chairs, desks, paper. It's all trashed. And there's—"

"Lauren?"

"Oh my *God*."

"What?"

"There's blood. *Lots* of it. Like something's—"

She stops again. I expect her to pull away but she only presses her face closer to the glass.

"What's going on?"

"There's something in there," she says, and only now does she pull away and look at us. "Something moving."

42

LAUREN TAKES A FULL STEP BACK FROM THE DOOR, A REFLEX OF FEAR AS MUCH AS to allow me to look inside. There's no choice but to slide closer. Draw my hands up the cold steel and stare into the darkness on the other side.

Not quite darkness.

There are half a dozen glowsticks, each of them radiating the greenish yellow of streetlights in fog. They reveal a wide corridor leading straight ahead through gaps of shadow to a wall at the far end, maybe sixty feet away. Doors on either side, most of them ajar but at least one still closed. Office furniture, leather-bound log books and files along with random metal equipment of some kind, boxes overflowing with spiraled wires, power cables, most of it overturned and scattered.

"I don't see any blood," I say.

And then I do.

So much of it I think at first it's part of the vandalism, cans of paint thrown against the walls and left to congeal in pools on the floor.

Something dragged through it, leaving a diminishing trail of lines. A kind of haphazard musical staff that approached the door before fading.

Not something. A body.

This comes instantly, certainly. It could be nothing other than a human body. Lying at the end of the hall.

"How about now?" Lauren asks from what sounds like a great distance behind me. "On the walls? Spread out—"

"I see it."

"What do you think went on in there?"

"Just a sec. I'm trying—"

The body moves.

A moment ago it had the jagged outline of a figure lying on its side—the jutting shoulder lowering to the elbow, the rounded hip—and now the line is bending. Rising up from the floor. Its head. Turning and locking into place when it finds me.

"Aaron?"

"There's someone in there."

"*Someone?*"

"Yeah."

"Okay," Bridge moans. "I want to go now."

The figure stands. A woman. The hair so long and straggled it appears like a hood around her face. A face that comes into greater detail as she takes her first step forward, then the next. Moving into the light from one of the glowsticks.

"It's her," I say, but it comes out sounding like someone else's voice entirely.

"*Please*, Aaron. Let's *go*."

The old woman from the woods. Now lengthening her stride the closer she gets to the door, a bare foot slipping as it touches down in a pool of blood but immediately recovering, leaving new prints behind her.

"Aaron?"

I'm already moving back from the window. Not triggered by Lauren or Bridge's demands but so as not to be close to the door when the old woman reaches it.

But we don't leave yet. The three of us watch the porthole, waiting. Telling ourselves we're safe and convincing ourselves just enough not to run.

"You said it's 'her,'" Bridge says. "Who's in there?"

I'm about to answer when the old woman's face appears against the glass.

Lauren utters a low exhalation in place of a scream. Yet even now the fear nudges me forward instead of turning me away. Compelled by a force stronger than curiosity, a need to know and see and feel so great it's as if my life turned on my experiencing all of it.

"Who are you?" I ask, and the old woman cocks her head as if she registered my voice but couldn't make out the words.

I try again, louder this time.

"What's your name?"

She closes her eyes. I take it as a flinch against pain. But the longer she stays that way I read it instead as an effort to concentrate, to remember. The eyes open. Her mouth stretched into an uncertain grin.

"Do you know who you are?"

She frowns, as if suspecting a trick.

"Are you alone?"

The old woman looks behind her, then back at me. Both what was left of the grin and the suspicious frown disappear. Replaced by wide-eyed worry, her arms hugging herself as she starts to rock slightly from side to side.

"Let me in," I say.

She might be shaking her head no. She might just be shaking.

"Maybe you can do it from your side. Put your hand on the handle and turn."

"What are you doing?" Lauren says.

"We need to get inside." I turn to her, then to Bridge. "Everything that's happening to us—it has to do with what's already happened in there."

"Already happened? I can make a guess," Lauren says. "Someone was *killed*, Aaron. That's human blood on the floor. And this woman wasn't the one who did it."

"So how is she still alive?"

Lauren doesn't answer. She looks at me as if I'm the one she should be scared of, and takes another step back.

But Bridge stays close to me. "You're right," she says before looking back at Lauren. "The only way out is in."

I look through the window at the old woman once more, her expression unreadable because it keeps changing, sliding from anxiety to confusion to suppressed mirth.

"Try the door," I tell her. "I'll make sure—I'll protect you from whoever else is in there with you."

She almost laughs at this.

"How do you get in and out?" I shout at her. "I've seen you. Out in the woods. Is there another way?"

She's afraid now. Her head looking over her shoulder as she backs away.

"Don't go!"

The old woman walks backward from the door. Her eyes held on mine in pity, as if I'm the one locked underground, not her. What did I say that made her go away? Nothing. It *wasn't* me. It's something she's heard. Inside. Something that's coming.

"What happened to you?" I shout into the glass, and the question blasts back at me, demanding the same explanation of myself.

The old woman is ten feet away, fifteen, walking through the same pool of blood as before, leaving a new line of footsteps.

As she goes, she does something odd. Every time she passes a glowstick she bends to pick it up and tosses it into one of the open rooms. Each time she does the hallway darkens in grades, swallowing her.

"What's she doing?" Bridge asks.

"Putting out the lights."

"Why?"

"Because there's—"

"There's something she doesn't want you to see," Lauren finishes for me.

The old woman reaches the end of the hall. Only one glowstick remains on the floor, but she doesn't reach for it. Her head turned to the right, watching, as a new shadow plays over the wall.

A shadow that bends down and picks the glowstick up.

For a second, the two of them stare down the hall at me. The old woman and the Tall Man floating in a circle of underwater green. His one gloved hand on the glowstick and the other on the silver hatchet, the corner of its head notching into his thigh over and over without him seeming to feel it. The steel coming away shining and black.

"Oh no. Oh *Jesus*—"

He hides the glowstick behind his back and it turns them into outlines. Paper cutouts you'd see taped to school classroom windows at Halloween.

The two of them start forward. The bogeyman and the witch, coming for the door.

43

THE STAIRS HAVE MULTIPLIED SINCE WE CAME DOWN THEM. NOT ONLY MORE OF them in number but also stretched out like an accordion, so that each step demands something near a full leap.

Lauren reaches the top first, then Bridge. By the way they stand there, I assume the freezer door has been closed. *Entombed.* The word arrives like the name of an old girlfriend or childhood pet, intimate and particular.

Once I join them, I see that it's still open, and we start forward again. We rush out into the kitchen and, for the first time, one of us speaks.

"Wait," I say. "We should close this."

I throw the freezer's door into the latch and it locks shut with the loud *pop* of a pistol shot.

The three of us listen for a voice or pounding from the other side. There's nothing for long enough that I start to believe that we *are* hearing something. The Tall Man listening for us just as we listen for him.

• • •

When we're in the forest again I tell them what I saw. I'm as quick as I can be about it, because the falling dusk has me worried about the Tall Man coming after us and also because I want Lauren and Bridge to agree not to tell the others what we found.

"I don't think I can do that," Lauren says as we make our way along the trail. "And I don't understand why I should."

"Because they'll see it only as a threat. They'll go hunting. But they'll fail. And that place—it's not just where those—" I almost say *creatures* before correcting myself. "Where those people live. Whatever we need to know is in there."

"You want to keep this a secret so you can play detective? Satisfy your curiosity?"

"No. I want to keep this a secret so all of us have a chance to survive."

It doesn't make a lot of sense as I hear myself say it, but there's not another way I can come at what I believe. I can only hope that Lauren feels the same way Bridge and I do.

"If you're right, how do we get around the guy with the gloves?" she asks.

"We know he and the woman are out in the woods most of the time."

"So we go in when they're not there?"

"That's it. We have to find the other way in—because there has to be a second exit that—"

"Quiet."

Lauren and I look at Bridge. She nudges her chin, pointing along the trail. The lodge is now coming into view, the kitchen windows a band of yellow like a monobrow. It's not the structure itself she's alerting us to, but the figure standing at the bottom of the steps by the front door.

We turn off our headlamps. It makes it harder to not step on anything that might make a sound, but we crouch low and proceed closer.

"I think I heard something out there," the figure says to someone just inside the lodge's door.

"It's Ezra," Lauren says. "Ezra!"

"Lauren!"

The three of us come out of the trees, and Lauren runs to her brother, briefly inspecting him as if to make sure he's whole. Jerry joins them, his eyes on Bridge and me.

"Anything?" he asks.

"We didn't find her. You?"

"No. I'm so sorry."

Lauren looks back at us. She's going to tell them about the camp and she's silently apologizing. Then she looks at Bridge. I can't see my sister's face but whatever it conveys changes Lauren's mind.

"Let's get inside," she says, slides her arms around her brothers' waists, and guides them up the steps into the light.

We gather in the kitchen but none of us eat. There's the inspection of the last few apples and oranges in a bowl on the counter, the shaking of a bag of bread crusts—all the rituals of food inspection without the appetite. Jerry is the last to hold an apple in his palm and replace it before he speaks.

"I think we should talk about where things stand. Aaron, maybe Bridge shouldn't be here for this?"

"It's up to her. Bridge, you want to—"

"You don't think Mom is missing," Bridge says. "You think she's dead."

She stands on her own closest to the dining room. For a moment I'm worried that she's ill. Her cancer has returned and I'm seeing it before she can feel it. But I look at her a moment longer and recognize that I'm wrong. She's recharging. Her body folding inward. Readying.

"I don't know anything," Jerry says. "I'm just trying—"

"But that's what you *think*," Bridge says. "My mother is gone and isn't coming back."

Jerry glances at me, sees I'm not going to bail him out. "Yes, that's what I think."

"Because it's been too long?"

"And because we know there's someone out there who is—look, Elias was killed. It happened at night. And it's night now."

"So we shouldn't look for her anymore?"

"We should do what we need to for those of us still here." He reaches for an orange before pulling his hand back, seeing the emptiness of the gesture for what it is. "These search parties we're throwing together and arming with cutlery and flashlights—it's not going to work. If your mom knocks on the door tonight or tomorrow morning or whenever, great. But for the sake of all of us, we have to assume she's not going to."

"Fine. Okay, fine," Bridge says, her lower lip curling out.

I go to her. My pride in her so great it pushes back against the first plumes of grief blowing up from within, and when I open my arms and she steps into them, it's me drawing strength from her more than the other way around.

We talk about what our plan should be. Some radical options are put forward, including Franny's idea that we climb the fence while wearing oven mitts (nobody goes to the trouble of pointing out all the ways that wouldn't work). We hypothesize how we might go on the offensive and take down the Tall Man ourselves. But we don't know if he's alone. And there's no question that when it comes to killing, he's better at it than any of us.

The conclusions we eventually come to are the same we started with.

Everyone stays inside.

Keep all doors and windows secure.

Ezra, Lauren, Jerry, and I will keep watch in shifts through the night.

Only then, before going to our rooms, sofas, or chairs to attempt sleep, do we eat.

44

THE DREAM OF BLACK WATER.

Of all the ways it is unique and strange—how it's passed between us, how it enlarges in scope each night—the strangest and most unique is how it announces itself as the product of the subconscious and, at the same time, feels more acutely real than anything experienced in our waking hours.

Another odd thing: I have this thought even as I dream the dream.

I'm in the water, fighting to stay up. There's no boat in sight. Remembering the descriptions the others gave of a sinking vessel, I rotate and find it behind me.

Outlined against a sky pinholed with stars, nosing down so sharply the rotator blades poke up through the surface at its stern. A blink of electric light behind the windows of the bridge, brief as lightning. It shows I'm not alone. Other bodies riding the thick swells around me. Some treading water, chins up. Some facedown longer than a held breath would allow.

Bridge is one of them. Still swimming. I see her, try to go to her, but the water hardens into icy slush.

When a wave washes over my head, the world is muffled, replaced by the mute simplicity of the water. The alien singing rising up. The voice of the ocean itself.

Then I'm breaking through again, snapping at breath. The night shattered by screams. A voice that doesn't belong to the dream.

It belongs to Belfountain. To my sister.

45

IT'S COMING FROM THE KITCHEN. FRANNY.

I'm off the sofa and rounding the dining room corner when she crashes into me.

"It came in!" she shouts into my chest. "It came *inside*!"

Whatever she's referring to isn't visible in the kitchen. There are the broken plates and a saucepan I'd heard her fling off the counter as she came my way, but nothing else.

Franny breaks away from me and runs down the elevated walkway toward the bedrooms, where she huddles with Bridge at the far end. I signal to her to stay where she is as Jerry comes up from the great room to join me.

"What's going on?" he asks.

"I don't know. Franny thinks she saw—"

"Saw *what*? I thought it was your shift!"

"Is it?" I glance over at my watch on the coffee table, the timepiece we were using to designate our turns to be awake, but it's too far away to make out what it says. "I was—Ezra didn't wake me up. What time—"

"*Shit*, Aaron."

Jerry is about to curse me out, or maybe throw a fist my way, when he looks behind him. "Where's Ezra?"

He'd been on the other extension of the sofa from me before the start of his shift when I drifted off. Not there now.

Jerry and I turn to look at the far end of the kitchen at the same time. The pantry door is slightly ajar. I start toward it with Jerry at my shoulder, his breath whistling and catching in his throat.

"Hold up," he says. He looks in the drawers, the sink, opens the dishwasher. "All the knives are gone. Everything."

"Someone took them?"

He shakes his head. "There's sure as hell nothing here we can use."

"Oh my God."

Lauren stands at the entry to the kitchen. Her eyes held by something neither Jerry nor I have noticed.

And then we do.

Jerry's breath doesn't whistle or catch anymore. It just stops.

I lean my body over the blood on the floor. A wide line pushing out from under the door and around its edge, tonguing around the corner, coming faster along the grouted crevices in the floor than over the tiles.

My hand on the knob. Pulling the door open through the crimson pool.

Ezra's blood. Easing out from his stomach as it had his brother's. His body in a self-defensive posture, arms crossed over his front and knees curled up, a question mark on the pantry's concrete.

Jerry nudges me aside. "Oh, *shit*."

It came in. Franny's conclusion after finding the body. *It came inside*.

Which means it might still be.

The kitchen door, the one that opens to the garbage bins outside. It's the most likely way the Tall Man would have gained entry. I start down the short hall and flick on the light.

The door is open. Not forced. Unlocked.

I shoulder it closed. Turn the bolt.

"Was it—"

"Yeah. I'll check the front door and make sure the others are safe," I tell Jerry. "You search the rest of the place."

Lauren has joined Franny and Bridge outside the bedrooms. None of them are speaking but it's clear Lauren has told them about Ezra. Even after I confirm the front door is secure and stand with them none of us say anything. None of us touch.

When Jerry returns, he comes at me.

"You were supposed to be on watch," he says, raising his index finger and jabbing the air inches from my chest.

"I know that. I—"

"It was up to *us*!"

"Jerry, listen. Ezra didn't wake me up. That was the way it was supposed to work."

"Or you don't remember him waking you up. Like you don't remember how to be a doctor."

"No, not like that."

"Oh for *fuck*—" He slides a hand over his face as if wiping a set of darker intentions away. "You've got so many excuses, you'll have to forgive me for not being able to keep up with the bullshit."

"What's just happened—you're hurting more than I could ever imagine. But everything's changed now, so we—"

"You're right about that, Dr. Quinlan. It's all changed." Jerry circles his hands in front of him, his body searching for something to do, something to strike at. "I don't have brothers anymore. It was *your* turn to make sure nobody got in, but they did. And unless that psycho has his own goddamn key, somebody opened the door for him."

I hear what Jerry is saying. We all do. His accusation isn't that I might have welcomed the Tall Man inside, but that I killed Ezra myself. I might suspect the same of me if I was in Jerry's position, reeling off the cocktail of his rage, his fear.

The thing is, I *am* feeling his fear. It's what allows me to see how all of us are standing at a point where everything will be decided. Yet I have no idea how to direct this moment, how to bring us back to a place where we can preserve the narrowing chance of saving ourselves.

"I would never hurt Ezra," I say.

"That's *wonderful*. What am I supposed to do with that, Aaron? Because here's the thing: you're not my family. I don't *know* you." He swings around to take in Franny and Bridge. "Any of you."

Jerry is bouncing on the balls of his feet. A boxer's dance.

"Don't hit him."

He looks over at Bridge, his fingers curling into fists.

"Please don't hit him," she says.

Her words add invisible sandbags to his legs. The hands stop circling the air and loosen, but only a little, his fists now opened to show their hollow cores.

"I'm not staying here," he says.

At first, I take him to mean in this spot, this chilly, slate-tiled foyer with the rib cage chandelier hanging above us. But he moves to the door and it's clear he means he won't stay in the lodge.

"Lauren?"

He pauses for her to join him. I'm anticipating his disappointment when she refuses. But as Jerry starts for the door, she goes after him. When I put my hand to her shoulder, she spins around.

"This is a mistake," I say.

"He's my brother."

She looks into me. It allows me to see something too.

This is how families operate. They forgive, they bail each other out. But they can't forget the walls that define them, how they decide who's allowed in and who must be kept out.

"He's my brother," Lauren says again, and is the first out when Jerry opens the door.

46

EZRA'S GRAVE ISN'T NEARLY AS DEEP AS HIS TWIN'S.

Franny and Bridge help as much as they can with the shoveling, but they're as tired and broken as I am. After singlehandedly pulling his body from the lodge to the spot next to where Elias lies, it's all I can do to fit him into the long groove in the ground and cover him with loose soil.

That night, we're putting away the dishes when Bridge points out that Jerry and Lauren didn't take any food with them.

"They'll be hungry," I say. "Which means they'll come back in the morning when it's light out."

This doesn't come out sounding particularly believable. But all we have is the performance of hope and we stick to the script.

• • •

I stay awake all night. It gives me time to form the lie I plan on telling Franny in the morning. The announcement that Bridge and I are going to the fence's gate to check for new supplies, when in fact we'll head into the woods to find another entrance to the underground hallway where we saw the Tall Man and the witch.

But at sunrise, when Franny shuffles into the great room and I tell her this, she does the opposite of what I thought she would. She insists on coming along.

"We can't leave the door open," I say. "Someone has to stay."

"It's not going to be me. I *won't* be left alone, Aaron. I won't."

"We should tell her," Bridge says, appearing in the bedroom hallway behind her.

"Tell me what?"

I step up onto the dining room's platform, pull out chairs for the two of them.

"Have a seat."

The story of the camp, the key, the murderous beings that live inside. How Bridge and I believe whatever was going on down there is connected to Dad. Franny listens to all of it with her head lowered so that I vacillate between thinking she's crying or sleeping.

"Our father," she announces when I'm done. "I'll be honest. I wasn't too blown back to find out about the secret second family thing. But this? Didn't see it. You got me there, Dad."

She slaps her knees. The only thing that's missing is actual laughter.

"It's why we're here," Bridge says.

"I don't doubt that, honey. But here's my one reservation. Why should we do what he wants us to?"

"Dad brought me here. Before."

Franny looks the way I probably did when Bridge told me the same thing.

"Why'd he do that?"

"I think it was to show me everything he'd done. Show me the truth."

"Couldn't he have just sent us postcards or something?" Franny asks, her exasperation reddening her face into an eraser atop a thin, yellowed pencil. "'So sorry for being evil and insane. Move on with your lives and don't look back. Love, Daddy'?"

"I didn't say he was *sorry*," Bridge says. "I think he just wanted us to *see*."

This stops Franny. Her body transformed to a wax figure in the first stage of its melting.

"It makes me crazy too," I say to her. "The idea of submitting to Dad's plan—whatever it is—it makes me sick. But this is his place, Franny. Belfountain is his brain. Which means we have to find out its language. We need—"

"We need to find out who he was," Franny says.

"We need to find Mom," Bridge says.

47

BRIDGE LEADS THE WAY ALONG THE GREEN TRAIL WITH ME AND FRANNY BEHIND her. I don't like having her exposed as the first in line but she's got the compass and she's the only one who can read it right.

"This way," Bridge says, striking out off the trail where I wouldn't have guessed we should.

I've been here twice before, yet this part of the forest feels particularly unfamiliar. The trees appear closer together than elsewhere, the trunks of the birches peeling and huddled. It prevents any view farther than twenty feet or so. It also throws every *crack* and *crunch* our feet make back at us.

When we reach the camp we stop to figure where the second underground entry point might be. Bridge thinks it's some distance beyond the clearing.

We walk through the high grass of the camp's grounds trying to imagine the children who would have run here, laughed, and played Capture the Flag, but nothing comes.

"It's like a cemetery," Bridge says. And even though it's not like a cemetery in any obvious way, it seems to me that she's right. A place of markers for the dead, stand-ins for lives of unguessable shape.

As we go, I estimate that if the hallway we saw through the porthole window runs more or less straight, we're passing over it now. If I'm right about that, the most likely second entrance will come at the opposite end.

We're into the forest again. I'm about to suggest we've gone too far when a ridge rises up from the ground like a partly collapsed wall. Fern covered and leaning away from us. A dozen feet to the top.

In the center of it, a gaping mouth. Nearly perfectly oval, perfectly dark, the stones on the visible part of its floor black as coal nuggets. A cave.

We climb up without a word between us. It takes longer than the modest slope of wild thyme and jutting limestone would lead you to believe. At the top we look back the way we've come, and I'm so ready to see the Tall Man at the base that for a moment he's there, starting after us, effortless and swift. And then, in the next instant, he evaporates like a shadow when the sun goes behind a cloud, and there's only the bunched trees that, from this elevation, look oozy and squat.

The entrance isn't large, only twice my body width and a foot shorter than I am when standing. I know because I'm upright now. Walking to the edge of the darkness and peering inside. A trickling rivulet of water rushing toward my shoe as if it recognizes something.

We turn our headlamps on, revealing circles of yellow on the damp stone floor. The illumination only works to make the walls feel closer than they were in darkness. The bulbs and joints of the rock wall. The sharp fins that jut down from the ceiling. As we advance, the motion of the beams lend the rock a lurching animation, its arrowhead edges and zigzagged cracks grabbing and retreating.

It's why we almost fall into the hole.

An opening in the cave floor that marks its farthest point. It appears to be a natural formation until we gather close to its edge. See the concrete steps heading steeply down into its depths.

"Doesn't look too stable," I say.

"And I don't feel too stable, so maybe I'll go first," Franny says, and starts down.

The stairs are so narrow and steep it requires us to descend in side steps. We have to hold our beams down at our feet to prevent slippage, as any of us falling would take out those below.

While clearly built by industrial means, these stairs are far more basic and hastily constructed than those that led to the door with the porthole window. I try to occupy my thoughts with how it was done, holding at bay the claustrophobia that sounds in my ears as a shrill ringing of tinnitus. A noise that hides, just beneath it, the breath and scratch of a human shriek.

"Wait," Franny says, farther below than I thought she was. "There's something here."

Bridge and I join her, and the three of us take up the entire breadth of the tunnel that is now level and starts away into a hallway with concrete floors, walls, and ceilings. But there's also something else. A barrier that separated where we are now from the rest of the hallway. A square of plate metal smashed off its hinges, now leaning up against the wall.

"Somebody fought their way in," Franny says.

We study the metal as if reading it. And in return it relates an episode of violence and desperation.

"All the dents and scratches are on the inside," I say. "It was a fight to get out."

Not that it makes a difference now. This is the page of Belfountain's story we least want to turn but have to. A trail of blood, not bread crumbs, has led us here. And inside is where the witch lives.

48

THE CEILINGS ARE LOW AND COMPOSED OF PERFORATED PARTICLEBOARD THAT looks like domino tiles. On the walls, randomly placed landscape paintings (some higher than eye level, some at the waist). Oils of frothing seashores and sunlit groves, all unsigned but probably the work of the same artist, considering the consistent palette of colors. The first rooms off the hallway are bedrooms of identical size, not quite prison cells but equipped with only the simplest comforts: single beds, corkboards spotted with thumbtacks over foldout desks. Put together, it suggests a place that's part bomb shelter, part Siberian hotel, part mental hospital.

"You think Dad did those paintings?"

You'd think that Franny would be more urgently interested in what might have gone on here. Yet her question is the one I'm most curious about too. There's the overwhelming sense that we are closer to our father now than we'd ever come in our lives under the same roof with him. No matter how awful or strange the things that occurred here, these halls were his true home.

"They're his," Bridge answers before I can.

"Why are you so sure?"

"Because he thought he was an artist. Just not the normal kind."

"So the paintings—"

"A hobby," she says. "His real work is what he made here."

Once we're past the bedrooms, the hallway meets another running off to the left. We shine our lights down its length and see that it's the same one where we'd seen the old woman when we'd come down from the walk-in freezer. There's the blood on the floor and walls, now dried into footprints like a choreography map. The metal rim around the porthole window where I'd pressed my nose glints sixty feet away. Which makes where we're standing now the exact spot where the Tall Man had appeared.

The hallway we'd entered through continues ahead before coming to a wall. The entire complex, from what we've discovered so far, is shaped like a T.

"Straight, or down that way?" I ask.

"This room looks bigger than the others," Bridge says, starting down the hallway to the left and slipping through the first doorframe.

"Bridge!" Franny calls out, but I'm ahead of her, almost tripping over a nest of wires and some kind of electronics component of black dials and knobs. I lurch through the doorframe and my headlamp flashes over Bridge's back, standing rigid, a few feet inside.

"You okay?"

I bend and pick up a steel strip of the kind that houses power cords and wield it in front of me. But as I stand and play my light over the space we're in, I can't spot the witch or the Tall Man. Yet what I can see stops me the same as it stopped Bridge.

"It happened here," she says.

The room is double the width of the ones with the beds but much longer, maybe forty feet from one end to the other. Aside from a few desks and toppled office chairs, the only furniture is a number of similarly shaped boxes set upon stainless steel platforms, each set waist-high, their legs on wheels like gurneys. The boxes themselves are made of brownish metal, with electric cables feeding out of their sides, some of which lead to outlets in the wall and others to computer terminals on the worktables (or used to, as most of the computers lie smashed on their sides on the floor).

The number of boxes, angled and body-sized, puts me in mind of a showroom in a discount funeral home.

"There're names on them," Bridge says, walking between the boxes and letting her hand stroke their curved metal lids.

Eight. The same number as the combined Quinlan families.

"This one says Jerry," Bridge says.

Franny passes me to join Bridge before she too stops at one of what, considering their metallic smoothness, I don't think of as boxes anymore, but pods.

"This one's yours," Franny says.

She's looking at me strangely. Her mouth hanging open in a consuming, skeletal way that reminds me of the Tall Man.

I can see my name on the pod even before I start to approach. *AARON*. Spelled out in those adhesive letters on a gold foil background you see stuck on roadside mailboxes.

My hands are on the edges of the lid before I'm aware of moving close enough to reach for it. The idea that, if I lift it open, I will find myself inside arrives with such force it holds me still. I'm here, breathing in the bunker's filtered air, my body at my command. Yet the unseen contents of the pod have overtaken these formerly reliable tests of reality. If the cool metal at the ends of my fingers is a coffin, the dead man within is more present and alive than the one who is about to look down on him.

"You have to," Bridge says.

The lid rises and it's me doing it. It's me, aware of how I'm about to be ruined like the child who nudges open the door to his parents' bedroom to witness who they truly are, the things they do that cannot be understood.

There is no body. Only water.

So lightless in its steel container that it appears black as bitumen, reflecting my headlamp without allowing any illumination to penetrate the surface. I place my palm on it and I feel its resistance, the whole weight of my hand held up as if it were no more than a sheet of paper. The lid falls fully open, and the vibration sends a half dozen silver ripples inward from the sides that blend and diminish within seconds, leaving the liquid smooth once more.

I've seen isolation tanks on TV, read magazine features on spas that feature individual tubs filled with saline water so that you rest on the surface and meditate or sleep or, as I'm sure I would, bang on the lid and demand to be let out. The pod in front of me is like those in some respects, but unlike them in others. The screen, for instance. How the whole interior side of the lid is transparent plastic, semicircular, glowing faintly blue.

"Here," Franny says, picking up a narrow console from the floor. Two cords run from it to the side of the pod. "Maybe these do something."

The console has three dials on its face and two switches. She tries the first of these. Nothing. When she flicks the second, it begins.

The pod's curved screen comes to life. Images—some moving, others still—sharpen into focus. The quality of the visuals is unlike anything I've ever seen: three-dimensional but without the cutout fakery of the effect when seen through the glasses they hand out in cinemas. This has a genuine suppleness and veracity. There's a soundtrack too. Speakers I can't see but must be located both in the pod's lid and beneath the water's surface, as it comes from all around, causing the water to tremble slightly so that the motion gives it the appearance of an oil slick sliding and spreading over its surface.

It takes longer than it should to recognize what it is. Once I do, I watch. Franny and Bridge come to stand on either side of me.

"What is it?" Bridge asks.

"It's the movie of my life," I say.

49

IN FACT, IT'S SOMETHING BETWEEN A SLIDESHOW AND A MOVIE. A COMBINATION OF images appearing for differing lengths of time—some remain on screen for close to a full minute, others flashing so quickly I can hardly make them out—and a similarly varied range of sounds. Phrases of music, effects both quiet and deafening (a shattered glass, crashing tide, orgasmic moan). Pieces of random-seeming facts conveyed in a neutral, androgynous voice, like excerpts from AM radio advertising. Together it's disconcerting, transfixing. Simultaneously unlike lived experience and an amplification of it. Like a dream. Like art.

Some of it is shaped as scenes with compressed beginnings and ends. Lisa Gerber breaking up with me at my locker in eleventh grade. Mom letting me hold Bridge for the first time in her maternity-ward room. A fistfight I lost to some guy who thought I was looking covetously at his girlfriend (I was) from the other side of a pool table.

Most of it, though, is vaguer, less coherent than a story. Snapshots. Pictures of faces (friends growing up, a favorite med school prof, ex-lovers) and buildings (the Cape Cod–style house where we grew up, my high school viewed from the parking lot). Younger versions of Franny and Mom. Images that are discernible but also muted in some way, blurred or fogged or bleached. The thudding machetes and gurgled screams from *overseas*. Places on bodies where surgical steel split skin but never the patients' faces. Close-ups that are too close up to take in the whole.

The picture that takes my breath away most is the fuzziest of all of them, but it remains on the screen longer than the others.

There are the tortoiseshell glasses set upon a small, bluish nose. The hair finger-combed to the side. The cheeks, round and smooth. Harmless.

His voice too. Subdued, slightly Southern flavored, polite. Speaking some of the words and sentences I remember best.

Strong enough for a spoon to stand up in it . . .

A castle in the middle of an endless wood named Belfountain . . .

Have to go, have to go. I'll see you when I see you.

"Daddy," Bridge says.

When his image is replaced by another, I'm finally able to pull my attention away from the screen. The other pods all have cords running out of them connected to consoles with dials and switches. All of them individual movie houses to float in. Each with their own show, their own life.

Franny scans her headlight over the other pods as Bridge and I do, as if measuring to see if any have moved on their own since we entered.

"What are they?" she asks.

"I don't know exactly."

"You think I—you think we were *made* in those things?"

"No. Not physically, anyway. But maybe in some other way."

"*What* way?"

"Our past. A version of it. The stuff we think makes us who we are.

It's all here." I point to the pod two over from us labeled *FRANNY*. "And that's you."

As Franny approaches the pod, horror reshapes her expression in a rictus of anticipated pain, but her body shuffles closer anyway. Her limbs advancing with the terrible need of the undead.

"Aaron?" Her hands grip the pod's lid as she looks back at me.

"You don't have to do this."

"I'm not sure that's true."

"We can wait. Come back later. We can walk away and—"

"I'm going to be *inside* here, aren't I?"

Franny stares at the pod and I honestly don't know what she will do next. I'm not sure she will ever move again.

"I always knew you could fit me in a box," she says finally. "I just never thought I'd be around to see mine."

She starts to shake with the same wracking, noiseless sobs as Bridge and me. As I watch her, I can see that, for all of us, it's equal parts confused emotion and panic.

She opens the lid.

Over Franny's shoulder I watch a few seconds of her slideshow-movie on the pod's screen before looking away. It feels like an invasion of privacy, or something even deeper than that, more perverse. There are things I know will be there that I don't want to see. All the years of doing whatever she had to do to buy a fix, the pornography of addiction. The long stretches of nothingness mistaken for bliss. Nate will be there too. The fragments of a brief life poorly recalled, a child loved and neglected and lost.

"None of this is real, is it?"

Based on her words alone it isn't clear whether Franny's question is asked of our being here or the authenticity of the images played out over the screen. I can only tell what she's referring to by how shattered she is.

The "real" is her. The Mr. Turtle pool she loved. Eli Einstein, her middle school crush. Nathaniel Quinlan, her son.

"He can't—he can't take my *baby* away from me! Not a second time. He wouldn't do that, would he? He wouldn't do that to his *daughter*?"

She closes the lid on her pod and backs away from it as if expecting something to push its way out from inside.

I open my arms to Franny. She enters my embrace as accidentally as a ghost ship floats sideways into harbor.

We only separate when we hear the soundtrack of Bridge's life.

One-ah, two-ah, three-ah . . . diarrhea!

Air rushing past ears, then the crash. Bubbles squirming up to the surface, followed by the density of the water, muffled as the grave.

The Day My Big Brother Saved My Life. More coherent than any of the other memories contained within my pod or Franny's. The movie playing on the screen looks and sounds more vivid, more simultaneously poetic and terrifying, than what I carry with me.

Tick-tock! Tick-tock! Tick-tock!

Jump to: Me and Bridge playing Hook and Wendy, dill pickles for swords.

Jump to: My face, twisting, at the realization that my sister can't breathe.

Jump to: The X-Acto blade in my hand. Bridge's point of view looking up at me, her breathing calm, and whatever she conveys through her eyes settles me, lets me bring the blade to her throat.

Jump to: Darkness.

The screen and speakers are lifeless for so long I assume the show's over, that this is how Bridge's story begins and ends for her. But then there's a voice that comes up out of the black water of the pod. Dad. Walking next to her through a breeze-cooled forest, speaking against a backgrounded concert of birdsong.

Where does the path lead after it ends?

Bridge closes the lid.

Both of us look around. Franny isn't here.

We scan the long room with our lights, both wishing for and dreading a glimpse of her rising up from behind one of the pods where she'd been hiding.

I can tell Bridge is holding herself back from calling out for her the same as I am.

We back away from Bridge's pod and turn to face the doorway where we came in. Stepping as quietly as we can over the scattered wires and equipment, our beams concentrated on the wall on the opposite side of the hallway like a spotlight awaiting the appearance of a stand-up comedian.

We're paused in the doorframe, stretching our necks forward to peek around the corner, when a figure steps into the spotlight.

"You need to see this," Franny says.

50

WE FOLLOW HER TO WHERE THE BLOODIED HALLWAY MEETS THE ONE WE CAME in through. She heads to the left, the direction we didn't go, where there are only two rooms. One is a kitchen: cupboards ripped from the walls; a still-running fridge that emits a rank, meaty odor as I pass; a table and floor littered with the empty packaging of frozen waffles and corn dogs.

"Eggos and Pogos," Bridge whispers.

The other room is an office. Filing cabinets lining one wall, and on the other side a wooden desk, heavy and broad as the kind school principals sit behind. This is where Franny goes. Spreading out a number of files over its surface like a magician showing a set of oversized cards before impossibly revealing the one you'd selected while her back was turned.

"I found these in that first filing cabinet," she says. "The one marked 'Subject Summaries.' "

She's been crying. But as before, her tears make no sound, as if her feelings come from a deeper place than that.

"We should go," Bridge says.

"She's right, Franny. We've been here too long. We can think this through and—"

"Read this," she says, picking up one of the files and offering it to me.

The file's blank cover opens on its own like the fairy-tale books at the beginning of the kids' movies of my youth. The narrator's voice-over reading aloud the opening words.

FRANNY QUINLAN

Subject Profile

Birthplace: Seattle.
Current residence: Seattle.

SUMMARY

Frances Quinlan ("FRANNY"), 31, sister to AARON and younger sister, BRIDGE. Middle child of the Eleanor Quinlan family. Troubled, restless childhood. Initially shoplifting, school truancy, allegiance to rebellious social groups. As early as middle school: drugs. Daily pot use escalating to heroin and crack cocaine after high school. Adulthood of severe addiction.

Son, Nathaniel ("Nate"), born five years earlier from START POINT. Father a fellow addict (unnamed), moved east, no contact since prior to birth. Nate is recalled only vaguely but powerfully: sweet-faced, angelic. Asthmatic.

Nate dies in rooming house while being overseen by fellow addicts as FRANNY was out seeking crack cocaine. Even after her return to the rooming house, it takes over two hours—following a hit from her pipe—for FRANNY to remember the child and find his body.

This latter fact is KEPT SECRET by the subject.

FRANNY employs various coping mechanisms that allow her to appear "recovered." In addition to her (so far) successful drug-free life since Nate's death, she has resolved to devote her remaining years to helping other addicts. She insists that she's "changed." She sometimes believes this, but at other times her inner weaknesses remind her—

Franny reaches over and turns the page, and the next one. When she stops, she stabs her index finger into a page with the header "Origin Identity."

"Now this," she says.

LYNN WEST

Origin Identity of FRANNY QUINLAN

Birthplace: Sacramento, CA
Current residence: Los Angeles

SUMMARY

Lynn West ("WEST"), homosexual, unmarried but since 2012 in on-and-off relationship with Nadia Pender, San Diego high school teacher. Long-distance relationship resulting in multiple breakups and jealousy. Currently works as sound editor in film production, primarily animation. Non-drug user. No children.

Raised as one of four children in fundamentalist Christian household. Only West child to remain committed to her faith.

Historically, WEST has dated exclusively using Christian social media apps. Seeks husband (see: Facebook feed)—a posture presumably for the benefit of her parents/family (possibly also employer?) to whom she has not "come out."

WEST recently purchased bungalow in Silver Lake. No pets.

Hobbies: hiking, reading, movie buff (mostly kids films, foreign animation, Studio Ghibli, etc.). Fondness for out-of-doors. Devotes vacation time on outings to—

Bridge pulls the file out of my hand. Replaces it with one she's picked up from the desk.

"Let's read this one together," she says.

BRIGIT QUINLAN

Subject Profile

Birthplace: Seattle
Current residence: Seattle

SUMMARY

Brigit (called BRIDGE by family and close friends), aged 14. Emotionally intuitive. Academically average, athletically inclined (dance, soccer).

Keeper of a journal she believes no one but her father has read. This is why he seems to understand her at a level more precise than even her brother, AARON.

Father brought her alone to Belfountain when she was 5. This leaves her with conflicting feelings of being CHOSEN as well as CONFUSION about the event itself. She has the strong sense that her father is not a good man. But she remains divided in her theories on the possible NATURE OF HIS CORRUPTION.

Personality (and her physical self) marked by a previous episode of survival. Her brother, AARON, a medical student at the time, performed an emergency tracheotomy on her using an X-Acto blade from a fishing tackle box (see: IMAGE INVENTORY) while on holiday at the Quinlan lakeside cabin. BRIDGE's feelings about this are complicated. She is grateful to AARON, but blames her father's absence at the time of the event. Where was he at the most frightening moment of her life?

Above defines her operating mode as one of DISTRUST.

It's my turn to flip ahead to the second set of paperclipped papers in the file the same way Franny pushed me. This is what Bridge is most terrified of. She reads with her cheek pressed against my arm, her lips moving as they mouth the words.

OLIVIA GOLDSTEIN

Origin Identity of BRIDGE QUINLAN

Birthplace: Tacoma, WA
Current residence: Seattle

SUMMARY

Olivia Goldstein ("GOLDSTEIN") is the eldest of three daughters of Barry and Lee Goldstein. Father: Corporate finance. Mother: Recent return to employment at private accounting firm.

GOLDSTEIN deemed academically "gifted" according to school assessments. Additional proficiency in athletics, primarily track (state finals).

Accomplishments understood as particularly notable given GOLDSTEIN's history of periodic, severe depression. Episodes of self-harm, including hospitalization following suicide attempt (scissor wound to throat). Note: This injury to be accounted for by BRIDGE as the scar from the emergency tracheotomy performed by brother, AARON (see above).

Currently on daily dosage of Sarafem. Talk therapy has yielded no previous trauma or sexual/physical abuse. Assumed chemical imbalance by psychiatric evaluations.

Stated career goal: marine biology. Love of marine life—whales, dolphins, sharks. Maintains extensive aquarium in home bedroom.

Bridge closes the file. Looks up at me with her finger tracing the outline of the scar on her neck.

"I did this?" she asks. "I did it to *myself*?"

"I don't know, Bridge. I don't—I can't put it together."

"There are two people," she says, the back of her hand slapping at her file. "Two people! But which one is me?"

"I think we need to slow down—"

"One is me, and one is somebody else," she carries on, not listening to me or anything other than her own thoughts. "Except I'm the fake. The other person, the one I don't know—the one who is *so sad*—that's who I really am."

I have no idea how it was done. I don't know what it means for us in anything other than this moment. But the thing is, I feel certain that what Bridge has just said is true. My little sister, the one person in the world I would die for, have wanted to make proud, is a forgery. Franny too. Which means I'm no more real than they are, no matter that the story that played out on the screen of my pod is the only story I've ever known.

Franny staggers back from the desk. The paperclipped pages falling from her hand and fluttering to the floor like a graceless, multi-winged bird.

"Something was done here," I say. "Done to us. I'm not—"

"Dad was—he was *never* real?"

I reach out to Franny in case she's about to pass out, but she jumps back from contact.

"My *child*," she says. "Nate never *existed*?"

"I don't know. I don't know," I say, and would keep saying forever rather than tell her the thought that is gaining weight in my mind, in the very core of me, more certain than the face of the girl I lost my virginity to or my first day leading a procedure in the surgical theater.

No, you never had a son. Nate was never born. Never lived, never died. He's haunted you your entire life but he's even less than a ghost.

Franny sifts through the other files on the desk. I see Jerry's name on one, Lauren's on another. She pulls out the one with my name on it, but I don't touch it.

"Aren't you going to read yours?"

"Not now."

"What? Don't you—"

"Not *now*."

I fold the file in half and stuff it into my pocket. When Franny hands all the others to me, I do the same with them.

"He'll be coming back soon," Bridge says.

I start away but Franny grabs me by the arm.

"Why are we leaving if everything is here?" she says.

"We don't know what this is."

"It's us. It's all we have."

"That doesn't mean we have to stay."

"Then what *does* it mean, Aaron?"

We're flesh and blood. We feel and remember and love. Even if none of us are who we think we are.

"It means we have to go," I say.

51

WE MAKE OUR WAY BACK PAST THE AMATEUR LANDSCAPE PAINTINGS. FRANNY AND I keep our eyes ahead when we pass the other, bloodied hallway that leads to the room of pods. But Bridge flashes her light down its length.

"Mom?"

Franny doesn't go back but I do. And see the same thing Bridge does.

The old woman stands in front of the door with the porthole window. Then she steps closer. Her feet bulging and bare. The pale blue hospital gown open at the front, a peepshow of folds and moles and dried blood.

The witch.

I hear this. Think it's Bridge before realizing it's me.

Our lights brighten her features as she approaches. The pockets of yellow in the corners of her eyes. The pair of scissors held in her hand.

"Go," I say.

The skin of the old woman's feet meeting the cracked concrete floor like the slap of meat on the butcher's board.

"*GO!*"

52

THERE'S A CATEGORY OF FEAR THAT DENIES YOU THE AIR TO SCREAM.

It's why we're so quiet as we run through the steel portal that's been wrenched from its hinges. The only sound that reaches us is the old woman's breath. Rattling and semi-verbal, as if searching for names or curses that have slipped her mind.

The stairs were difficult to come down and are now almost impossible to ascend. I've situated myself at the end of the line so that I'm able to put my shoulder to Franny's back. We advance like a worm. Stretching thin and muscling tight, over and over.

The air reaches me before the light. A chestful of weightlessness. It doesn't last long. Once we've emerged from the cave, the effort we've made arrives in a thousand needlepoints of pain.

Franny is the only one to look back. Whatever she sees makes her jump.

Spilling and sliding but never quite crumbling altogether; she makes her way down the ridge like a skier losing and regaining control, over and over.

Bridge goes next. I'm about to follow when I feel the witch's touch.

The cold scratch of her hand on my cheek, the fingers hard as bone.

Falling down the ridge after leaping from its edge.

Getting up after blacking out.

Making it back to the gravel parking area outside the lodge.

I can only confirm the last of these because that's where I am now. Blinking away the light after being shielded by the forest's canopy, watching Bridge and Franny rush to the lodge's front door. My eyes catching on something on the edges of what they can see.

He's standing over the twins' graves. His height accentuated all the more by his head being lowered. The stillness of a ceremonial moment of silence.

Bridge seems to sense the Tall Man, not see him, as she slows even with her back to him.

"Get inside!"

It's my voice, but it comes out stronger than I am, more aware of what is happening and the things most likely to come next. It doesn't appear that Bridge hears me. But the Tall Man does.

He raises his head, and the silver hatchet, glinting and slick as if carved from ice, slides up his pant leg. His mouth hanging open as before, but now it reads as anguish instead of hunger. Or perhaps it was always this way. These two absences combined as one suffering.

"*Run!*"

I tell Bridge this. I tell myself.

I catch up to her at the same time we join Franny already pounding at the door.

"Open it!" I'm shouting even as I grasp the handle and find it locked.

"We *left* it open!" Franny says.

Bridge is the only one of us keeping up with the facts of the moment. The only one watching the Tall Man.

"He's coming," she says.

The pruning shears. The ones I took from the shed. Is there time to fish them out of my windbreaker pocket and—and what? The thought goes nowhere. I keep pounding at the door. Franny joins me with her brittle fists.

The door hears us. The wood gives way to the gray space behind it.

I let Franny and Bridge in first, bracing for the hatchet to swing into my back.

"Aaron!"

Bridge has my hand, pulls me in as the door clicks shut.

"Is it him?" Jerry asks. "*Aaron!* Is it—"

"Yes!"

"Does—"

CRACK.

All of us jump back as the silver line of the hatchet's blade cuts through the door. It stays there like the tip of a tongue, tasting the difference between inside and outside, before it's pulled away.

CRACK!

The second strike meets the first at an angle, slicing an X into the wood. Weakening it.

We'd been quiet until this. Now all of our voices come together in a chorus of pleading. I don't see her but Lauren's voice joins in too. Only Bridge maintains anything resembling a coherent thought.

"Leave us alone!" she shouts through the door.

The rest of our voices fall off, waiting for the next strike to come. It doesn't.

We don't hear him leave. There's no way to see him as none of us dare go close to the side windows to look, yet we feel him go as if we do.

"Why'd he stop?" Lauren asks nobody in particular, and nobody answers her.

It prompts me to reach into my pocket. Pull out the files we'd taken and hand Lauren and Jerry the ones with their names on them. They hold them without opening them.

"What's this?" Lauren asks.

"It's what Dad kept in the cellar of the gingerbread house," I say. "It's us."

53

"THIS IS BATSHIT," JERRY SAYS, SLAPPING HIS FILE ONTO THE COFFEE TABLE.

We've retreated to the great room, deciding that being away from the door is worth being visible to the forest outside the giant windows. Without being asked Lauren tells us how they came back to the lodge for something to eat. When they found us gone, they lingered, guessing something was wrong.

"So what is it? Other than that thing out there?" Lauren asked us. "What's wrong?"

Bridge and Franny did most of the talking. The discovery of the summer camp, the second cave entrance, the pods, the old woman with the scissors. As they traded the story back and forth between them, Jerry remained silent. Until now.

"Are you *listening* to this, Lauren?"

"Yes."

"So you agree it's bullshit."

"I don't think I do."

"Can I ask why the fuck not?"

"Because it explains so much."

"About why Dad locked us in here?"

"No. About me."

Jerry looks around for someone to return his exasperation. "How about you, doc? You think we're all clones or something?"

"Not clones," I say. "Just not ourselves."

"Because you saw a bunch of tanks with our names on them? That's a hell of a leap."

"I know it's hard to grasp. But think of the scale of this project, Jerry. They've gone to great lengths to keep it secret. So yes, what we're talking about is pretty far past the boundaries of what we know. Far past what's legal too. That's why it's been built way out here. Why there's a fence."

"Why we can't get out," Franny adds.

Jerry shakes his head at me but doesn't have an immediate reply. He's trying to not go where the rest of us have and it's draining him right before our eyes.

"So these isolation tanks," he says eventually. "They put ideas in our heads?"

"They put our whole lives in our heads," Franny says.

"Fake memories."

"Yes, but they don't just overlap with our real memories," I say. "The fake ones are all we have."

"How'd they *do* that? Kill us?" Jerry laughs uncomfortably. "Are we *dead* right now?"

"Maybe," Bridge says.

"So what's that make *this*? A dream?"

"It's not a dream," Franny says.

"One part of it is," Bridge says.

Jerry looks at her. "What part?"

"The dark water. The sinking boat," she says. "The music."

Jerry doesn't shake his head at her as he had at me. It's because he believes her, even if he doesn't believe the rest of it yet.

"How do I know you're not making this up?" he says, addressing this to me.

"You think we're in on this?"

"Could be."

"You're arguing with yourself," Lauren says.

"How's that?"

"You're trying to hold on to your disbelief but you don't have any. It *is* insane. It's also true."

This does it. Jerry has nothing left to fight with. He sits next to Lauren. Opens his mouth and closes it again.

"I didn't bring the twins' files, but I read some of it when we were underground," Franny says. "There was no Delta commercial. They weren't even actors."

"Who were they?" Lauren asks.

"Dentists. They had a practice together in Fort Lauderdale. Two kids each. They had *lives*."

"What about *Better Together*?" Bridge says. "We all saw them on TV. Well, you guys did. 'Ah poop.' That was their *thing*."

"There was no *Better Together*. They must have put that into our heads as part of the background to make Ezra and Elias fit in."

"I can only remember a couple scenes they were in anyway," I say.

"Me too," Franny says.

"No. Only one," Jerry says, and it's true. When I think of either of the twins as TV stars, I can only see them—or the one character they played—in a single sequence. A kid wearing pin-striped shorts, covered in chocolate ice cream, delivering his trademark line to his dad whose anger melted away at his son's overwhelming cuteness as the studio audience uttered a collective *awwwww*.

There's a moment as we take the measure of one another, trying to read who is having the toughest time of it. But we're all equally bewildered. We all look ill.

"I guess it's time to see who I really am," Lauren announces, and opens her file.

It's like watching someone sleep through a nightmare. There's the same twitches, stretches of stillness, winces. A whimper of recognition before she raises her glistening eyes to us.

"My name is Kayla Thomas," she says.

She was a pediatrician in Chicago. Her area of specialization was cancers of the blood. Work that meant everything to her, particularly following her divorce and the loss of her only child. A daughter, Addison, who died in a car accident with her grandfather—Lauren's dad—behind the wheel. She never remarried. Never spoke to her father again.

"I had a daughter," she says, drawing Bridge close against her. "I don't remember anything about her. Not her face, her laugh. Nothing."

Jerry is about to put his arms around her, but stops and pulls away.

"What about Dad?" he says. "The will, the lawyer, the estate. None of that is real either?"

"We can't be sure about that," I say. "There must be someone behind this. It might be him."

"What about the hatchet man? The old woman who came after you," Jerry says. "How do they fit?"

"I have no idea," I say.

"I do," Lauren says. "Belfountain. The haunted forest. It's a fairy tale."

"And every fairy tale needs monsters," Bridge says.

All at once Jerry stands as if discovering the sofa is smoldering under him. He grabs his file off the coffee table and opens it to the first page.

"This is a description of me," he says.

"Keep reading," Franny says. "The second section tells you who you were before."

He turns the page to the Origin Summary memo. Scans what might be the first paragraph or two before closing the file.

"I'm not doing this," he says.

"Who are you?" Franny asks him. "You saw, didn't you?"

"I'm Gerald Oliver Quinlan."

Franny reads his face as if it were the pages from the second part of Jerry's file. "You hurt someone."

"What are you talking about?"

"I thought I had a son who died, but I never did. You thought you were a wounded football hero, but you're not."

"Shut up."

"You did something awful."

"Shut the *fuck up*!"

Hatred. Decisive and boundless. Jerry is capable of it. He shows a flare of it now, directed not just at Franny but all of us.

That's not all I know now that I didn't ten seconds ago.

I carry the same rage in myself.

Whatever I was before this, I was a man familiar with violence. Not the controlled kind of surgery, nor the isolated episode of *overseas*. It happened in my life, gave shape to that life.

I don't know what side I was on, but I had a stomach for it.

More than that. I was good at it.

54

JERRY SWINGS HIS FIST AT ME AND MISSES. MY FIST DOES THE SAME. FINDS THE side of his face, his mouth, his ear.

Bridge and Lauren have to pull us apart. Then the shouting and taunts. The spitting of blood on the rug, the calls for a bandage that Jerry insists he doesn't need.

It all distracts everyone from the fact that I alone didn't read my file. It wasn't intentional. But now that we're all slumped in different chairs, catching our breath, I decide I don't want to know.

Franny is the first to speak.

"There's something more," she says, rising to pull what looks to be a folded, glossy brochure from her back pocket.

"What is it?" I ask.

"I'm not sure. I took it from the same room we got our files."

She unfolds the thick paper and smooths out its creases over the coffee table. The cover page has a diagonally stamped *DRAFT* over its front.

"Why don't you read it for all of us," Lauren says.

YOURSTORY

It's time to be free from history.

It's time for . . . YOURSTORY.

PROSPECTUS

Overview for Investors

Talk therapies. Meditation. Mood-altering pharmaceuticals.

The demand for a new self—a new future—has never been greater than today. But how do we get there?

The problem is that we always return to remembering who we are.

But what if you could change that past? What if you could trade the life you've led for one that's new?

Yourstory is a memory alteration therapy that can literally change the story of our lives.

And in these challenging times, the market for deleted pasts and new beginnings is unquestionably vast.

WHAT IS YOURSTORY?

FOUR STEPS TO A NEW PAST

STEP ONE: Erase

The first step of Yourstory's process is what we call Induced Endpoint, or IE. IE is achieved by a surprisingly simple exercise: physician-controlled euthanasia.

Our research has determined that termination of life, combined with a neural protein "bath" of our own patented devising, is the only method that fully erases our connection to the past. But don't think of it as the

End. Think of it as a light switch. *Flick!* You're gone. *Flick!* You're safely returned to life and ready for a new future.

STEP TWO: Introduce

There are generally two kinds of memories: semantic and episodic. Semantic memories are a baseline of common knowledge, including cultural and historical reference points (how a cell phone operates, who won last year's World Series, the outcome of the Second World War, etc.). These are preserved in the Yourstory process. Episodic memories are the details of personal recollection (your first love, family experiences, the inclinations and aversions created by emotional response). These are erased in IE.

In the second step of Yourstory, patients are introduced to the new lives they've chosen. The physical means by which we achieve this is a combination of cutting-edge technology and ancient meditative tools. Once IE is completed, clients are mildly sedated and placed in specially designed flotation tanks. In this embryonic state of blank—but waking—consciousness, they bear witness to their new lives. Our research has yielded a method of Memory Introduction (MI) that is completely seamless, convincing, and effective.

STEP THREE: Stimulate

The hippocampus. When it comes to memory, this is the control booth of the brain. It's here that our minds link new information together and encode it into memories. By using various techniques of optogenetics, the brain can be artificially stimulated in the same way it would be if experiencing something new or momentous in "real" life.

To make a memory a lasting one, our brains must be attentive to all the senses. That's why with Yourstory, while the MI program is underway, the brain is simultaneously stimulated by neural implants to excite our sense of smell or touch, even our emotions.

STEP FOUR: Implantation Erasure

Of course it's crucial that our clients not be aware that they've been the subjects of a therapeutic procedure (particularly one involving a death experience). The fourth and final step of Yourstory, therefore, erases the memory of the process itself.

Fortunately, this is the easiest part. During the IE, MI, and Stimulation stages, the client is kept in a state of semiconsciousness, so that whatever memory she may

"That's it?" Jerry says.

"There was more, but the pages have been ripped away."

"They *did* that to us?"

"Seems so," Franny says. "Though why I'd pay anybody to change me from a lesbian sound editor into a heroin addict is anyone's guess."

"We weren't clients," Lauren says. "This brochure or whatever—it was for a stock offering. They were planning to go public but still had trials to do. They had to prove it could work."

"Not public trials," I say.

"Experiments," Jerry says. "Us."

"Yourstory," Lauren repeats, weighing the viability of the word itself. "How much you figure people would pay to be someone else? Artificially reincarnated. To die and come back different?"

"A lot," I say.

"More," Jerry says. "Everything they have."

55

SHE TOLD ME SHE WASN'T HUNGRY, BUT I HEAT UP SOME FISH STICKS FOR BRIDGE and me anyway. We take our plates to the farthest end of the dining table, the others in the great hall so far off they appear as figures on the opposite shore of a lake.

"You want to talk about any of this?" I say, drawing a fish stick through a pool of ketchup.

"I think I'm too freaked to talk about it."

"We're going to get out of here, okay?"

"Are you saying that as my big brother? Or just whoever you are?"

"It doesn't matter. I'm saying it. Me."

Bridge picks up a fish stick. Crams the whole thing into her mouth.

"I remember more than just the dark water from before," she says after she swallows. "Not dreams. Memories."

"How can you tell the difference?"

She looks away at some point over my shoulder as if lip-reading someone standing there speaking. "It's like meatballs," she says.

"Okay."

"So meatballs all look the same, right? But if you had two different people make them and put them into spaghetti sauce and you ate them, you could tell they didn't come from the same place. They'd *taste* different."

"You're saying these thoughts you have from before—they were made by someone else."

"They weren't made by *anyone*. The memories we have now—the cabin at the lake, our Tuesday dinners together—those were put in our heads. But the memories I'm talking about were lived."

"Homemade meatballs instead of frozen."

She laughs. A sound that's so good to hear I almost gasp.

"Yeah," she says. "Like that."

She clears her throat. The humor replaced by something she's summoning into words out of the darkness.

"There were soldiers. Police. Or men who used to be police," she says. "Men in uniforms who came to our school and took some of the kids away. I remember our teacher crying. Everybody was crying."

"Did they hurt you?"

"No. They asked us questions though."

"Like what?"

"Like 'Do you love your country?' and 'Where were you born?' None of it made sense. And they didn't *seem* mean. They smiled and called us 'buddy' and 'sweetheart.' But that just made them scarier."

For the second time I attempt to eat, but the ketchupped fish stick looks wounded with the others gathered around it in sympathy. I push my plate away.

"Me too," I say. "I remember the police too."

"What happened, Aaron? Was it a war? Were we invaded?"

"I think it was us. Us against ourselves."

"Did we win? The people on the good side?"

"I don't know. I'm pretty sure, whatever it is, it's still going on."

• • •

I'm awake.

I know because Bridge is kneeling next to the sofa. I know because I can smell her fish sticky breath.

"There's something outside," she whispers.

I'm on one of the sofas in the great room. All the lights are off, but I can see the outline of Jerry sitting up in the chair closest to the hearth, staring out the wall of glass. I take a quick scan outside but can't see anything other than the impenetrable tree line.

"What is it?" I ask him.

"I can't tell," he says, his hands whitening with his tightened grip at the edges of the armrests. "Something that wasn't there before."

As if his words enact an external reality, I look outside again and see something that wasn't there before.

It doesn't move. A limbless sapling. A halved flagpole. But those things don't transport themselves into a place where they didn't exist before. They don't watch.

"Go to the bedroom," I tell Bridge. "Lock the door."

"I'm not leaving."

"Bridge, I'm not asking, I'm—"

"It won't make a difference."

Now that she's said it, I hear it as something I've known all along. The lodge's open-concept layout, high ceilings, wall of glass. There's no hiding in Belfountain's castle.

"Okay," I say. "Be ready."

I get up and slide toward the windows. The shape outside detects my approach—I can sense this without it changing position—but even as it comes into clearer focus, it doesn't reveal itself, doesn't respond.

"What are you doing?"

Jerry has come up behind me.

"We can't just wait until there's nothing left," I say, and as I do, I realize that what I believe to be outside, the thing I fear most, isn't the thing standing there, but the forest itself. All of the estate, reaching out from here to its walls as a single organism.

I sidestep to the left, all the way to the wall. Feel for the light switch and turn it on.

The mouth. This comes first. The Tall Man's lips stretched over gray studs of teeth.

He comes at us.

There's an apron of grass between the trees and the window that's been untended long enough that some of it is patches of dirt, some of it grown to ankle height. The Tall Man passes over it soundlessly, a quiet that reaches out from him like an odor.

He comes into the stark illumination of the floodlights and shows himself to be more corpse than phantom, a marriage of decay and grace. And unlike a ghost, he doesn't pass through the wall of glass but stops at it. His eyes, white and bulbous, moving between me and Jerry.

They only stop when they find Bridge.

I back away from the glass and feel Jerry do the same, both of us seeing what he's going to do before he begins to do it. The silver hatchet gripped in both of his gloved hands. Its head rising up over the waxy snarl of his hair.

The sound of it comes a fraction before the impact, as if a glitch in the soundtrack. Not a crack but an impenetrable wash of noise. A wave that drives your head into the ocean's floor.

"Bridge!"

The wall of glass smashed into diamonds, falling over us, biting our skin. I try to find her but I'm blinking through darkness. I bring the back of my hand up to swipe something sharp from my face and it lets me see. The sharp thing was a shard embedded in my forehead. The darkness was blood.

Jerry is shouting. At once close by and in another world. Trying to ward off the Tall Man who is walking into the castle. I don't look back but I can hear him coming. The crunch of his feet over the glass.

Bridge is here. Backing away from the Tall Man, the cold air that blows in and brings the smell of the woods with it.

"Run!"

It's me telling her this, but it's only my grip around her forearm that makes her move. Pulling her over the shards that reach all the way to the stairs up from the great room.

The lodge's front door is already open.

Outside, Franny is there, urging us forward. Lauren is there too. Already running, already gone, a few strides ahead of Franny.

Bridge is out first, then me. The hardness of the air holding us back, a freezing weight in our lungs as if we'd taken a breath of lake water down the wrong way.

The last thing we hear before we throw ourselves into the trees is Jerry's voice. A wordless shrieking coming from inside the lodge. It wavers between a signal of bravery and agony, an unreadable human utterance, animal, prehistoric.

It goes on longer than you'd think a held breath would allow. And when it stops, it doesn't come again.

56

WE DON'T MAKE A CHOICE TO TAKE THE RED TRAIL AWAY FROM THE LODGE. IT'S THE one we start for because it's the one that none of the three of us have gone down so far.

The trail curves more than the others. A meandering through the trees that will play to the Tall Man's strengths. I ready myself for him to plow onto the trail ahead after taking a straight line from the lodge. What will I do when it happens? There must be an attack I could attempt, a self-sacrifice. But nothing occurs to me.

"There!"

Franny is ahead of the rest of us. Now she plunges off the trail, leaping like a deer, gangly and flailing. Bridge goes after her, then Lauren.

I hold my arms up against the thrashing branches, but it doesn't stop them from cutting into the side of my neck, the sharp ends stabbing at my eyes. Even after I've broken through and the cabin is there, I come to the door with my hands up as if in surrender.

Once I'm inside, Bridge locks the door.

The cabin is like the others in layout, though with slightly different furnishings. This one is more committed to a hunter's retreat theme. A camouflage-pattern blanket laid over the top of the sofa's back, oil paintings of ducks flying in formation over marshes with rifle barrels poking up from the reeds, the mounted head of a buck over the archway to the bedrooms.

Bridge follows me into the kitchen and watches as I go through the drawers and cabinets. All the utensils, if there ever were any, have been removed. There's nothing to defend ourselves with any more useful than a salad spinner.

When we return to the living room, Franny is stepping away from the front window. She turns to look at us.

"He's here," she says.

A shattering smash against the cabin door.

"Open up!"

It's Jerry.

"Open! The . . . *door*!"

I'm not going to. I'm thinking about seeing if Bridge could fit through one of the bedroom windows. I'm thinking about charging into whatever is outside and wrapping myself around it, buying some time. But none of this happens. Because Franny goes to the door and opens it.

"Sorry if I *disturbed* you," Jerry says as he strides in and kicks the door closed with the back of his heel.

"Is he after you?"

Jerry looks at Franny as if this is exactly the sort of question he'd expect her to ask. The contempt that comes from being surrounded by weakness, by an entire world of weakness.

"Why don't you take a look for yourself?"

Franny doesn't move.

"What happened back there?" I ask, and Jerry turns his attention to me.

"We had a *problem*. Which you left me to handle."

He opens his hands, stretching the fingers as if to crack their knuckles, but it's only to draw our eyes to his palms. The lines and creases a map of white lines drawn through blood.

"We need to *know*, Jerry," Lauren pleads. "Are you saying—"

"I'm saying you don't need to worry. It's just us now. Just family."

His right hand reaches behind his back and pulls something up from where it had been tucked into his belt. A knife. The chef's blade from the lodge that was among the ones we thought the Tall Man had taken away.

"Where'd you find that?" Franny asks him.

"Where I put it. Along with all the others."

"I don't—"

"You *wouldn't* understand."

He trades the knife from one hand to another. There's an audible click as the handle pulls away from the red glue of his skin.

"That's why when the shit hits the fan you turn to people like me," he goes on. "But God forbid if somebody breaks a nail or a skull, you forget that you were the ones who asked for help in the first place."

"I never asked you to do anything," Franny says.

"See, *that's* what I'm talking about! *That's* the kind of thing I've heard come out of the mouths of entitled bitches like you my whole goddamned life."

"You remember," I say, coming between the two of them as I use my hand at my side to signal Bridge to move away. "Who you were before."

Jerry sees what I'm trying to do, and he grins his toothy grin at me in mock congratulations.

"You're no doctor, Aaron," he says. "But you're not a total shithead either."

"The watch," I say, voicing my observation at the same time I take note of it. "The one Dad gave the twins."

"What about it?"

"You're wearing it."

Jerry looks cross-eyed at the Bulova on his wrist. "Nice, right?"

"Ezra left it with Elias when we buried him."

"And I dug it out," Jerry says. "No point leaving one of the only souvenirs from dear old Dad in the dirt like that."

Jerry shifts focus from the watch to us. Grips the knife in his right hand and waves it in front of him. It pushes the three of us back deeper into the cabin's living room. When the backs of our legs hit the sofa's edge, he holds up his hands for us to stop.

"Seeing as you're *curious*, I don't remember everything," he says. "But yeah, I've got some ideas."

"Who were you?" Lauren asks.

"A serviceman. Maybe a cop. But then I was given another assignment when the priorities got switched up. Domestic security."

"What did you do?"

"The *good* stuff. Illegals. We were given quite a bit of latitude. And what I mean by that is we could do absolutely whatever the fuck we wanted."

Jerry shakes his head as if at the recollection of a college stunt, an accomplishment that, while perhaps foolish, demonstrated the boldness and stamina of his younger self.

"I remember *them*, that's for sure," he says, his amusement now curdling with something else, poisonous even for him. "How terrified they were. Some of them saw us coming and literally shit their pants. And we hadn't even *done* anything yet."

"Why?"

This is Bridge. Her voice firm but without accusation. The steadiness of a prosecutor bringing a witness to the place they must go.

"Why what, sweetheart?"

"Why kill your brothers?"

Jerry shakes his head and gives Lauren a *Can you believe this?* look.

"Well, first off," he says, "they weren't my brothers."

"But you didn't know that when you did it."

"You got me there," he says, making a sucking pop with the inside of his cheek. "I guess I'm just exercising my rights and freedoms. It's what smart people do. So when we got driven up here and I saw there was thirty million on the table and that there was nobody to tell me what I could and couldn't do—well, I seized the day."

"By killing Elias."

"You got to start somewhere. And I started when I walked into that big house and saw that pretty little hatchet by the fireplace. All polished up like this designer feature. I figured I could put a few scratches in it. And I did. But then Ezra heard me working on Elias out in the woods, and I had to leave the blade in him. When we all came out and it was gone—that's when I was sure."

"Sure of what?"

"That the homeless guy—or whoever he is—he'd be my cover. That once he took the hatchet you'd all figure it was him. I mean, I would have done it all anyway most likely. But sometimes the breaks go your way, know what I'm saying?"

He shifts his hungry gaze from Lauren to Bridge, and for the first time I see the potential in him for actions worse than killing. Ways of hurting intended only for the pleasure in delivering the hurt, watching what it did.

"Why did you let us go to the fence?" I ask him, drawing his attention to me instead of them. "It looked like you wanted out as much as the rest of us."

"I couldn't take you all down at the same time. So I had to go with the flow. But even if that gate opened, I doubt any of you would have made it through."

Jerry straightens his knees, stands at his full height. A motion that is the precursor to something else.

"Listen to me," I say, and he does, but only partly. "There's no money. No estate. We didn't know that before. But we do now. Getting rid of them—of us—isn't going to make your cut any bigger."

"Maybe so. Maybe not."

"Jerry, please. We won't say anything—"

He comes at us as I speak and Franny sees it all before I do.

Sees the blade drive into her. Hears the screech of the steel as it grinds against the bottom rung of her ribs. Screams the second before it happens.

The knife is pulled away almost as quickly as it goes in.

Once it's out Franny goes quiet. As if her pain was activated by a circuit that's been broken, leaving her puzzled and then, when she looks down to see what comes out of her, astonished.

She sidesteps away. An attempt to recover her balance but she can't, and she slams against the wall and slides down the paneling to the floor. Nothing moves but her hands. Scrambling into the pouch sewn into the front of her hoodie like a pair of spiders trying to find shelter from the rain.

The four of us watch her.

"How's that?" Jerry says to himself. At first intrigued, then awestruck. "How's *that*?"

I'm moving as he speaks. Going at him. A good-sized man slamming into a smaller, thicker man who remembers how these things go.

But I remember too.

Something from my life before that is familiar with the shifts required to throw a body to the floor. The simultaneous struggles to get on top. To hold arms under the weight of knees. To push down with the thumbs into the cradles of bone that hold the eyes.

I remember this but forgot he has the knife.

He's under me, pinned at the shoulders. It allows him to bring the blade up but limits the arc to the length of his forearm. Still, it's a good enough reach to cut me.

The pain rolls me off him and I end up next to Franny against the wall. Her eyes frozen, mouth agape. Her characteristically mocking face.

I look up in time to see Lauren starting toward Jerry where he still lies on the floor, her leg pulling back to deliver a kick to his head. The knife stops her. Raised and warding her off like a crucifix holding a vampire at bay.

He takes his time getting to his feet. Blinking, rolling his shoulders.

"That shouldn't be too long," he says, referring to my wound. The slice he made to the soft flesh at the top of my chest.

He will make more cuts now.

There will be nothing I'll be able to do as he steps over and brings the knife down where I'm slumped, my legs jerking at the knees. He'll do it again and again.

What he actually does is worse.

"Let's go," he says, turning to Bridge and Lauren.

Lauren takes Bridge's hand and opens the door. The two of them wait there in the pale light that blinds me nonetheless.

Before she goes, Bridge looks back at me.

The dark is coming. It could be death, it could be one of the increments along the way. All I'm sure of is how the core of me has gone prickly and cold.

Jerry is nothing but a smudge of shadow in the doorframe, leering in and out of focus. But I can still see his teeth. The upper row of perfectly aligned slabs like a miniature, marble wall.

"You look like all the others," he says, an observation that provokes what sounds like pity in him, but it's not that.

There's a throbbing in my throat that wasn't there a second ago. Something trying to come up. Hard as stone, turning and scratching.

I open my mouth and what comes out is my sister's name but I'm the only one to hear it. And then even I'm not here anymore.

57

I REMEMBER EVERYTHING.

A July afternoon so hot it thickened the waves to syrup. Standing at the edge of the shore's highest boulder—

One-ah, two-ah—

Then everything went dark.

Thinking you'd been under too long—

My sister. My little sister.

Broken phrases. Coming to me out of the air. Trying to recall how they fit together, the precise wording, helps bring me back. Lifted into consciousness by threads of meaning.

The little sister is real, even if the memory isn't.

Bridge.

He took Bridge.

Moving hurts but not as much as I'm expecting. I'm able to sit up, straighten my legs. I've made the same mistake that Jerry had in overestimating the extent of the damage his knife did. He thought I would bleed out, but the cut isn't so deep. I slip my hand under my shirt and feel the skin below my shoulder. It's almost dried, the bleeding mostly slowed. If it opens up again, it may still bring me down. Just not now.

Before I attempt to rise, I notice how one of Franny's hands has slipped out of her hoodie's pouch. The fingers wrapped around the baby rattle Dad left for her. The hand-painted birds flying over a Japanese lake.

I stand up. Franny seems to congratulate me for this simple triumph with her look of mock amazement.

"I'll find her," I say.

A promise made to the dead. A stranger I've known my whole life.

I wonder if it's the lack of food or water or blood that makes the air feel so cool on my skin. In typical Pacific Northwest fashion, it has never been outright hot nor cold in Belfountain. But there's a damp weight to the place now, a pressure, like a drizzle of soil falling over me.

I'm curving back along the Red trail. That maddening switchback feels like it's only inching me closer to the lodge when I see something up ahead.

The witch laughs when I spot her.

"Where did they go?" I shout, my voice so hoarse it's on the verge of evaporating.

The old woman flaps her hands with the excitement of a child.

"Where did he take them?"

She plows away into the deeper bush.

It's all I can do to keep up with her. It's not her speed so much as the way she doesn't seem to feel the thrashings and bites of the branches and roots. I let them thrash and bite me too.

She's leading me nowhere. I see this too late.

We aren't going to Bridge or the lodge or a secret passage through the fence. She's a madwoman doing a mad thing and all it means is I've wasted time I don't have.

"Wait!" I call to her. "Wait!"

She keeps going as if she hadn't heard me. It makes me even more furious. Rushing up to her and, when I'm close enough, grabbing her arm so that she looks at me.

"Where is she?" I gasp at her. "Where's my sister?"

There isn't anything in her face to indicate comprehension. All that reaches me is the smell of her. Salty and mineral like a creature of the sea.

Her free arm lifts up. Points through the trees.

It can't be there. But it is.

The house I grew up in. The Cape Cod with a red-brick chimney and the Stars and Stripes hanging limp from a pole out front. Exactly as I remember it except it's here, gardenless, in the middle of Belfountain's woods.

The front door opens.

I back away, but now it's the old woman's turn to hold me by the arm, her grip strong. She knows who's opened the door. She wants me to see too.

A figure steps out. It takes a second to match its identity to a living person, because the person who's there isn't alive.

She waves.

My mother. Welcoming me home.

58

SHE KEEPS STANDING THERE. KEEPS WAVING.

I go to her and the old woman follows just behind me. When I reach the porch, Mom seems to give a signal, a half wink I'm not sure has even happened, and the witch stops at the bottom of the steps.

"Come in, Aaron," she says, backstepping deeper into the front hall.

It's my mother speaking. Telling me to do something, which means I do it. But this moment, one that ought to provide familiarity and comfort, delivers only the opposite. Walking over the threshold into my home to approach my mother in the hallway is the most frightening thing I've done.

"What happened to you?" I ask her.

"I was here," she says, not sounding like herself, not like she did before. A barely masked impatience, the hostility that comes with seeing others as standing in the way of where you alone can go. "And there."

"This is wrong."

"What is?"

"You." She backs away from me. A retreat that instead of making me feel safe communicates a threat. "Who are you?"

"Well, you know who I'm *not*."

It comes to me then. How Mom's file hadn't been among the others Franny found. How there hadn't been a pod with her name on it.

"Who are you?" I ask again.

"Aaron. Don't move, okay? Don't—"

"Where's Bridge?"

"There's no need—"

"*Tell me where she is!*"

She reaches for something around the corner behind her. A countertop that, from memory, held the notepads and mug with pens and pencils. When her hand returns to view, it's holding a revolver.

"The living room," she says.

The interior here is as I remember it too. But I can also see the evidence of haste in its construction: nailheads poking out where they hadn't been entirely hammered in, sections of exposed plywood wall, the way the Laura Ashley wallpaper doesn't reach all the way to the ceiling. In the corners there are stray crates marked *'80s* and *'90s* and inside them random items: a rotary-dial phone, packs of Marlboros, a Rubik's Cube. On the glass coffee table a variety of magazines from different periods of the past: Michael Jackson on the cover of *Time*, a *Sports Illustrated* with the Blue Jays winning their second World Series in a row, a stack of yellow-spined *National Geographic*s.

"It's something, isn't it?"

"No," I say. "It's nothing."

She considers this, then nods in the manner of a teacher congratulating an unpromising student for his effort.

"In fact, it *was* rather unnecessary in the end," she says. "We built this place for the photo shoots, the home videos, but we could have done that in any studio. The idea to do it *here* was to have you and Bridge and

Franny spend a little time walking around the space, absorbing it all. But it didn't work. Even half out of it, each of you could tell it was fake. So we ended up having to erase *that* from you as well."

The gun looks alien in her hand, a thing of magic, as if she wields a hissing snake or glowing wand instead of a Beretta. How do I know what kind of gun it is? I feel sure it belongs to a set of knowledge not given to me in the pod. Another piece that's slipped through. More and more of it is returning. Held back for a time but now too powerful to be resisted, forcing its passage like the tide dissolving a wall of sand.

"Are you going to kill me?"

"What a question!" she exclaims, and flutters her free hand over her heart. Yet her expression doesn't match the horrified intent of her gesture. She remains detached, observing me.

"Are you going to tell me or not?"

"I'll confess to improvising at this point, Aaron," she says. "My current thinking is that I need to find the others, particularly that half brother of yours, once he's done with whatever he's up to. You may well be helpful in accomplishing that. You're *motivated*, aren't you? A surprise. Your profile didn't suggest that you'd be the most emotionally involved of the group, but I'm rather proud of the impact that the imprinting had on you."

She moves to stand with her back to the bay window so that to look at her leaves me squinting to see her through a corona of light.

"We have a little time," she says in the brisk tone of an executive heading up some marketing spitballing session. "I'd be curious to know how you're responding to all this."

I want you to suffer. I want to squeeze your throat closed and never let go. I want you to feel what it is to have not just one but two lives taken from you.

"Not well," I say.

"Do you have any specific queries?"

"Where's Bridge?"

She rolls her eyes. "Really? You're sticking with the devoted big brother arc?"

"Where *is* she?"

"With Jerry somewhere. Care for me to speculate?"

She's clearly bored by this—the concern of one doomed subject over the fate of another doomed subject—and there's a risk of losing her interest.

"Please don't," I say. "Tell me about Yourstory instead."

"You found your files, along with some of the promotional documents. Were they not clear?"

"What I don't understand—how all this—what do you call it? The business model. If you take this to market, how do you get away with destroying people like this?"

"*Destroying* doesn't strike me as remotely the right term, Aaron." She clears her throat to articulate a string of words she's said before so many times they come out by rote. "People *want* oblivion, Aaron. It allows them to carve something new out of the ashes. It's what will make Yourstory possibly the most important, transformative therapy since early humans devised their first god to pray to."

"And you own it," I say, the words prompting a wave of physical illness that almost silences me. "You're the 'Dad.' Ray Quinlan. The workaholic with all the secrets. You fashioned him after yourself."

"I gave him some of my best lines too."

"So this place—Belfountain—it's all yours."

"It's special, isn't it? There were a few parcels like it elsewhere—some I could have set up with more straightforward construction, to be honest—but it was the old summer camp that sold me. All those Bible-thumpy messages about forgiveness, new life. Born again! Not to mention the additional advantages of having Camp Belfountain already marked on the maps so all the excavation that had to be done could happen under existing structures. Dig a hole right under the old dining hall and connect it to a cave system. If you happened to be looking at the site from a satellite, you wouldn't think anything had gone on down there in thirty years."

"It must have cost a fortune," I say, and it comes out with unintended admiration.

"Fortunately, I was in *possession* of a fortune. I sold some neural implantation patents a few years ago—really interesting stuff, emotional variation, antidepressive stimulation, amazingly lucrative pharmacological alternatives. But making sad people less sad wasn't my real interest."

"That's killing people and giving them fake memories."

The hand holding the gun stiffens.

"What is a self other than a past?" she says.

In the pictures they showed me in the pod, the view outside the bay windows Mom stands in front of revealed a tiered garden leading up to a crabapple tree. Now there's only the rain forest, thick and close.

Along with the witch. Staring. She wants in but isn't allowed, and she holds her eyes on me, dark buttons, empty and shining.

"It gets rid of the bad things you've done—or have been done to you," I say, forcing my attention back to Mom. "A shame remover."

"That's clever! A stain remover for the conscience. Thank you. I'll have to remember that for the rollout." Something rueful passes over her features. "It was always going to be a self-improvement tool. But *now*, after what's happened—the clampdown, the internment programs, the whole unpleasant pageant—well, we *all* have so much we'd like to forget. The things we did. Didn't do. The things we stood and watched."

There's a creak in the floorboards upstairs. A single crunch from the shifting of weight. Mom (I can't stop myself from thinking of her as this) doesn't appear to hear it. Her mind elsewhere, reflecting, self-congratulating.

"I've learned so much these past few days, despite the many difficulties. I've learned so much *from* the difficulties," she says. "But what genuinely startled me was how few gaps Yourstory left in all of you. Next time I'll put even less into the MI. Turns out it's better when what we provide isn't much more than scant suggestions. And then, once you come out and start to be around other people again, you tell your stories and they tell theirs. Mix and match. The brain is so hungry for memories it'll take some from others if it has to. Make them up out of next to nothing."

"Jerry is the only one who doesn't know who he was before this," I say, wagering there's no way she'd have a way of detecting my lie. "Who was he?"

"You don't really want to know that. You want to know why he killed all of you."

I note the past tense as well as the inclusiveness—*killed all of you*—but push it away to pursue my first point.

"So it was him," I say. "It wasn't the man in the woods?"

"No, no," she says with what may be a note of sadness. "That's why I left the lodge. I knew he was out there, and that someone other than him was a murderer. Things were quite far off the rails at that point. That's when I turned on the fence. And when more of you started to die, I had to secure myself."

I'm tempted to ask more, but she's become distracted by the mention of the Tall Man in a way that threatens to pull her away.

"What about Jerry?"

She approaches a chair—a plaid upholstered La-Z-Boy I remember being Dad's favorite to sit in while hiding behind the newspaper—and I'm hoping she sits in it, perhaps putting herself at a disadvantage. She appears to have the same thought and merely leans against one of its arms.

"He was what, these days, they call a patriot," she begins. "Fearful, taste for violence. A deportation squad officer right from the early days. All of which made him a fascinating candidate. Could we cleanse him of not only what he'd witnessed of cruelty but being cruel himself? I honestly thought we'd been successful until—well, we don't need to be forthcoming about that in the research we release, do we? I mean, who's going to know?"

I'll know, I think of saying but stop myself. *I'm probably the only one alive who does, and soon there won't even be me.*

She studies me as if reading my thoughts. There's a flicker of something I mistake for pity, but when she speaks, I hear as only her curiosity.

"Do you know who you really are, Aaron?"

"No."

"Shall I tell you? You're not a doctor, as you've already discovered. Not a runner, either. You—"

"Stop."

"A leader of a kind. Defiance! One of the few who didn't get scared off even after—"

"*Stop!*"

She raises her eyebrows. The gun too. Aiming it at my head instead of my chest.

"All right," she says. "But would you like to know how you died?"

She takes my silence for acquiescence. Or maybe she doesn't care what I want to know or not.

"I was confident of Yourstory's methodology. But it was unproven. And I confess that some of the initial trials were, well, *less* than successful. Memories are stubborn. Pharmaceutical cleanses, protein sponges. The past came back no matter what chemical manipulation we applied. I knew, deep down, that only a total shutdown would do the trick. Death. But my financial backers were rather nervous about experiments involving, you know, the real thing. Even now. Even them. You should have seen their faces when I brought it up! I knew I would have to proceed on my own. And that called for human subjects."

There's the creaking in the floor upstairs again, directly over our heads. This time Mom definitely hears it too. Her eyes glance up at the ceiling as if it were glass and she's confirming what she knows to be there. But she doesn't mention it, only looks back down to the gun, and along its barrel at me.

"It was essential that all of you be taken at once," she goes on. "Hiring goons to drive around snatching people—a common sort of crime, but it offered patterns to be discovered. And in any case, it was important that I know *who* was being taken, to have an idea of their profiles so that I could evaluate the efficacy of their transformation."

As she speaks, I feel the cold water lapping against my chin, my lips, as I struggled to stay above the surface. The twins, Bridge, and the others around me doing the same. The alien song reaching up to us from the deep. Not a shared dream, not the sensation of floating in the pods. The last moments of our lives.

"We drowned," I say. "You drowned us."

"We could have done it a different way, of course. Something controlled in the lab. Lethal injection. But I felt it needed to be organic."

"Mass murder isn't organic."

"Really? How do you think you were *born*, Aaron?"

I try to think of the answer. Try to envision who my real mother might be, where she delivered me, the faces of those who first blanketed me, held me. Not even the vaguest guess comes to mind.

"In water!" my false mother exclaims in reply to herself. "The most intimate darkness. I recreated that as best I could. Do you see the circularity? Birth and death? Mother to ocean? No? Well. Perhaps the elegance of it is outside your grasp at the moment."

"Why a boat? Why not drown us in a tank here at Belfountain instead?"

"Missing at sea. One of the last ways to truly disappear. You've *already* been declared dead. A swift turnaround. With an abduction on land? It would take *years*."

Once again her words make my head swim. *Declared dead*. Which makes me what? An error. A monster. Nothing.

"How was it done?"

"The old-fashioned way. A bribe. I can tell you, the whale watching business isn't what it used to be," she says, her free hand picking at a thread in the chair's armrest. "So the captain of one such vessel was quite amenable to a new identity in a foreign country and more than enough money to see him through the rest of his days. Because you'd all booked your tickets in advance, we had time to find out who you were, the broad strokes of your personalities. Then, an hour out—an explosive charge below decks. Enough to sink the ship but *look* like the engine blew. Our boat recovered your bodies, then revived you on board—a successful process in all cases but one. We sedated you, brought you here. The Coast Guard's search for survivors was predictably brief and fruitless. And all the while I had you here, becoming something new."

"What was the music we all heard? Under the water?"

"I was interested in that too. I assumed it was some aural hallucination triggered by the compound we administered on the rescue boat. But my subsequent investigation suggests that it was something else altogether." She grins, a pause to lend emphasis to what comes next. "The whales," she says. "A choir of humpbacks, serenading you into the afterlife. Isn't that remarkable?"

I can hear them now. Another true memory, the last of my life. Sounding up from the endless dark.

"Well," she announces, straightening. "Perhaps we should proceed to—"

"What about Fogarty, the lawyer?"

"An actor. Apparently well regarded in the San Francisco theater community, but I personally thought he overcooked it a smidge."

"And the limo drivers? They were actors too?"

"They were *limo drivers*."

Through the window, the old woman steps closer. At first I think it's to press her face to the glass, but then she veers off toward the front door. A moment later I can't see her at all.

"Were you ever going to let us go?"

"You know, I hadn't decided on that. It was possible—well, I certainly *liked* the idea. A united family, getting together for Sunday dinners and summer holidays."

She flinches at this. A flare of discomfort that comes from a place she normally has safely contained. But only for a second. She arches her back in a yogic pose of strength.

But it lets me see something. We weren't the first prisoners at Belfountain. There had been others before us. Two of them.

"Who is the Tall Man?" I ask. "The old woman outside?"

"I admit that working mostly on my own, as I was forced to do, led to a number of mistakes. Not anticipating the danger Jerry brought, for instance," she says, nodding to indicate that she's heard my question but that the answer must be approached indirectly. "Also leaving the key to the lab in the shed—I'd simply forgotten about that one. So many *stages* to the construction, so much *Here, you'll need this*. And yes, the escapees. The ones you call the Tall Man and the old woman."

She sighs at the thought of them, wistful and strangely girlish, as if at the memory of some lost intimacy.

"You haven't told me who they are."

"Who are they *now*? Failed experiments," she says. "But *before* that? They were my only family. My mother. My son."

The sound of a foot coming down at the top of the stairs. From where I stand, I'll only be able to see who it is when they've completed the descent, but there's no question that it's a person up there, deliberate and slow.

"Over the time I was developing Yourstory I was losing them, bit by bit. My mother to Alzheimer's. My son to—well, they gave it a number of different diagnoses," she continues, louder than necessary, before pausing with a sigh. "Acute bipolar disorder. That's what most of them hung their hats on. But what's that *mean*? A defective mind. Faulty wiring. True for both of them. It's why I rushed my work so much at the end. I thought I could save them. Wipe their bad brains clean and reboot them. A second chance at sanity for my son, at memory for my mother."

"Your family," I say, catching up.

"Yes."

"We thought they might have been ghosts."

"*We're* the ghosts, Aaron. Sentimental hangers-on, wishing we could go back to the good old days. Ghosts are my prime market."

Another step on the stairs. If I turn my head, I might be able to see the legs of whoever it is, but I sense that to do so would be the end of the agreement I have with Mom to not shoot me dead here and now. She's pretending not to hear the person on the stairs. So I must do the same.

"Every obsessive is motivated for personal reasons, and I'm no exception," she says, as if in reply to a point I've made. "My father left when I was a child, which perhaps explains why the one I created for you was such a cold spot. But you must believe that I *wanted* you to have a father. Everything I've done here—it's always been about family. I tried to save my own because I loved them. And after they slipped away, I loved the memory of them. I still do. Because memory is all there is."

The weight on the stairs seems to be actively growing, now sounding great enough to crack them. To fall through the floor altogether.

"I *wanted* to be your mother," she says to me, blinking. "Wouldn't you agree that, in some sense, I always will be?"

The steps reach the base of the stairs and pause.

"Steven?" Mom says. "I'd like you to meet someone."

I look. The Tall Man doesn't appear to hear her or understand her words if he does. He doesn't move other than his heaving torso, as though he's drawing breath through a hole in his back. He's without the silver hatchet. Stooped and bleeding. His mouth pulled open in silent agony.

"Aaron, this is my son, Steven," she says, and steps closer to him.

Whether it is to embrace the Tall Man or guide him over to shake my hand or whisper her command for him to attack, I can't say, because in her approach she lowers the gun a few inches, momentarily forgetting it's there at the end of her arm, and I'm rushing at her, leaping into the space between us even after the crack of the shot.

59

SHE'S SO LIGHT. BIRD-BONED. AND LIKE A BIRD, SHE FLIES.

Her head hits the window behind her. At the impact, she utters a single grunt and lands on the floor, arms crossed over her chest as if a stubborn child refusing to play a game.

Seeing Mom there delivers two pieces of information I hadn't grasped the second before.

The bullet missed me.

She's not holding the gun anymore.

It's there on the floor where she dropped it when I connected with her, just beyond her right foot. I'm bending to pick it up when she sees it too. But instead of reaching for it she starts screaming.

"*Help* me*! Steven!*"

Her voice unlike any of her previous tones, frantic and shattering. The strangeness of it prevents me from understanding its meaning.

"*Steven!*"

I feel the Tall Man moving. The vibration of his bulging feet on the shoddy floorboards. One more step and he'll be on top of me. If I look, I can confirm it. If I look, I won't move before he's here.

The gun is there and it's the only thing in the world.

I fall onto my side next to it and pick it up at the same time that Mom pushes away from the wall and stretches out her leg, kicking my face. But it's something I'm barely aware of. There's only my hand slipping around the gun, lifting the gun, raising the gun to my right, and firing once, twice, a third time.

The Tall Man attempts to close his mouth. To speak? To spit? It doesn't work, whatever his intent. The gray lips shiver and fall open again, his eyes not on me, but on his mother. There's no recognition in them. There's nothing I would identify as emotion. It was her voice he responded to, not her, and now that he can't hear her, he topples onto his back, his spine and knees locked so that he comes down like a felled tree.

"What did you do? What did you do?"

She's getting up. I figured she'd broken something. Maybe she has. But it doesn't stop her from rolling onto her knees, reaching for the arm of the recliner, fighting her way to her feet.

"Don't move," I say, and point the gun at her face.

"You *hurt* him. You—"

"I didn't hurt him. I shot him. Now don't fucking move."

She stays where she is.

Her eyes dart over to see whoever walks in through the front door. Soft padding over the carpet, the steps tentative as a child's.

I try to find whoever is there in my peripheral vision but the angle won't allow it. It requires me to look away from Mom, though I keep the barrel trained on her.

The old woman. Peeking around the corner from the front hall, her eyes flicking from the body on the floor, to Mom, to me.

By reflex my arm swings the gun over and aims at her.

"Don't," Mom says.

Pleading. Not as startling as her shrieked appeal to the Tall Man yet it's the most genuine sound I've ever heard her make.

"She doesn't *know*. *She doesn't know*."

I don't understand what she means and for a moment I consider firing if for no other reason than she's asked me not to. Then I see how the old woman looks at me, confused but seeking approval, the wish to not cause any harm, to please. *She doesn't know*.

"I'll take you to them," Mom says.

60

MOM GOES FIRST.

As she passes the old woman, there's the briefest glance between them I worry might be some kind of secret signal, and I stay back another stride in case one of them comes at me.

Once Mom is out the front door and down the porch steps, I look back at the old woman. Through the semidarkness of the hallway, her eyes glint at me like black pinheads pushed into a dried apple.

"Don't come after us," I say.

Her head lowers an inch in the way of a dog disappointed to be told it won't be coming along for a walk. Other than this she doesn't protest, doesn't advance or retreat. I pull the door shut, and there's only the pinhead eyes, as empty of the future as they are of the past.

I tell her to take me to Bridge and Lauren first. Then she has to turn off the electrical charge to the fence and open the gate.

"This way," she says.

At first I think I can figure out where she's going, a backtrack toward the lodge that takes one variation, then another, each successive branching off the trail we're on more abrupt than the last. Soon I'm turned around so completely I'm free of even a guess at which way we're headed. Not that it matters. Either Mom is taking me to where I have to go or she's not. To be freed from choice is a liberation, and I can feel the lightness of it now the way I suppose it is with soldiers following orders.

"How far is it?" I call ahead to her.

"It's here."

And it is.

We come out of the cover of trees and into the shaggy yard around another suburban home in the middle of the woods, this one a boxy split-level with a rooster weather vane on the rooftop. The Kirkland house where the second Quinlans believed they grew up.

I expect Mom to head for the front door but instead she veers to the left, starting for the side.

"Aren't they in there?"

"Inside," she says. "But not in the house."

I don't like how she's in charge again, even with a gun pointed at her, but there doesn't seem to be a way to swing control back my way. She knows things, can do things. She is my mother and father rolled into one.

We pass around to the back where there's another structure, this one not trying to look like anything other than what it is: a cement block, flat topped and windowless. It frightens me.

"What's this?"

"It's sort of the control center of the whole place," she says. "You said you wanted the fence turned off, right?"

At the narrow end of the building, there's a steel door with an entry code pad next to it much like the one next to the underground porthole door. Mom places her hand onto the screen and the door latch clunks opens.

"You want me to—"

"What's the code?" I ask.

"What difference—"

"Tell me."

She barks out a laugh. "Your father's birthday," she says without turning around. "Do you remember?"

"July 4, 1951."

"Very good!"

"Open the door."

There's something to smell before there's something to see. Acrid urine, wet fur, animal waste.

"What's in there?"

"Your sister," Mom says, and steps into the dark before I tell her to.

61

I LIFT THE GUN HIGHER AS IF IT'S A FLASHLIGHT THAT WILL SHOW THE WAY. AS soon as the shadow of the structure's interior falls over me, the weapon feels all the more useless. A dead weight in my hand as meaningless as a bundle of keys.

It takes a moment to realize I'm not following Mom, but the whimpering.

"Is that a dog?"

"Poor thing," Mom says, dimly visible ten feet ahead of me, the light from the partly open door showing her working at the buttons and dials of a power board against the right wall. "Not my idea. The security contractor thought it would be sensible in case external conflicts reached all the way up here. A *guard dog*. And wouldn't you know it, I've completely forgotten to feed the creature. I'm frankly surprised it's still alive. I mean, *look* at it."

To her left, a fenced pen. Inside, pacing through mounds of its own filth, is a German shepherd mix of some kind, its hackles raised and head dipped so low it could be crossbred with a hyena. It never stops whimpering. Somehow the tenor of it makes it clear that it's not voicing its loneliness but its simulation, a bluff meant to get one of us to open its cage door. It looks at me when it comes my way, and when it turns, it swivels its head to keep staring at me.

"The howling," I say. "It was the dog."

"That was part of why I had to slip away. I was concerned that one of you might follow the noise it was making and find the house and this place and—well, you *did* find the lab, so my coming here to feed the beast was a waste of time, as it turns out."

I keep watching the dog as it watches me. It pulls me away from why I'm here, what Mom is doing.

"There were two originally, you know," she says.

"Two what?"

"Dogs. This one and one at the lab. When I left my mother and Steven down there after their unsuccessful therapies, the two of them decided to let the animal out. God knows why. Well, there wasn't food for all of them so—oh *dear*. Steven had to take care of it. That was all the mess on the floor you no doubt discovered. That *dog*. There was a fight. The dog lost."

Mom squeezes her chin as she works the keys on the board, recalls some sequence in her mind, starts clicking again.

"I suppose the smell of it got to him eventually," she goes on, "because Steven knocked that second door down, hammered it down with such—"

"You left them down there to die?"

She looks at me. "There was food."

"But you closed the doors on them. Your mother and son. You locked them down there."

"They *weren't* my mother and son anymore. Nevertheless, I didn't have the heart to—"

"Where's Bridge?"

I shake my head as if pulling myself out of an attempted hypnosis.

"She's close."

"You said she—"

"You wanted me to turn off the fence," she says, and punches a button on the board. "There. It's off."

She's counting on me to speak next. The back-and-forth rules of conversation are a powerful convention, as some study of hers has probably told her, because what she does is so straightforward it takes me completely by surprise. Instead of honoring the gun, instead of waiting for my words, she shifts away from the control board and slides back the bolt on the dog's cage.

It stops whimpering at the same time it comes at me.

I was right.

This occurs to me in the fragment of time of the dog's advance, its claws scratching on the hard floor, the show of its teeth like the raising of a pink curtain.

It was faking.

It's not the only thought I have either. The animal has been trained to not hurt Mom, only others.

Which means she was lying about having nothing to do with it.

Which means the dog was her idea.

"On!" she shouts, which makes no sense until the dog's teeth wrap around my ankle.

The gun cracks. A deafening noise inside the concrete crypt, so loud it comes to me with the same as the pain of the bite: a flash of brightness, sickening and yellow.

I manage not to fall. Yanking the dog forward and back at the end of my leg. All of which means the bullet didn't hit the animal.

A few feet away, I'm aware of Mom moving away. Her arms wheeling back, a hand slamming down on the control board.

"Oh . . . oh . . . *oh*."

An escalation of polite astonishment, as if she's pulled a soufflé out of the oven to discover that it's not only fallen, it's burnt.

The bullet found her. Her body folding under itself. I don't know if I aimed at her or the dog or if it was a stray shot that found the base of her throat. I don't know how it happened, but even through the searing pain, there's satisfaction that it did.

The dog releases me. Leaping straight up, jaw snapping, looking for the soft flesh of my inner thigh. Part of its training too.

I don't aim this time either. I just shoot down as the dog comes up.

It comes close enough that I can feel the rancid heat of its breath as it yips once before tumbling backward. The animal rolling onto its side, opening and closing its mouth as if testing to see if it still works.

I limp for the door at the same time I think I should shoot it again. But the gun isn't in my hand anymore. I must have dropped it after taking the shot. If I did, it must be next to the dog.

My ankle feels like there's an iron shackle that's been left in a fire for hours fused tight around it. That doesn't stop me from dragging it along at my side, learning how much weight it will take. It buckles when I'm not more than ten feet out.

I turn to find the dog having the same trouble I am.

The shot must have got some part of its hind leg. It comes out of the bunker and blinks against the light. Not a powerful animal, underfed and greasy, the head so low it appears shrunken with shame.

I've seen people like this before. Experiences from my previous life, breaking through now in a solid cluster. Despite their appearance, the weak, the desperate—they're the ones you ought to be afraid of. The ones who won't listen, won't reason. The ones with nothing to lose who'll come and keep coming.

62

A HOBBLED RACE BETWEEN MAN AND DOG.

If it was observed from the trees, it might appear comical, a Chaplinesque dance of limps and hops. So long as you didn't see the terror on the man's face you might assume it was an act.

I make it to the house's back door, and when it opens, I scream for the first time. If it had been locked, I was so ready for the bite against the back of my good leg that another second's reprieve only doubles the panic.

It's not a good idea to go upstairs. I think this once I'm halfway up the stairs.

I can hear the dog throwing itself at the first step but scrabbling to lift itself to the next. I'm lucky there's no carpet on the varnished wood, leaving it slippery. Lucky too that the dog's leg is making it hard to bound up at me as it otherwise would.

I'm at the top of the stairs when my luck runs out.

The dog figures out how it's done. Lifting with its front legs and jumping with its uninjured back one. Once it's got this down, it rushes up, leaving a looping signature of blood over the steps behind it.

I look down a hallway with three open doors off it and throw myself through the closest one. Kicking the door closed at the same instant the dog slams into it.

A moment's pause before it starts scratching at the wood. The whole time it's whimpering just as it had in its cage.

I slide over and put my back to the door. It gives me the time to look around and see that it's Lauren's room.

Judging from the *Purple Rain* movie poster on the wall and the volleyball trophies lined up along the top of her dresser, it was designed to look the way it did when she was in high school. Aside from the rain forest crowding close to the window's glass it's the absence of any human scent that gives it away. It also makes the room feel unbearably lonesome.

The dog stops.

I can hear it panting, the wet smack of its chops. I wonder how the thing on the other side might be killed. Animal and man waiting for each other in the loneliest house in the world.

Eventually I hear it go away. The thump of its hindquarters down the stairs, the startled yips of suffering as it goes.

Bridge is out there. I need to find Bridge.

But that won't happen if the dog is at the bottom of the stairs or hidden in the living room, ready for when I come down. There's no way of knowing when the right time might be.

I open the door. Slide over to the stairs. Nothing there but trails of blood. The dog's coming and going, and one of my own.

At the back door, I look out over the tall grass, the trampled courses we'd made through it, the concrete outbuilding. I can't see the dog, though it could be anywhere. Would my chances be better if I reversed, walked the length of the house's interior and tried the front door? Maybe.

Maybe not, if the animal is also inside and can corner me as soon as I make the move.

I'm at the bottom of the back porch steps when I hear the growling.

Echoed and hollow, coming from inside the concrete bunker. I watch the dark rectangle of the open door but the animal doesn't come out. It's busy. I can tell from the ripping and tearing. The clack of its teeth as it eats.

I start away to the right and enter the woods. Straight for a time, then left, straight again, right. Trying to make myself difficult to follow. It would have left me totally lost, except I know where I have to go, even if it will be hard to find from where I am. But I'm starting to understand Belfountain now. If I just keep going, I will come to one of its trails. Once you've followed it to the end, take another step and you'll be there.

63

I HEAR THE HOWLING WITHIN MINUTES OF COMING UPON WHAT I'M PRETTY SURE is the Green trail.

It's on the move. Following my scent with greater certainty than me following the trail to the spot where I hope to head off and find the camp, the hole at the end of the cave beyond it that will take me down.

Jerry could have taken Bridge and Lauren back to the lodge or to one of the cabins or found a place in the woods it would take hours to discover. But I don't think he's in any of those places. For one thing, he assumes I'm dead. For another, he's not hiding. He's learning all he wants to learn, satisfying his wants, before leaving this place a grave behind him.

The place Mom called the lab would allow him to do all of these things. And Bridge could take him there.

• • •

I come to the camp sooner than I expected. Limp through the grounds, keeping my eyes straight on the trees on the far side. Then I'm into them. Keep going until the ridge.

The climb up is harder and higher than the last time. With my gnawed ankle it hurts a lot more too. When I reach the cave mouth, I roll over the ground and into the darkness. Eventually the tunnel's narrowing width forces me up.

At the hole I pause before descending, listening for voices below or howls from the woods, but everything is quiet. Even the moist breeze that I've been grateful to for cooling the sweat at the back of my neck has stopped, thickening the air into broth.

When I reach the bottom and step through the battered metal door I see how the Tall Man broke out. He used the heavy fire extinguisher that's missing from its box inset on the wall and now lies battered on the floor. Swung it into the steel door until it started to bend, pulling away from the bolts. Once he could get his hands through, he must have put on the oversized gloves and pulled until it came off altogether. And then the two of them had come up into the forest and wandered like spirits, drinking from rain puddles and eating leaves and roots without any way of knowing how they had come to be abandoned in this way.

I slide my back along the wall, careful with each step not to disturb any of the wires or files on the floor. When I'm at the T-junction where the other hallway runs left to the porthole door, I notice how there's the same kind of keypad on the wall next to it on the inside just as there is on the outside. Locked both ways.

There's something moving in the shadows straight ahead. But it's not something I can see. It's something I can hear.

A chair being dragged over the floor. A male voice. Coming from one of the rooms along the hallway to the left.

I come around the corner and freeze.

Lauren. Lying on her side in the hallway outside the pod room. Her body behind a console on the floor so that I didn't see her at first, one arm out in front of her like a swimmer stretching to touch the end of the pool.

The blood, her stillness, the frozen eyes. Then the eyes blink. Look up at me.

She whispers something and I bend close to hear.

I died.

I understand her to mean her life before this. That everything that happened at Belfountain doesn't count because she'd already lived, already passed.

She glances down. She wants me to check under her. I roll her halfway over as gently as I can and she stifles her pain. It's a steak knife. One she must have pocketed before Jerry took them all.

I tried.

Her lips say this, soundlessly. The same word she had whispered a moment ago. Telling me that she'd resisted as best she could, she'd been brave.

I pick up the knife. When I stand, her eyes remain open, but they are still now in a way they weren't before.

" . . . all the time in the world . . . "

In the pod room, Jerry is speaking and Bridge is sobbing, but even without seeing her, I can tell she's trying not to.

" . . . can be friends, or we can be something else. It all amounts to the same thing, so you might . . . "

His voice is drowned out by the blood in my ears. An escalating expression of force, what remains of me. The body telling the brain it will take it from here.

I come around the doorframe. Jerry is standing with his back to me ten feet away. He's holding the chef's blade in his right hand. A comma-shaped puddle of blood on the floor, the tip of it dripping, adding to its size. He's talking to Bridge, who sits in a metal desk chair—has been *told* to sit there, *told* not to move.

She sees me. The quickest dart of her eyes that she instantly corrects but Jerry detects it anyway. He starts to turn around. It lets me notice how his belt is unbuckled, the top button of his pants undone. Readying himself.

I'm thinking about all this as if it's already happened, already become the past, because it arrives from the mind and the mind is far away from things, as far as someone reading about a war compared to the ones fighting it.

The body is doing something else.

The body brings the steak knife into the top of Jerry's shoulder, pulling it out and doing the same to the middle of his back. When he spins around to defend himself, it goes into his side.

He drops to his knees, but his arm is moving, the one with the chef's blade at the end of it, a wide arc intended for the back of my knee. It's slow though—slower than me—and I'm able to kick the blade out of his grip before it gets close.

Jerry's mouth is moving.

Cursing me, showing me he's not afraid. I can see that without hearing the words. But he's in the past now too. His threats, the intimidating confidence and handsomeness. He's behind me. The body wants only to go to Bridge, help Bridge up, get her out.

She's out of the chair before I reach her. Taking me by the hand and pulling me past Jerry, who's weaving from side to side while remaining on his knees as if screwing his body into the ground.

"Leave him," Bridge says.

We're starting back toward the tunnel when both of us hear the click of claws on the concrete. Bridge and I back away from the corner, but we don't take our eyes from it, as if so long as we can't see the animal it isn't actually there.

"What is it?"

"A dog," I say.

“Will it—”

“Yes.”

We’ve backed up far enough that the dog stands at an equal distance from the pod room door as we do. There’s just the iron door to the cave behind us, the one with the porthole window.

“We run on three,” I say. “You ready?”

“Ready.”

“One. Two—”

Jerry comes out into the hallway.

For a second we watch him just as the dog does. Jerry’s pants are undone and his belt buckle is clanking against his hip, a look of groggy irritation on his face. If it weren’t for his wounds, he would appear hungover, rising from a fitful rest to tell somebody to turn the music down or get him a coffee.

He looks one way and sees us. Looks the other way and sees the dog.

We never get to *three*.

64

JERRY COMES AT US FASTER THAN I WOULD HAVE THOUGHT HIS INJURIES WOULD allow. I get in front of Bridge and widen my stance, preparing myself for the blow, then see from where he's looking that he doesn't care about reaching me or Bridge. It's the door at the end of the hall he's going for.

Bridge is ahead of me. She would have made it to the door before any of us if Jerry hadn't shoved her against the wall as he passed. It doesn't take her down though. She regains her footing and has caught up to him by the time it takes me to reach my top hopping, jumping pace.

My target isn't the door. It's Jerry. I launch myself at him, grabbing for any part to hold on to. My fingers pull into fists, gripping the fabric of his untucked shirt along with folds of his skin, and throw him behind me.

Bridge slams into the door. Tries the handle.

"It's locked!"

I think of the different ways to numerically express Dad's birthdate. Month, day, year? Day, month, year?

"Enter 07041951. See the keypad?"

She presses some buttons. "Didn't work. What's the number?"

"July fourth, 1951. Dad's birthday." I say the numbers again.

Bridge finishes the sequence. Pulls on the door. It eases open with a depressurizing whoosh, popping my ears.

"Go!" I shout at her when she looks back.

She slips out the door and it seals shut again.

I suppose it's relief in knowing that Bridge is free, that at least she is out of Jerry's reach even if there's only the enormous forest waiting for her outside of the cave—whatever it is, the exhaustion hits me now, a few feet short of the door. I wouldn't move if I didn't hear the dog behind me. The animal paused, watching the three of us struggling against each other and now seeing the two wounded humans left behind.

It was the body that pushed me forward when I was in the pod room. But it's the mind that does it now.

You're so close.

I take a dainty skip with my good leg.

You can let all of it go on the other side.

Another skip. Another and another and I'm there.

The door sucks open with a blast of fresh air, hard as water. Something is behind me—the dog, a rush of motion, the sense of weight about to crash into me—and I squeeze myself through the gap. The door clicks shut.

"The number worked on this one too," Bridge says. She's standing by the external keypad, blinking the sweat from her eyes.

A soft *thump* against the door.

"Open it."

Jerry's face. Three inches from mine through the porthole window's glass. Not shouting, not reasoning. He's giving me an order.

"Open the *door*, Aaron."

I keep my shoulder to the metal surface. Stare at Jerry through the glass, his skin pallid and buttery.

"Let me the fuck out!"

There's no refusal other than my staying still. Jerry reads it in me before I'm certain of it myself. I won't open the door. There is no order or plea I will listen to. A realization that brings a nauseous smile to his lips.

"I read the file. I know who you were before. I *know*," he says through the glass.

I look past him and he turns to see the dog approaching. It holds its head higher than before, nourished and emboldened.

Jerry turns back to the window and I can see him consider begging me to help him, but he changes his mind. There's no way he can stop the fear from showing. But he can keep his mouth shut.

Even so, he appears about to say something when the dog scrambles forward and rips into the back of his leg. After that there are only his screams.

The door trembles. When I peer through the porthole again, Jerry is down on the floor, the animal upon him.

"Can you walk?" Bridge asks.

"I'll be faster if you hold my elbow."

She cradles my arm in both her hands and the two of us start up the concrete stairs. I came down the same stairs only two days ago but it feels like months. It makes me think how Belfountain, as with all fairy-tale places, is no more constrained by time than by geography. The characters in those stories—Hansel and Gretel, Rapunzel, Cinderella—the way they existed as only names on paper prevented us from feeling the horror they would have experienced as they were enslaved, imprisoned, baked into pies.

A whistle.

Not the kind made with pursed lips, but a sports whistle, loud and shrill. The one left for Jerry as a gift and that he'd put in his pocket.

I wait for the dog to growl or whine before silencing him, but there's only the abrupt interruption of the whistle, then nothing.

65

IF WE HAVE A CHANCE OF GETTING OUT, IT'S NOW. WE COULD TRY TO GO BACK TO THE fake house to find the gun. But I don't know how to get there. We could spend hours wandering around before we found it. There's a good chance we never would.

Eventually, the dog's hunger will return.

Eventually, it will come for us.

We stumble through the camp and into the forest to join the trail again, start back toward the lodge. When we get there, we see where Jerry had been digging at the twins' graves, a group of smaller piles of soil next to the two larger ones. We proceed into the lodge where I pull a quarter-full jug of orange juice from the fridge, and then the two of us walk out through the smashed wall of glass.

Bridge takes a drink. Hands the jug back to me. The juice is too sweet, too cold, too good. And then I remember that I'm still alive.

"You found Mom," Bridge says once we start out along the road.

"Yes."

"She wasn't who we thought she was. She knew."

"Yes."

"What about the Tall Man?"

"He's gone. They're all gone."

"The dog?"

"It'll come for us. But we've got a little time, I think."

When we reach the fence, I tell Bridge that if it's still electrified I might not get up again after I touch it. If that's how it goes, she shouldn't stay with me but go back to the lodge. Secure the food, barricade herself in one of the rooms. Wait for help.

"Sure," she says. But she's only agreeing because there's no point in arguing. She knows there's no help coming. Either we get out now or we never do.

I walk up and place both hands against the metal.

There's a tremor in my arms, but it's only me, anticipating the jolt that doesn't come. I slip my fingers through the holes. Then I pull back hard to the left.

"Still locked," I tell Bridge, looking up at the barbed wire. "There's one thing I want to try."

It's been a long time since I've climbed a fence. Not that I remember having ever done it; it's only how my body feels pulling itself up while negotiating the too-small footholds and finger locks that tells me I have. Once at the top, I use my free hand to pull the pruning shears from my pocket.

The wire isn't thick. Clamping the blades firmly around a point is half of the challenge, and pressing through the cut without the sharp burrs gouging into my face is the other.

I can only do it with my right hand. Soon my left is numb, and my bad ankle won't stay in the hole in the fence, so I have to choose between coming down again or falling. Whatever cuts I've managed so far will have to be enough.

"Watch out," I call down to Bridge before letting the shears drop to the ground.

I start dividing the wire to the sides. When it has yielded the widest gap I'm ever going to get—a couple of feet, no more—my hand is so bloodied it looks like I wear a single, shining glove.

I pull myself onto the top of the fence. Shimmy into the gap between the razor wire, the sharp ends snagging into my skin on both sides. When I'm halfway, I hold myself in position as firmly as I'm able.

"Climb up," I tell Bridge. "Up and over me."

"Are you crazy?"

"Do it."

I'm worried she's going to refuse. But then the fence is shaking, and I have to hold on hard as she makes it up to where I am.

"Put one leg over me so that you're sitting up on my back," I say.

"The wire—it's *in* you—"

"I'm all right. Can you do it?"

She doesn't answer. She's doing it.

"Ow!" The burrs find her on the way up and again at the top "*Ow!*"

"Now slide over to the other side."

"I'll fall!"

"Hold on to me with your one hand. Your foot will find the fence if you lean over far enough. I won't let you fall."

When her foot comes into view, I guide it into a hold in the fence. Bridge slides over my back until her other leg is free. Then she grips my jacket and lowers herself until she can hold the fence on her own. I watch her scramble down to the ground. Once she's there, she looks up at me.

"Now you," she says.

"It's going to be messy."

"You're already messy."

I try to climb down the other side head first. My hips are barely past the top bar and I'm tumbling through air.

The meeting of body and ground takes my breath away. For a good while all I do is try to find the air again, coax it down my throat until my lungs accept it.

"Does it hurt a lot?" Bridge says.

"Not much."

This is true. It may ultimately be a bad sign, but for now there isn't much more than a burning here and there on my skin that I keep waiting to dull but never does.

"Look," Bridge says.

The old woman stands on the other side of the fence. Maybe she followed us here and only now arrived. Maybe she was here the whole time, watching.

She makes no appeal to be released, doesn't speak. She remains more still than the trees around her. It's as if she had always been there. An object—pickup truck, corroded bed frame—you sometimes come upon in the woods and mistake for a living thing because it's halfway between the two, a piece of the human past losing its identity as the vines and branches pull it deeper and deeper into the green.

OCEAN

66

NEITHER OF US IS SURPRISED TO FIND THERE'S NO SATELLITE PHONE INSIDE THE metal box. Even if there was, we couldn't let whoever answered know where we were.

We walk all the way to the interstate. None of the few pickups or military vehicles that pass stop to check on us. Our hope is that we look like a problem. To inquire how we came to be shuffling along this remote road, a bloodied man and teenaged girl, would be to involve yourself in that problem. We're counting on the self-preserving calculations that go into minding your own business.

By the time we collapse in the prickly grass next to the on-ramp, it's almost nightfall. The highway groans behind us. We need help. We cannot ask for help. The paradox of prison escapees or refugees or wounded animals.

Bridge's questions reach me through the near dark, and somehow because she is only a graphite silhouette, it's easier to answer them directly. She wants to know about all the things Mom told me in the house-that-wasn't-our-house. Who Jerry was in the life before. How we were chosen, left to drown, returned from the dead.

She doesn't ask who I really am. She can tell I'm not ready for that, and like an actual friend, an actual sister, she lets it go.

When I'm finished, it's dark. The passing headlights almost touch us but not quite, so that with every passing vehicle Bridge is briefly stretched out, a shadow that bends and rushes over the grass.

"I think I know why the Tall Man came after us," she says.

"Tell me."

"He saw us and recognized something from before. He saw a family and he wanted to be closer to it. Part of it. He was *lonely*, Aaron."

I nod but I'm not sure she sees me do it. It makes me feel invisible. A spirit observing its final glimpses of the world and trying to memorize it, holding fast to the vague outline of this one person sitting next to me.

"My file," Bridge says. "Brigit and Olivia. Neither said anything about my cancer. What do you think that means?"

"It means it's not true."

"Is that what you think, or what you hope?"

"I'm doing my best to make them the same thing."

"But some of it you can't hope away. Like me cutting myself. That part was true."

I reach out for her but I can't find her in the darkness. "You're different now," I say, and imagine casting a spell toward her through my fingertips. "You can make yourself different."

At the earliest sky-bruising of dawn an older model Sunbird rattles onto the shoulder. An arm appears from out of the driver's-side window, waving us over. Bridge starts toward the car. A woman's arm, no other passengers.

"You going into the city?" the woman asks once we're stuffed into the back seat and she starts us rolling onto the blacktop.

"Yes," I say.

"Need a hospital?"

"Yes."

"Any preference?"

"A busy one, I guess."

None of us speak over the next couple hours until we reach the outerlands of the city, the sound barrier walls separating the lanes from the malls and housing developments and schools. Then the low-rise office buildings, the software developers and makers of parts that go into fighter jets and submarines.

"There're checkpoints along here sometimes," the woman says. "You two have ID?"

"Not me," Bridge answers.

"I do," I say, feeling the wallet in my back pocket but not pulling it out. "But I'm pretty sure it's fake."

The woman looks at me in the rearview mirror.

"Don't tell me anything more. The less I know the better," she says, returning her eyes to the traffic ahead. "Most days I wish I didn't know a goddamn thing about any of this."

A few minutes later we're downtown, stopping on the edge of the university campus, a block from the Swedish First Hill Hospital. When we thank her, she waves at us with her fingers as if shooing away the very concept of gratitude.

"We've got to stick together now, right?" she says.

Once she's driven off, I tell Bridge to wait under an elm on the Union Green. I warn her not to talk to anyone until I come back.

"Who am I going to talk to?" she says, trying a smile and getting it halfway right. "You're the only person I know."

• • •

In the emergency room the doctor doesn't ask any follow-up questions when I tell her I was injured in a dog attack. A neighbor's rottweiler that jumped the fence. She doesn't believe me, but decides the truth isn't necessary. There's an administrative nurse who asks for my insurance information, and when I assure her my roommate is bringing my health card from home, she laughs in my face.

It's a chaotic, bad-smelling place I've never been to before, yet this is the hospital where I worked as a surgeon. In the life I never lived I would have been treating these shouting, pain-twisted people around me, not been sitting among them, waiting my turn. I wish at least this one aspect of Mom's made-up story had been true.

When my wounds have been swabbed and bandaged, the doctor tells me an orderly will come soon to take me to get some X-rays done. Once she pulls the curtains closed, I count to thirty and slip through them, heading right and going straight the way someone who knows where they're going might.

There's the certainty that my doing this will trigger an alarm. But I make my way out a side door without any of that. I might have gotten lucky. They might have been aware of my leaving but happy to see a case like mine walk away, a number they could wipe from the board.

Bridge is waiting for me. I hoped she would be but figured there were a dozen good reasons why she'd be gone. Police spotting her and sweeping her up. Passersby noting her soiled appearance and offering help of either the genuine or false kind. There's also the possibility that she would leave on her own.

"You're still here," I say.

"I didn't stay the whole time."

"Where'd you go?"

"I borrowed a phone. Called the police."

"Bridge. Do you know what—"

"Not for us. And I didn't tell them who I was. Where we were."

I look at my sister and instead of telling me she waits for me to see it in her.

"You sent them to Belfountain," I say. "To find the old woman."

"Yes."

"Because you didn't want to leave her there."

"No."

Bridge starts to walk and I follow her. Part of me wants to ask her who she borrowed the phone from, if they could have reported us. Part of me knows it won't make any difference in where we have to go next even if they had.

"How are you?" Bridge asks after a stretch of silence between us as we make our way along Pike Street toward the waterfront, the mountains a watercolor in progress.

"Aside from feeling like a pincushion covered in duct tape, I'm fine. You?"

"Tired. But I think I'll always be tired, you know?"

We pass a group of National Guardsmen at a corner, then a similar clutch of men—not army, not cops, just uniformed militia, the official-looking patches and stripes down their pants stitched on at home—holding mismatched rifles. None of them question us. They're too occupied by striking the right pose, trying to find the balance between menacing and bored.

At the park by the waterfront we sit on a set of concrete steps and look out over the harbor. In the distance tankers slide over the horizon as if cleaning it.

"I don't know if I've ever been here before," I say. "But the water—it's so familiar."

"Maybe it is."

"Maybe. Or maybe I was born in St. Louis or Des Moines or Toronto. For all I know, this is the first time I've ever seen the ocean."

Bridge looks directly at me and waits until I turn to her.

"I have this idea," she says. "There're some things we're born remembering. The ones that are always there no matter what. The stars." She shifts her eyes back to scan the blue horizon again. "The ocean."

We remain like this, the tide distant and massive as a crowd marching in the streets.

"What about you?" Bridge asks after the sun slips behind a wayward cloud and a coolness returns us to wakefulness. "What do you remember from the beginning?"

"Just one thing," I say. "Just you."

67

IT TAKES A LITTLE OVER AN HOUR TO PANHANDLE THREE DOLLARS. ENOUGH TO PAY for a half hour on a computer in an internet café, but it turns out we only need five minutes to look up the news stories about the missing Olivia Goldstein and figure out where she lives.

We share a chocolate bar with the leftover change and walk over the course of the afternoon. Neither of us says much. Olivia has a mother and a father and a brother who are about to have the dead returned to them. The thought of this, the startling, frightening joy it will bring, takes hold of our thoughts.

It's a fancy neighborhood, but in the Seattle manner. Which is to say it's not about the grandeur of the house, but how well it's hidden, in this case obscured by a wall of hedge and the junipers behind it.

The two of us stand at the end of the curving drive, peering up at what we can glimpse of the Tudor facade: the basketball net over the closed garage, the uncollected newspapers wrapped in plastic on the front walk, the neglected lawn growing wild.

"They must be so sad," Bridge says. "You can feel it from way out here."

"Not for long. You've come back."

"Yeah. I've come back."

I wait for her to move but she only looks at the *GOLDSTEIN* stenciled on the mailbox and then back up at the house.

"They're strangers," she says.

"They're your family."

"But I don't remember them."

"It'll come back. And if it doesn't, you'll learn. They'll help you."

"What about you? What are you going to do now?"

"I don't know."

"Are you going to go away? Will I—"

"I'm not going anywhere. Nowhere far."

Later, I'll try to recall if she was crying when she put her arms around me, gentle as she could so as not to disturb the bandages over my cuts. It's because it was hard for me to see her face through my own tears, which came without warning and wouldn't stop.

When she pulls away, she squeezes my hand twice. Our code.

I squeeze hers back. One time. One more.

"See you Tuesday?"

She doesn't understand for a second, and then it comes back. Our standing dinner arrangement. The secrets shared over tables in Chuck E. Cheese or downtown oyster bars. She laughs without making a sound.

"Tuesday," she says before she turns and starts up the drive.

I stay there for a time. It's hard to say how long.

Piece by piece the world tells me. The spinning leaves of an oak in a neighbor's yard. The distressed yowl of a cat. The smell of the sea. All of it asking the same thing.

What now? What now? What now?

Maybe freedom always feels like this.

My file is still folded in my pocket. The answer to who I really am that, with each breath, feels more disposable.

Where does the path lead after it ends?

I take a step. And another. Each one a little faster than the one before, testing my strength. Nameless and unhistoried and light.

I'll go on.

I'll run.

ACKNOWLEDGMENTS

Thank you to Anne McDermid, Peter McGuigan, Chris Bucci, Jason Richman, Kevin Hanson, Laurie Grassi, Crissie Johnson Molina, Siobhan Doody, Nita Pronovost, Catherine Whiteside, Sarah St. Pierre, Randall Perry (and the whole team at Simon & Schuster Canada).

To my children, Maude and Ford, and to my wife, Heidi, thank you for listening to the idea early on and nudging me in the right directions.

ABOUT THE AUTHOR

HEIDI PYPER

ANDREW PYPER is the author of *The Only Child*, which was an instant national bestseller in Canada. He is also the author of seven previous novels, including *The Demonologist*, which won the International Thriller Writers award for best hardcover novel and was selected for *The Globe and Mail*'s best 100 books and Amazon's top twenty best books. *The Killing Circle* was a *New York Times* best crime novel of the year. Three of Pyper's novels, including *The Homecoming*, are in active development for feature film and television. He lives in Toronto. Visit **AndrewPyper.com** and follow him on Twitter **@andrewpyper**.